Escape Into Rain

A Rick Blaine Novel

J.P. Robideaux

For Lorrie, Shakespeare, Lewis Black and my weekly golf partners.

Pend Oreille Lake region, North Idaho

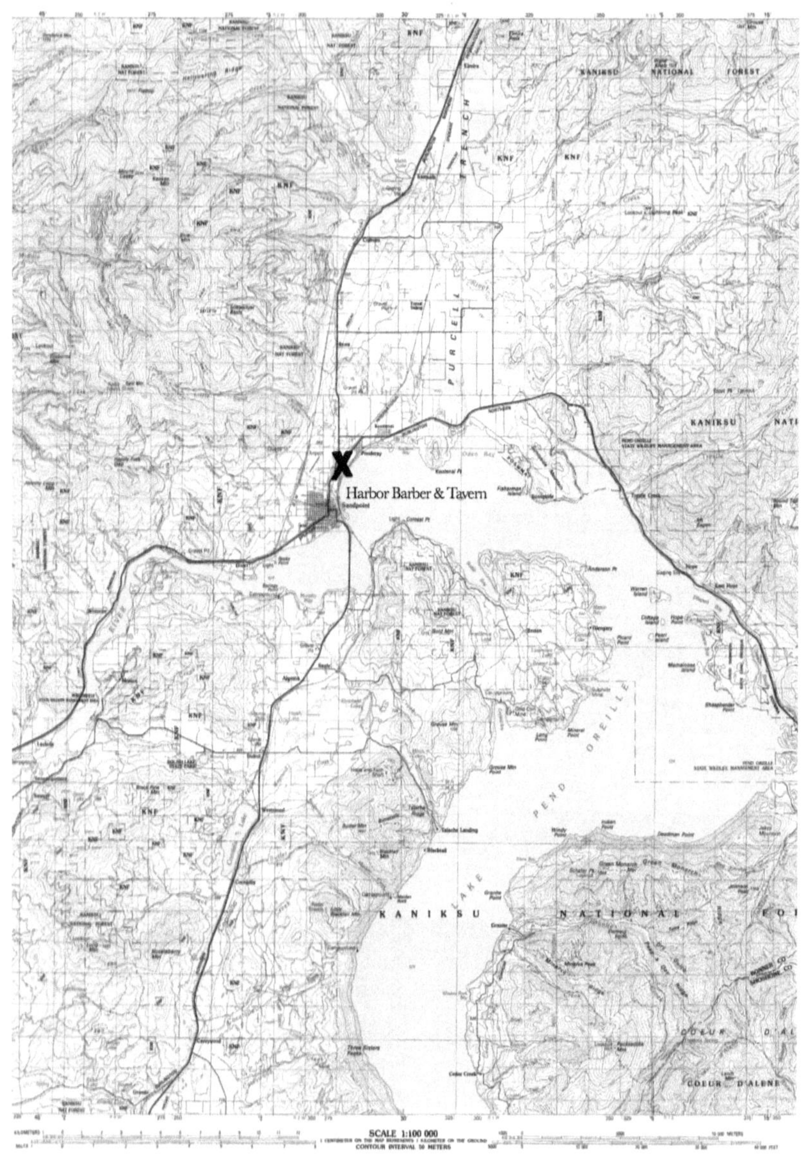

Santa Monica, Venice Beach, and Los Angeles area

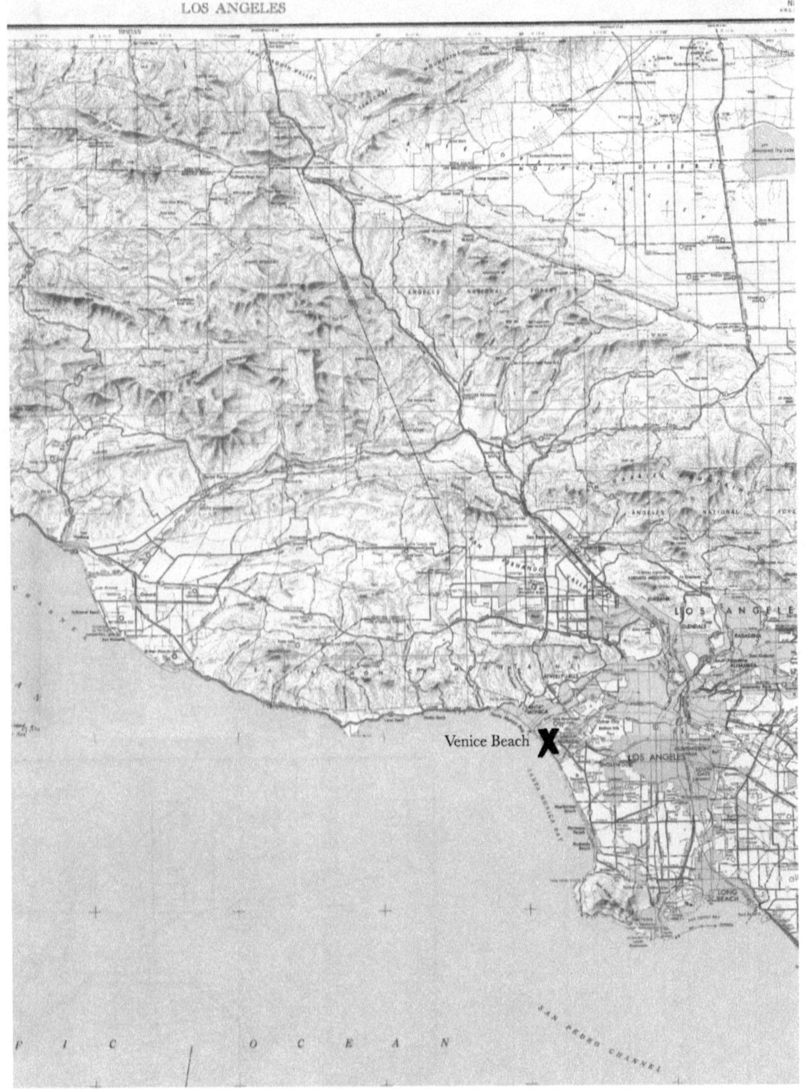

We can't do much about the length of our lives, but we can do plenty about its width and depth.

-Evan Esar

Prologue

The throbbing in my head began to subside, but I knew it would return soon like the sun setting outside my office window here in Silicon Valley. The past days and weeks jammed together in one giant collage of headaches now pounding at my skull. That was my last clue. The time had come. There was no getting around it — I had to go.

After dropping a note on Brenda's desk, then waving to the cleaning lady, I left out the exit, heading down the concrete stairs. The brightly colored orange steps ran for six floors to the parking garage. Each step down, some taken two at a time, felt like a therapeutic massage to my temples as I quickly rounded a corner halfway to my destination. I picked up speed as the blue door at the finish line came into view.

My new lightweight briefcase containing a laptop and several files swung out in opposition to my pace-setting turn, its leather strap pulling, tight, tighter around my neck. The choking sensation was not going to slow me down as I came crashing, palms first, into the blue door at the bottom of the stairwell.

I made the descent in just under three minutes, my new world record!

Turning my back to the door before opening it, I caught my breath. Leaning there for a full minute, taking deep breaths, felt so good I had to shout. As the echo faded, I checked my bag to make sure the daily journal my therapist suggested I keep was still with me. It was there along with my phone, wallet and keys. After gathering myself, I opened the door and walked calmly to my car, smiling to myself, having just run my personal best. I popped the trunk on the vintage 911 and removed the car cover, draping it carefully over the sleek body. Better to leave this classic ride here than at the airport. I finished tying down the cover just as my Uber ride pulled up.

1. "Gone with the Wind."

LAKE PEND OREILLE, NORTH IDAHO

The storm came on faster than either one of us anticipated. For once, the weather forecaster was right, leaving me no choice but to batten down the hatches, reduce the main, and change the jib. My crewman for the day, Joe Parker, father of a good friend and a member of the local Fire and Rescue Unit, skillfully managed to make the jib change without falling overboard. Sailing came easily to Joe, a fifty-something, full-bearded outdoorsman. This was our race to lose, and we were having the time of our life.

"Bring it in, Rick."

The starboard winch sang out as I pulled the sheet tightening the slack on the smaller jib Joe had just raised.

Waves, producing a stinging mist, forced my head to roll back and forth as if being punched in the face. The other boats in the regatta were scrambling to make adjustments as the storm quickly moved past us, headed in their direction. One after another, the thirteen other boats copied our adjustments, attempting to gain on us. It was like putting first in golf and revealing the best path to the hole. Success comes by doing it better – even if you show others how it's done, you just have to cross the finish line first.

We were fighting hard to maintain our lead in this mid-season regatta on the lake. So far, Joe and I were able to maintain the lead in the fourteen-boat competition.

We'd been at it for just over an hour, thanks to the great wind. Sometimes, when the wind seemed a distant memory, the boats would just sit and we'd wait it out. That wasn't the case today. I was on my last legs but trying not to show it. One last buoy to pass and then homeward. Suck it up, I told myself.

The timing had to be perfect as the orange and white homeward buoy came racing toward us. Joe and I were positioned on the starboard side of the boat, maintaining a balancing act, as I made the call to tack our twenty-one-foot Hobie Cat and run with the wind pushing us to the finish.

"Jibe ho," I shouted out. The helm was over, and the buoy shot past like a bullet.

The other hobbies were in pursuit and closing fast. Lannie Watkins, a local tavern owner, had her boat in second position and was running hard at us. She popped a larger jib to use as a spinnaker, which was daring in this wind, but the maneuver appeared to work. She swung her boat wide past the buoy. Lannie and her crewman were having a hard time bringing the spinnaker to life until they finally set the spinnaker pole in place. We watched as the maneuver knocked Lannie backward, nearly carrying her overboard. She immediately sat up and gave us the finger as her boat gained speed.

We had a different strategy, using a smaller jib out front because of the heavy wind. Our best course of action was to split the sails and hope we could maintain enough speed. A fifty-yard gap between Lannie's boat and ours was shrinking with two hundred yards remaining until the finish line. Both Joe and I were facing each other close to the stern, he on the starboard sponson and me on the port side. We were two drowning rats smiling at each other, holding on for dear life. The wind was gusting to twenty miles per hour, causing our smaller jib sheet to strain against the starboard cleat.

Lannie's boat and one other were gaining on us with less than a hundred yards to go.

"This is going to be close, Rick!" Joe yelled through his grey beard with a big broad smile.

We managed to hang on for a close win and enjoyed hoisting the trophy one more time in a brief dock ceremony. Two hours later, we were center stage at Harbor Barber and Tavern.

"You bastards! You did it again."

Lannie was serving up beers with lunch and letting us have it.

"All I needed was another twenty yards," Lannie shouted as she placed twenty-ounce mugs of cold Kokanee on the table and hugged us both.

It was nearing four in the afternoon by the time we all said our goodbyes. Thunderstorms were reportedly arriving later that afternoon and into the evening, with threats of lightning strikes. Or maybe not. Weather forecasters' predictions are suspect at best. And unpredictable forecasting creates dangerous situations, not only around here at the lake, but in life. Especially in business. My whole life depends on business predictions, updates, reposting, and changing production volumes. Up until now, business has taken up most of my life, which is why I occasionally escape to North Idaho.

Only one person knows my location when I'm here. And she understands what a uniquely special place Lake Pend Oreille is – a place with four seasons, pine trees forever, and fresh water. It's also where the U.S. Navy declared, and local folklore supported: There is no bottom. Someone may find the bottom of this lake one day, just take your time and don't hold your breath.

Sailing in the regatta today, plus all the preparation that preceded it and the celebration that followed, temporarily replaced endless business meetings, daily review of production schedules, and the ongoing rearrangement of sales quotas.

Important work, for sure, that always makes my days go fast, but also makes me wonder why I ever left the farm. I've been safely removed from all of that for nearly two weeks now, with a few days remaining, thanks to my pre-planned time away schedule carefully crafted by my closest confidant. Some people would call this time away a vacation; I prefer the more adventurous word: escape. In my estimation, it's a word more appropriately connected to taking to the road and disappearing for a while. The Ford motor company named a vehicle after it. Just like the one Chet drove into my driveway after the regatta. I hosted a barbecue that night in celebration of our sailing win; Chet brought the steaks. I feel life is measured by the amount of good times we have, not bad.

I was taught to take what life throws at you and make the most of it, constantly on the lookout for new partnerships, the pursuit of which can be misunderstood when coming from a bachelor like me. But the longer my stay here at the lake, the closer lake life and sailing become my trustworthy partners. Each one enables me to compete more effectively in a competitive corporate world. Being aggressive is a natural instinct because succeeding requires hard work. I enjoy success and sharing its benefits. What I have found as a result is that enjoying a win is no solitary matter.

Escaping has become an essential part of my life. I've divided it up into three parts that work for me:

<u>First</u>, appreciate the anticipation prior to leaving. It's like planning a vacation, only more intense and clandestine because no one can know, except one person, just in case. It appears to be mysterious and solitary, but it's not. It's personal.

<u>Second</u>, enjoy every minute, second, nanosecond of your time away. No guilt is allowed to infiltrate, ever.

<u>Third</u>, accomplish everything you set out to experience, including a safe and successful return. It may be easier for me; I'm the boss. I owe no one any explanations or details related

to my time. All I need to do is show up renewed and ready to kick it with fresh ideas with my team, safely tucked away in my briefcase. Those are mostly my expectations, not necessarily theirs. Achievement is what I'm looking for, and that leads to success.

Nurturing unique ideas keeps me sane, grounded, motivated.

My mother, along with my executive assistant Brenda, and Ted, my therapist, have helped me monitor my motivation over the years. Evidently, unbridled motivation can turn into bad habits. Who knew? In any case, each of them watch out for me in their own way. And just for the record, Ted would make an unbelievably cool weather forecaster. I know, because he's helped me turn personal, occasional cloudy skies into sunny vistas. No television weather prognosticator I watch can do that, not even twice a month like Ted.

Mom, my original grounder, will frequently share stories from parochial grade school years, whenever the family gathers for holidays and reunions. Days of future past. She usually begins with:

"You'll never believe what my Rick did with that chain saw. I can't believe he still has all ten fingers."

Let's just say that there were more than a few situations that challenged mother's rural common-sense rules. And for some reason, my reality didn't match that of the beloved Franciscan nuns. Sanctifying judgments, resulting from my actions, led to demerits, dismissals, and eventually, depression, which have lingered, and require regularly scheduled visits with Ted, the forecasting therapist.

"Evidently, sailing is the most therapeutic exercise for your brain, Rick," Ted realized last month.

Paying people to tell you what you already know can be frustrating, but I like Ted, so it doesn't matter. He's right, of course. Unpredictable Lake Pend Oreille offers a full range of therapy lessons, some smooth as silk and others rough and raging. That's what I like about this forty-mile long, gigantic pit of fresh water. And the lake at night reminds me of a beautiful lady, with a deep, dark secret, just waiting to be revealed. Maybe tomorrow night we'll be dancing together.

§

BLAINE MANUFACTURING, SILICON VALLEY, CALIFORNIA

"Rick Blaine's office, Brenda speaking. Yes, I understand. Mr. Blaine is looking forward to working with you on that matter, as soon as he returns. Yes, next week. Friday, but he will be in a conference. I will contact him and let him know of the urgency. Of course. Thank you for understanding. Good-bye."

§

SOUTH BOSTON, MASSACHUSETTS – 1989

Michael Castillino walked slowly behind his little brother, Anthony, as they rounded the corner at L Street and headed down Broadway to school. It wasn't that he didn't like walking with his third-grade sibling. Michael, now twelve, was always on alert, making sure no one followed or bothered them. Besides, Anthony walked faster. He liked school and couldn't wait to get there. That was not the case with Michael, who hated most everything about school, especially the nuns and priests. He couldn't stand their strange rules and regulations or depressing deep black dress code with uniformly matching attitudes. Whenever he saw a nun walking down the hall or between classes outside, they appeared to him like ghostly apparitions, floating, robes rippling in silence apart from the world around them.

"When I grow up, I want to be a priest who also plays

professional football," Anthony told Michael on their walk.

"That's not possible."

"Why? Dad says anything is possible if you work hard enough."

"Think. How are you going to say Mass and play ball? They both happen on Sunday, stupid."

"Oh, ya."

Anthony quickly moved on ahead, avoiding Michael's finger flick on his head, feeling a little embarrassed from his last comment. He didn't go too far though, remembering his mother's words after a big hug and kiss.

"You boys behave, stay together."

South Boston Catholic Academy had a very good reputation. SBCA had more alums attend college than any other academy in the city. Michael and Anthony's father insisted they attended and left the rest up to them, and their mother, to become educated and make him proud. His outlook for the boys was already taking shape, which, oddly enough, didn't necessarily include a college degree.

Mr. Castillino came from the old country, Sicily. Along with him, he brought a self-made determination handed down from father to son. To a Castillino, providing for your family meant that you convinced others to buy whatever you sold or not to buy at all. Early on, Carlo reasoned that buying and selling really happened through one source: Trucking. Nothing moved without something to haul it from the manufacturer to the distributor and, eventually, to the retailer. Carlo worked for others and quickly learned the business of short-haul auto freight around the Boston area.

Carlo had an engaging personality and a willingness to do whatever it took to complete his tasks. His current boss appreciated those qualities, which were hard to find in the trucking industry. What he didn't know was that Carlo had his own agenda. He'd given himself two years to learn everything his boss knew, then fill in the blanks with how to improve and change the service to fit what Carlo had in mind.

After two years, Carlo felt it was time to make his move. He had become an integral part of Petrulo Trucking, and now his employer became his target. Giovanni Petrulo started with one truck that he proudly drove around Boston looking for anything to haul. He enjoyed driving, meeting people, and making an honest living. When Carlo came to him with the idea of creating a partnership, he was surprised. Carlo was his best worker out of his three employees. But Giovanni had no idea that the guy knew anything apart from driving, loading, and unloading.

Carlo knew that a competitor was struggling with financial troubles. Gambling had become an obsession for the owner of a slightly larger firm, and Carlo suggested Giovanni consider buying the competitor out. Carlo's passion for expansion came through loud and clear. Giovanni consented, which triggered Carlo's next move. He made an appointment the next day to visit the competitor, after hours, to do some creative convincing. Years later, Giovanni would find out that Carlo had threatened to expose the competitor's gambling problems, and when that didn't work, he excused himself and returned with two associates. By the time the men had finished with the competitor, his ring finger on his left hand was the only one left unbroken. Why the ring finger? Because to Carlo, family was everything, and if the man didn't sell his business to Petrulo, his family was next.

As a result of the altercation, the competitor had a little trouble signing the documents Carlo had an attorney prepare. But sign them he did, happy to make the transaction, and Carlo, go away.

Within a few months, Petrulo Trucking had more than doubled in size. The operation continued to expand throughout the years with Carlo bringing in new business, offering prospective customers creative contracts the Sicilian Way. Giovanni and

Carlo enjoyed an equal partnership all through the years. Carlo eventually took over the day-to-day operations with Giovanni remaining as president of the company. Carlo made sure the company made money, not only in trucking services, but also with the addition of other business ventures that provided non-taxable income.

§

LAKE PEND OREILLE

Brenda, my executive assistant, just called with an urgent message. People are looking for me. It's time. I can feel it. As always, I won't be found until I'm ready. Some of those searchers work for me. It's a little game we play. Brenda has a name for it: The Runs. I run the company, Blaine Manufacturing, and when the pressure builds, I run away from time to time. Clever, Brenda.

Her explanation is simple, and I love it: No one person really runs a company with hundreds of employees. Plus, if you are in charge, and don't watch out for yourself, the company runs you. That's why escaping is so important to me. And none of my escapes would happen without trusting Brenda to keep things running while I'm away.

My name, Rick Blaine, has a funny anecdote connected to it. I'm also the accidental namesake of that same B-movie hero, Rick, in the classic movie, *Casablanca*, played by Humphrey Bogart. My parents never knew the name Rick Blaine had a Hollywood legacy when they named me. Not until an elderly uncle, a film buff, made them aware.

"You have to be kidding, you named your kid after a Humphrey Bogart character?" He laughed until he nearly choked to death.

Dad looked it up, and, yes, my uncle was right. The thought

made my dad laugh too. I didn't find out until I was a teenager. The Hollywood connection has never bothered me; in fact, the name similarity is one of many reasons that I'm motivated to do more and, more importantly, to be myself.

No surprise, *Casablanca* is one of my favorite movies. So much so that I installed an oversized *Casablanca* movie poster on the wall behind my office desk. People ask if I enjoy old movies, which I do, but I'm not shy when it comes to explaining why *Casablanca* tops the list. I tell people that I love the symbolism, which clearly shows "Rick's Place" in the background. Not only that, I say, but Casablanca in the movie is a city full of people waiting to escape. Insiders understand the symbolism.

A favorite line in the movie is sometimes heard around here at Blaine: Play it again, Sam. I sometimes use the expression to compliment a great presentation made by one of our employees. I'm thankful for my family ties every day.

My ancestors were a self-sufficient group of hardworking people, or so I've heard time after time, holiday after holiday, evening porch story after story. I remember an elderly grand uncle, Morris, telling me about covered wagons and how the Blaine family changed history:

"In those days, Rickie, the wagons would travel over hard terrain. Rocks and mud were a real problem. That is, until Josiah Blaine invented the larger wheel and axle on the back of the wagon, smaller in front. The slightly larger wheel in back allowed for larger loads and greater stability. He was quite a man, that Josiah."

Morris could have told me that the Blaines invented oxygen, and I probably would have believed him. Sure, there were plenty of stories to enjoy. Evidently, the Blaines pushed one another to do more, be more, and create more. That Blaine legacy was passed my direction over the years, though I was reluctant to accept it at first. But, after some soul-searching and chance-taking, I decided to create something. I attribute the success of Blaine Manufacturing Corporation, one of the most innovative and oldest technology accessory companies in the United States, to my heritage and my granduncles.

My grandfather, Eugene Blaine, homesteaded in North Idaho in 1946, following his honorable discharge from the Army. He and my grandmother, Betty, raised some of the first Angus and Holstein herds in that area. The ranch also included horses, and the appropriate amount of chickens, dogs, and barn cats. Once they had the homestead in place, they began raising a family of two girls and two boys. My father, Timothy James Blaine, or TJ, as he came to be known, was the eldest. Thoughts of the Blaine family home are an inspirational memory.

As a child, the homestead and surrounding landscape constantly engaged my imagination. I participated in all kinds of shenanigans with my siblings and cousins, riding horses bareback until the stars came out, then ending the day around a campfire.

As the story goes, my grandfather had worn out the seats in his '36 Chevy truck, which he let all the kids drive, way before they were of age. The coil springs were coming up through the upholstery, causing some embarrassing injuries, especially for those of us bouncing around like ping pong balls. Grandpa looked around for a repair shop, to no avail. He then came up with an idea and decided to fix the seat himself by recoiling the springs and using an old cowhide to re-cover the seats. After receiving compliments on his work, he referred to the job as: The Great County Seat Cowhide Cover Up.

Gramps didn't know it at the time, but that's the day a new business was born. And after a few years, he passed the process on to my dad, who did the same type of repair for a few neighbors until so many requests came in that he and grandpa decided to officially start a seat cover business.

Dad worked with gramps for a few years, then took the business to the next level and expanded production to cars and trucks, adding boat seat covers and eventually canopy covers for boats. Dad worked hard for years and developed the business until his health slowed him down. When he didn't show up for dinner one night, Mom went looking for him. She found him slumped over the front seat of our neighbor's Econoline van. He had died of a heart attack. That was twelve years ago. It all happened so fast. Mom inherited the business but had no idea what to do with it.

That's when my life changed.

Mom knew how to manage a home, which she does to this day. A seat cover business was another unwanted proposition. She took a week to consider her best options concerning the business. Two of my siblings had graduated from college and moved away from home and on with their careers. They were out. My older sister, Jess, who had a college degree, was busy raising a family with her husband, Ryan. Each of them had too much going on in their lives and showed no interest in the seat cover business. Selling the business was also an option.

When it came down to decision time, Mom asked me to consider taking over TJ's CountySeat Covers. After all, I worked there part-time, alongside Dad since I was a sophomore in high school. What I really enjoyed was organizing inventory and creating new business. So, even though I wasn't Mom's first choice, it fell to me to keep the business running.

My father's death was a huge blow to all of us. It hit me harder than I realized at the time. The seat cover business became a much-needed distraction for the rest of that year. Work became my life. Business was my first and second love. That included anything associated with it: business planning, drawing schematics, graphics, layout, and production. One seat cover project after another – covers , covers, and more covers.

Dad always encouraged us to follow our hearts. I did. It was that encouragement that kept me going strong, sunup to sundown. The thought of failure drove me to put my nose to the grindstone and keep it there. Then one night, after a particularly grueling day, a new idea hit me like the boom of a sailboat coming across the gunnels. What else could be covered? I went into the house and began making new plans. It was midnight, and ideas were coming like crazy.

The next morning, I sat at the breakfast table with mom, and shared my idea to sell our family's seat cover business, then use the proceeds to create an entirely new company.

§

BLAINE MANUFACTURING, SILICON VALLEY, CALIFORNIA

The company's administrative council convened in Blaine's main conference room at noon. Brenda Johnson looked around at the attendees and began the meeting.

"Mr. Blaine asked me to remind everyone to complete your report summaries by the end of day. Send them to me and I'll include them in the meeting agenda. Mr. Blaine will review each of your questions and ideas, and share some new ones of his own, this Friday, yes, Friday the 13th, at 3:30 sharp. I will be sending him those summaries along with the details of his agenda for the meeting with our British friends, the Lampersons. Again, we are set to meet this Friday, here at 3:30."

"Question," Eve said.

"Yes, Eve?"

"That meeting with the Lampersons is next week, right?"

"Yes, I'll have more on that by Friday. Anything else?"

"I have some critical changes that need to take place immediately on our social media," Eve continued. "Is it possible to conference with Rick before he returns?"

"I'm afraid that's out of the question," Brenda said. "What I can do is let him know and ask if he could contact you later today. Will that work?"

"Yes, of course. If he can't, you and I could meet, and you can pass along my thoughts."

§

It's been ten years of all-encompassing work. Initial Public Offering preparation, expanding operations to California, and my adjustment from a rural life to a more energetic and fast-paced lifestyle.

As a result, Blaine Manufacturing steadily increased business each year over the last decade, becoming an industry leader in the production of protective and decorative covers for cell phones, iPads, and anything electronic that needs protection. I never doubted myself and occasionally imagined my father giving me that supportive wave of his hand and thumbs up that suggested, "Hey kid, if you feel it, go for it."

My last journal entry on the dock last night:

"Just found out that Blaine's unique cowhide option is one of our most popular styles for direct-to-consumer ordering this quarter. Talk about farm to consumer."

It's funny how when you're on vacation you think about work, and when at work, you think about vacation.

Granted, it's been two years since my last escapade, but it wasn't just the pressure at work that justified the planning of this current time away. I need to work on cultivating relationships, too, maybe think about getting into a serious relationship.

Being here at the lake, mixing with the locals – real people who I enjoy – helps me appreciate life even more. My big sister, Jess, and Ryan, her husband, allow me to inhabit their spacious two-story log cabin on the lake. They graciously allow me to keep my sailboat here all year round. I call it my sanity supplier.

Relationships are very important to my sister. Jess would like to have more people around for the holidays, and lately she's been asking if I've found the right person. Right. Person. Commitment. It makes sense. Someday I'll be ready.

Ted would say, "What does your gut tell ya?"

Who knows? Is the right person up here in the northwest?

Could the Lake Pend Oreille area, in the panhandle of North Idaho bordered by Montana to the east, Washington to the west, and Canada on top, harbor the perfect person for me? Does she wear logging boots or know how to set a jib? The lake's several little townships and one small city take up sixty percent of its shoreline, extending over one hundred miles in circumference. The rest is wilderness.

And then there's California. Do you suppose she's out there in those woods somewhere? Or is she hung up in traffic on the Ventura Highway?

I have to pay attention and make this a priority. An open mind helps I suppose, but what does that really mean? Be ever watchful at Starbucks? Drive defensively and offensively at the same time? Smile more? It's obvious: From now on, I'll keep an eye out when sailing back and forth up here, and driving down south in the turmoil.

This escape has to be my most productive one to date. I've managed to prioritize my thoughts, which has led to two conclusions: A. My personal life has to come to life. I have to be open to taking time to be with friends, and B. Delegate more management decisions, providing me with more personal time. After all, our business potential at Blaine is as endless and deep as this lake.

My challenge is to manage the two options into co-existence. Like cream in coffee, Ted and his couch, and Brenda with her blue horn-rimmed glasses.

Hey, I got this . . . covered.

§

BOSTON, MASSACHUSETTS – PRESENT DAY

Boston Harbor is normally a very busy place, but not at three in the morning. The silence made it easy to hear, the backlit darkness challenging to see. And playing the waiting game made him nervous. Michael Castillino wanted that third cigarette but went for the doctor-recommended gum option instead. Michael was full of bad habits that were mostly unhealthy for other people. Anger, greed, violence. Off in the distance, a ship's horn sounded three long blasts, and then nothing. There they were, he and his brother, half listening, half watching, one hundred percent ready to pounce.

The harbor lights reminded Michael of people in his life, some brighter than others. He chuckled to himself at the thought as he unwrapped his second stick of gum. Cutting back on smoking proved a challenge, like trying to comfortably fit his six-foot three-inch frame in this economy-size sedan. The car was uncomfortable, untraceable, but most importantly, invisible.

They were following a hunch of his. Michael knew something odd was happening with his shipments at Petrulo Trucking, and he was going to find out what the hell was going on. Giovanni Petrulo and Michael's father started out together in the transportation business. They created a partnership that eventually became a cover for the movement of stolen and illegal goods on the east coast. One truck became two, and all of a sudden, they had a fleet of auto freight and long-haulers.

Michael's father, Carlo, immigrated from Palermo, Sicily to Boston. His mother was already here, her family having arrived from Calabria, the toe of Italy's boot. Michael's father used to joke about his wife "kicking his backside" because of where she came from. His father remained in charge of the family business, but his mother reigned over the home front. Carlo had some health challenges, the biggest problem being early-onset dementia. He had good days and bad, but he was finally convinced to retire after losing track of days in the week and his car one too many times. It became embarrassing. He was ready to turn things over. Michael was next in line.

After old man Petrulo retired two years ago, it was mutually decided between him and Carlo to hand over the supervision of their trucking operation to his lovely and efficient daughter, Lorretta. She masterfully changed the distribution system to include hair salons and barbershops which increased profits substantially. Her reputation for getting what she wanted went far beyond her beautiful Italian features, ones that rivaled a Hollywood starlet's. Her big brown eyes, olive-colored skin, curvy physique, and dark hair were among her most appealing features.

Michael did not suspect Lorretta of any wrongdoing in this unfortunate matter. His concern centered on the night shift manager, Rico Flemming, a half-breed Italian, charged with the storage and preparation of goods for shipment. Rico was the son of old man Petrulo's niece. He had the reputation of showing off by spending beyond his ability to earn. He went through money like ships passing through Boston Harbor. Rico claimed to know more than he did, and, as a result, he did not play well with others. Therefore, he was king of the night shift, where few employees had to put up with his antics.

"That's him," Anthony whispered as he handed the spotter's scope to Michael.

Flemming stood on the loading dock, in clear view, having a cigarette. Michael now had another reason to hate the rat he'd been sniffing out for the past few weeks. Anthony found out that Rico was mouthing off in a local dive called Johnny's about some side business he was starting with stolen goods from the Castillino inventory. Rico and some friends had been celebrating at the local bar after a Red Sox victory. He bragged about being able to adjust the shipping manifests so that some products "just disappeared." A friend of Anthony's passed the information on, and when Michael found out, he was livid.

"Someone needs to change his behavior," was all Michael had said then. He wanted to handle this unfortunate situation himself.

Working things out personally also meant that Anthony would be close to his brother's side. Each watched the other's back, as they had since grade school. They quietly left the car, both dressed in dark clothing, heading for the Petrulo trucking office. Michael gratefully stretched as he walked. Each packed their favorite weapons; Anthony concealed a nightstick while Michael held a nine-millimeter Glock special with an ivory handle. The gun was his pride and joy. As Michael made his way to the loading dock, he smiled at the thought of being fair with the kid. He would give the little prick a chance to confess before allowing his brother to beat the living shit out of him.

Rico Flemming was a Mommone, Momma's boy, who cared about his job only because she worked hard to convince Lorretta to hire Rico in the first place. The job provided him with a lifestyle that he never thought he would be able to manage. Now, after nearly a year, he discovered how he could generate even more from it.

The gold chain around his neck was the latest of five he wore with pride. His goal was to have one for every day of the week. He put out his cigarette, turned on his playlist, and locked the office door before starting his rounds. The last delivery truck just exited the gate, and he prepared to work his magic on some high-priced phones, modems, routers, and laptops contained in that last shipment. By Rico's calculations, this could be his most valuable heist to date. He was careful to cover all his bases. The thought of getting away with it made him smile.

Rico would wait to lock the gate. He was anxious to spend a few minutes in aisle three, with bin thirty-one. He skillfully steered the forklift as he took another long drag on his cigarette. He had all the time in the world now. He was alone; adrenaline was pumping. The surveillance video was off – he'd made sure of that. He had to remember to keep good notes so that he could change quantities on the shipping documents to accurately reflect what he was about to do.

The Castillino brothers moved like cats through the open gate and along the loading dock as Flemming, driving the forklift, went the other direction into the warehouse. Anthony removed two steel picks from his jacket pocket and worked the office door's lock with precision. Within a few seconds, they entered. Michael checked to make sure Rico was alone and watched on the monitor as the kid stopped, lit a second cigarette, then fired up the forklift and drove slowly while listening to his earbuds. They watched as Rico made his selections and carefully stacked the goods into a container on the front of the forklift. Anthony tapped Michael on the arm and pointed to the video control board. He smiled at Michael as he reached across and switched the video record button from "off" to "on." The screen now displayed the words: video record, in red.

After a few minutes of watching and recording Rico's misdeeds, Michael nodded his approval, turned the video record button back to the "off" position and gestured toward the warehouse entrance. Both men made their way to Rico's location and followed him into a back area where he set the bin down and backed away, smiling, as he shut down the forklift.

Rico hummed to his music as he carefully checked the items off his list. He was looking back and forth from the goods to the sheet when two shadows appeared from behind. The cigarette fell from Rico's lips as the shadows stretched further across the concrete ahead of him. Without skipping a beat, Rico turned and with a big, nervous smile, said, "I can explain."

Those were the last words he would comfortably say for the next four months.

Rico was found later that morning with a shattered right femur, six broken ribs, five fingers of his right hand broken, and a jawbone protruding out of a badly swollen face. A deep cigarette burn in the middle of his forehead made him look like he had a third eye. He was stripped down to his boxers, which smelled of urine and were stained with blood. Rico was strapped tight, horizontally, to the forklift with a note attached. It read:

Dear Lorretta, Check your security video. You'll find this employee of yours is a thief, and unless he can be rehabilitated, you should can his ass, the only part of him we didn't touch.
Love, Michael C.

The video that Lorretta watched later clearly showed Rico taking the items and storing them. It did not, however, contain any of the torturous moments that later ensued.

Two days later, Lorretta Petrulo showed up at Saint Elizabeth's Medical Center with flowers and a card. She waited outside the intensive care unit until the nurse showed her into Rico's room as a special favor. Normally, a patient in his condition was not allowed visitors for seventy-two hours.

After the nurse left, Lorretta carefully placed the flowers away from the bed, in the window. She walked slowly, taking in the poor boy's condition. The closer she approached, the madder she became. Lorretta was careful not to touch anything as she hovered over her now-unrecognizable relative. It would have appeared as though she was about to kiss him on the forehead, she was that close. Instead, she whispered: "You stupid little shit. I hope you choke and die on your own vomit."

Lorretta then straightened herself, and backed away from the bed. She stopped, almost forgetting, then unzipped her purse and took out the greeting card. It was one of those nice, heartfelt kinds, embossed with gold writing. At the bottom she signed her name below a brief message:

"Get well soon and find yourself another job. You're dead

to me."

§

The Pend Oreille general store, cafe, and post office is a place out of time with a vintage '40s style decor covering its century-old wooden floors and highlighted by an overworked cast iron wood stove. Pennelope Jane Parker runs the operation. She's generally the tallest woman in the place, slender, five foot, ten inches in her sandals, blue jeans and matching jean top. Penny is single, full of energy, and dedicated to her friends, garden, business, and handsome, white-haired golden retriever, Butch.

Penny's also an accomplished seaplane pilot. She proudly displays her pride and joy, secured to a dock close by. Her bright, orange-colored Beaver De Havilland is a sturdy workhorse and provides additional income during the tourist season, spring to fall. The plane is relatively new, but the design hasn't changed since the 1930s.

When Penny talks about her old and beautiful bird, she points out that it's hard to beat perfection.

Her orange bird is a familiar sight throughout North Idaho, and most especially here at Harbor Beach and the surrounding Pend Oreille area. The locals like to say that the tourist season begins when Penny flies. She also parks the plane on the beach, which is a thrill to watch during the spring and summer months. Part of her multi-faceted business is offering sightseeing tours around the area, and the beach provides the perfect space for advertising her service.

J.T. Small, the elderly and unofficial mayor of Harbor Beach, says that Penny is a natural marketer, a generous boss, and deserves every success. I couldn't agree more. Sometimes I'll just sit on the beach, relaxing with a cold drink, watching as Penny guides the public from her store to her plane and back.

Everyone enjoys watching Penny when she's at the controls

of her beloved plane. She'll tip the wings in a waving motion at people on the beach during take-offs and fly-overs. They love it. The tail of the craft has the offsetting color, blue, with the letter "P" reversed in white on both sides. It's an identifying mark you can see for miles, like the Eskimo on the tail of an Alaska Air jet.

One of Penny's best friends is my sister, Jess, dating back to their college days, which makes her mid-30 something. That's how we met, here at the lake, when our families routinely gathered for vacations and beach sports. You always wanted Penny on your beach volleyball team. She not only had the height; her athletic ability was off the charts. And she's so easy to be around, and at times flirty, so we do that dance on occasion.

Flirting with Penny, who is two years older, is more fun than serious. I remember once as teenagers we borrowed a canoe and paddled out to the center of the lake one night and went skinny dipping. We were having a blast until the sheriff's searchlight hit us. Our good time – laughing and swimming around the canoe, playing hide and seek – came to an abrupt end. Little did we know our voices could be heard on shore by our parents and half the Harbor Beach community. Busted but undaunted, we learned a valuable lesson: quietly enjoy canoe trips, especially at night.

That event, along with a few other young adult adventures, remains embedded in my mind as growth moments with Penny, Jess, and others, who helped us challenge authority, regardless of the consequences. In that regard, Penny is more like a dear friend. Ours is a relationship that provides fun times, so long as the sheriff doesn't get involved.

Last week, Penny posted a large eight-by-ten group photo of all the teenage "lakers," as we came to be known, in her store near the register. We knew we were cool, but Penny was the coolest. Her wide smile, perfect teeth, and Welsh heritage – which explained the dark hair, blue eyes and sharp features –

really stood out.

When she took over the general store, she remodeled to include a small cafe. Her menu was based on her Welsh heritage. Topping the list of culinary specialties is the most delicious Reuben sandwich on homemade bread. The old family recipe left me no choice but to eat at Penny's more than anywhere else in the county.

Travel has become part of my life, my business life. Traveling in my personal life these days is more of an escape. And only Brenda, my Executive Assistant, knows the location of my hideouts, and that I prefer the quiet reminders of life in North Idaho. Traveling north to the lake from Southern California is like being transported back in time to when people communicated differently. It's a place where people still talk face to face instead of on Facebook. People of my parent's generation were admittedly more laid back, though some would say gullible. Life was slower and less complicated. Whenever I share this sentiment with Brenda, she says: "It's time for you to go, isn't it?"

And I'm on the go plenty these days. I put more miles on the Porsche than I should, but it's out of necessity in California where the driving is much different.

Comparing the drive between Tiburon (where I live four and a half days a week) and Venice Beach (where I live on the weekends) to the drive between Spokane (where the plane lands) and Sandpoint (where I escape to) is laughable. The Northwest wins. And when I walk the endless hallways at Blaine, I convert them, in a crazy way, to the hike I take to Penny's store, with its grey-on-black slate steps, encased in moss, under a dozen sixty-foot cedar trees leading up to the front entrance. It's one of nature's most beautiful hallways.

Penny's outdoor sign reads: Harbor Beach General Store and Cafe - Where Hot Food meets Warm Conversation.

My sense of smell is constantly under attack up here. From

the surrounding pines and fresh-cut wood to the coffee aroma from the general store, each aroma attracts the locals like magnets to metal. They gather throughout the morning hours, beginning around six a.m. when Jimmy delivers the Gazette and the day's mail by boat from the State Park launch a few miles away. Jimmy O'Neill is a third-generation "delivery specialist" who makes his rounds six days a week. People ask him if he has ever had a vacation, and he just laughs and says: "This is my vacation. I've never had a regular job." Jimmy is one of those people who really do live the dream.

The pot-bellied stove, properly placed over one hundred years ago, is more popular than any Silverwood theme park attraction. Silverwood is a theme park designated as Disneyland north, located a few miles south of the lake. Silverwood has become a regional attraction over the last decade, though the lake has been the draw to this area for centuries. According to the Harbor Beach self-appointed spokesperson, J.T. Small, the stove in Penny's store was installed in the late 1800s. Consequently, there's plenty of history up here to share, including a stove.

"This here is a Jefferson stove. Designed by none other than Thomas Jefferson himself," J.T. stated in a low and slow tone in front of a few of us gathered before the last sailing regatta.

No one really knows if that's true, but who cares really. It's quite a show, watching as Mr. Small recites the story over and over, with conviction and dark fresh-brewed coffee in hand, trying not to spill as he embellishes. Watching J.T. and his audience of lake characters is just as good as witnessing a well-acted stage play on Broadway.

It's the old-fashioned way of life here on the lake at Harbor Beach that keeps a long-time visitor like me both mystified and grounded. In some ways, it also keeps Blaine Manufacturing's conveyor belts running. Connecting this place with industry may be a big stretch, but it's a stretch I believe in.

Life up here does have its challenges, however. For example, you never know how much you depend on your phone until you can't find bars, which, in the end, could drive you to drink more. How ironic. Cell phone service here is spotty at best, and the store's fax machine is considered the latest in technology according to Mr. Small.

Anytime an important call needs to be made, I either raise my phone high in the sky, standing on one foot at the end of the dock hoping for bars, or launch the sailboat as I'm doing now. Butch, Penny's retriever, is along for the ride too. Butch is good company, and he could care less about crewing or my cell phone service. Butch prefers his time in the wind; he barks at the gulls and keeps a constant vigil as we cut a path through the water. The cell service reappears right away, out here, away from shore and the hills surrounding Harbor Beach. Again, Butch could care less.

I've determined that maintaining a cell phone on a boat can be tricky. Because of a freak incident recently, the phone sails with me in a carefully placed "dry pack" located close by. Last week, as I sailed into a brisk wind with Penny's phone, it fell out of my jacket and onto the deck, outside the pilot sitting area in the stern. She let me use hers while mine charged. I watched as her phone slowly made its way around the deck, past winches, cleats, and the top of the cabin. It was like playing a wild game of pinball, by moving the helm back and forth and adjusting sails, instead of pushing buttons.

Eventually, the latest version of the iPhone – the one that didn't belong to me – circumnavigated the deck, then finally ended up within reach. Grabbing her phone was like golfing by yourself and sinking a hole-in-one. No one would ever know, especially Penny, the feeling of relief or accomplishment, but that's all that mattered as I slid her phone back into my jacket and zipped it shut. I made a mental note to send her a gift pack of our latest cell phone covers.

After a couple hours of comfortable sailing with Butch asleep at my feet, I change our heading back to Harbor Beach. Thoughts of returning to the dock are interrupted by feelings of work in California. One of my first business appointments, next week, will be spent catching up with some very special visitors from London. They are a bright spot on my wall-to-wall schedule. Brenda carved out two hours for the Brits, and I can't wait.

Butch's boat exits are not for the faint of heart. He watches me, then the dock, then back to me, smiles, and at the right moment, makes the leap. When he lands safely, I say a small prayer in thanks. Not necessarily because he makes it, but because no one was hurt in the process. I imagine he either can't wait to get back, or he had thoughts of never being on land again.

After getting back today, we – mostly me – tie the boat to the dock. Well, he actually licks my hands as I attempt to secure the boat. I assume his licking is a sign that he's trying to help, which turns out to be no help whatsoever. Or it's his expression of thanks for making it back safely. Good boy, Butch.

My first mate sticks around as I go below deck to pour a drink. The sky is turning a deep purple-blue – Venus appears first in the sky, and I salute her. Next, as is our tradition, Butch and I walk out to the end of the dock, scotch in one hand, throwing stick in the other, Butch leading the way. There are two lime-green Adirondack chairs waiting for us. Butch takes one; I sit in the other. I look up: "One . . . two . . ."

We're counting shooting, and eventually, all stars tonight. Butch is looking up. I'm convinced he's counting by twos. Great, now I have to start over, Butch. The lake is still and quiet . . . until I hear the faint snores from my friend in the next chair. So much for stick throwing.

2. "If the Song Keeps Playing in Your Head, Write It Down."

I decided to lay low for the evening. Pink Floyd's *Dark Side of the Moon* playing in the background helped me concentrate as I picked through the bookshelf while mouthing the words to "Brain Damage." My selection: *Think Like A Freak*, in lieu of sailing, or going to the bar for a late lunch and happy hour, allowed me to relax and sink into a title I'd been wanting to read for some time. The book turned out to be a page-turner, causing me to consider things I didn't know I needed to know. Know what I mean?

Sure enough, these freakish authors had a very different take on all kinds of things. Take gun control, for instance. I don't own a gun but believe people have the right to do so according to the law. Anyway, I gave it my best shot. The most intriguing story, however, concerned a new treatment for ulcers that used recycled poop. No shit. A study that I was happy not to have taken a part in, no matter how much it paid. Different, freakish thinking, is very appealing, if you have the stomach for it.

What would those freakish authors say about my management by escape?

The next morning at seven a.m., the weather looked clear, and the wind held steady at eight miles per hour out of the south. I set off for the dock to take a quick dip and to launch "Fore Sail," one of the prettiest sloops ever built. It makes my day when people can't help but comment about the name written across the stern. Playing with words is just plain fun. When the boat is moored in a public area, someone eventually asks:

"What a beautiful boat. Is it . . . for sale?"

After thanking them for the compliment, I don't leave them hanging for too long.

"Why, no. What gave you that idea?"

Then I wait and observe. Most people don't know how or if they should respond as I raise my eyebrows and turn my head slightly. Ted thinks I have a screw loose. Really? Just one?

Fore Sail is forty feet of the finest hull, wood-planking and teak decking. Built in 1939, the two white pine masts, a mizzen and a main, are as strong as they were when the boat was built in Nova Scotia. The two new sets of sails need to be given a hardy workout, which finally happened that day.

A good sailor works with all weather conditions. I was thankful that this day was perfect; the weather made for a more enjoyable ride for the guests that joined and for me. Penny, with Butch tagging along, stopped short of the boat. She said, "Hey, sailor. Permission to come aboard?"

She carried a picnic basket and raised Butch's dog dish. "Hey, we all need to eat," Penny gestured toward Butch as they climbed up.

"Wait, I haven't said, 'permission granted.'"

The hand that pushed me out of the way was expected and well-deserved. Penny knew my sense of humor and preparation routine for sailing. She also knew the ropes, so to speak. She helped untie the lines from the dock, as Butch does his thing next to me, announcing our departure by barking at the gulls. Penny hops in – Butch follows.

I started the small engine that worked to take us slowly out of the slip and out into the harbor into a slight and welcoming breeze. Just as we set the main, my phone rang. Penny took the helm. It was Brenda.

"You ready to return, Mr. Blaine?"

"How about two more weeks?" I said with a smile that caused Penny to laugh and Brenda to pause.

"Just kidding, I'm ready. What's up?"

She gave me the good news first before emailing the current business report and my updated schedule. The good news was from the sales team as they continued to set quarterly sales records. Part of the reason was our new focus on expanding our territories east, with the goal of achieving distribution coast to coast.

"Any surprises?"

"No surprises," she responded as if she was reviewing the sheet just to make sure. "Let's see, in addition to the sales report the new production line is up and running."

"That is good to hear." I paused for a few seconds. "How are you, Brenda? I mean, are you holding up okay?" I had to know how she felt. Brenda was the kind of person you could challenge and who would meet or exceed the mark every time. She kept setting records at Blaine; only no one was keeping score but me. Every successful CEO either has a Brenda at their right hand or is already their own Brenda.

"I'm fine. Everybody is doing their part. You leave a big hole, but you know we understand."

"Looking forward to Friday's meeting, good work. Can't wait to get a jump on the new quarter."

Brenda had someone in her office. I heard activity on the other end of the line, so we ended the conversation when I asked to be passed on to the head of production.

Brenda had things under control. After giving the production manager my congratulations for a job well done, I stowed my phone in the dry pack and stood, staring straight ahead at the water, watching for the wind.

"Hey, captain. Yoo-hoo, over here!" Penny shouted as the wind came up.

She and Butch had waited patiently. I handed her my bag containing the phone and asked that she stow it under one of the seating benches in the cockpit.

Even though I had never seen Penny give herself a complete day off during the season, I figured we probably had a few hours to enjoy sailing somewhere. She asked me where we were headed today, and I suggested Garfield Bay. Sure enough, she had to be back by four for a full flight scheduled at five.

Penny loved to sail. She learned from her father, Joe. He'd explained that if she knew how to sail, she could then learn to fly a plane since both used the wind to move. Penny looked like she was ready to relax a little and let herself enjoy this part of the day. We sailed in a light to moderate breeze, and after two hours, anchored in Garfield Bay for lunch.

"This is a classic day," Penny sighed as she sat up on one of the long orange cushions that ringed the cockpit area. She reached into her cooler and handed me one of her famous tuna delight sandwiches. I love tuna, which tasted even better in the shade on the water with lemonade.

We were only a mile and a half from Harbor Beach in a shaded cove naturally protecting us from the noon sun. There was no beach – Garfield Bay being one of the deepest on the lake.

"Hey, did I tell you about my baby?"

The look on my face must have revealed my wrong perception about Penny and a baby.

"My seaplane, silly."

Penny's seaplane had just been refurbished, with a new bright orange coat and blue accents. On any given day during the season, the plane sat stately next to her customized dock, lakeside, about fifty yards from the Harbor Beach General Store and Cafe. Every time I see the plane, a feeling of pride hits me. My friend, Penny, a laker, is the genius behind that service.

She learned to fly from one of the best, her father, of course. I'm not sure which she enjoyed most in life, flying or running her store/cafe business. If you asked her, she would shrug her shoulders, flash a playful smile, and say: "Flying back to the cafe."

"Dad just finished applying the detailing to the plane at the airport. Have you noticed?"

I had a mouthful and just shook my head.

"He added the pinstripe and my new slogan, all in blue. Took him three days in the hangar to do the application. He's the one that flew the plane back this morning."

"What's the slogan?"

"Come Fly with Me," she slurred as she sipped her water. "Dad is a huge Sinatra fan, and so am I."

Now it all made sense. Joe Parker serenaded us one night two years ago, after only two beers, on Penny's dock, with a few Sinatra standards. Lannie had made the request, and he was more than willing to treat the surrounding area with his talent. Her sense of pride when mentioning her father was clearly evident, although her blush was somewhat hidden by a nice tan she was working on.

"Not bad for a business lady."

"What?"

"Your tan."

"Thanks for noticing."

"I think it needs to get wet."

"Wait, what?"

I caught her off guard, and in one fluid motion I gently lifted her up, then carefully leaned just enough to slowly deliver the two of us over the rail with Butch close behind. Both Butch and Penny were on top of me in an instant.

"No fair. Two, *gulp*, against one. Help. Somebody, anybody!"

"There's no one to save you, captain, no one for miles. This is mutiny in the bay. Deal with it."

They ganged up on me. The water, cool at first, became even more refreshing. We swam around for the better part of an hour. I took a moment to do some snorkeling under the boat, checking the rudder fittings and making sure the hull's surface was clean.

Not long after the swim and lunch, we departed Garfield Bay, setting a course back to Harbor Beach. After saying our goodbyes, and a kiss on the cheek with a simultaneous pinch on my backside cheek, I playfully limped back toward the cabin as Penny and Butch made their way back along the beach. Before she left, I shared the fact that I knew about the detailing of her plane because of a random stop I'd made, two days ago, at the Sandpoint Airport.

§

TWO DAYS AGO AT THE SANDPOINT AIRPORT, HANGAR 14

I had some time on my hands and knew that Penny's plane was receiving a new facelift. So, I decided to stop by the Sandpoint Airport, only to find Joe Parker sweating bullets. The detailing on Penny's seaplane was taking longer than he anticipated. He'd hired a crew out of Spokane's Felts Field Airport to handle the majority of the work. They were experts in vinyl and aircraft paint applications. Although they came highly recommended, Joe acted as supervisor on the job. He knew to stay out of their way and let them do their work. His job was to supervise the project and approve the finishing touches on the aircraft. But the application work required more "drying time" than had been projected.

Unfortunately, Penny had a deadline to meet. Important clients were scheduled to fly thirty miles north to a lake closer to the Canadian border in two days. Joe split his work time on the project between detailing and engine maintenance. The rotation of work helped to make the time go faster, but the twelve-hour days were beginning to wear on him.

"Okay, we're ready to place the last of the decals. That gives us about thirty-six hours of drying time, cross your fingers," Joe told the man assisting him with the decals.

Joe told me later that when he left the hangar on the second night, dog-tired, he turned to look at Penny's plane under the glow of halogen lights. The old plane looked as though it had just rolled off the assembly line. The job turned out better than he envisioned.

"A classic look for a classy lady," he'd said.

I've watched Joe devote all his spare time to Penny since his wife, Penny's mother, passed away two years ago. He recently moved full-time to Lake Pend Oreille from Moscow, Idaho, where Penny spent her teenage years.

He had the time, having retired from the Air Force. Joe, and his wife, Lisa, had plans to travel the world. They enrolled in a class together to learn Italian. Her illness kept them closer to home, and Penny, who had decided to create a life at Pend Oreille, lived one hundred and forty miles north. After Lisa's death, Joe turned his attention to Penny, their only child. He knew she was serious about purchasing a newer seaplane, and asked if he could assist in any way.

"Are you kidding, Dad? I was hoping you'd ask," she replied.

Joe and Lisa had discussed helping Penny make the purchase of a new plane. Penny never knew.

Over the course of several trips to Seattle and Portland, a decision was made, and the fifteen-year-old seaplane became available when a new owner failed to make payments. Joe, who was cleared to fly amphibious aircraft, along with Penny, both flew the plane from Lake Union in Seattle to Lake Pend Oreille, landing several times, partly to refuel but also to sightsee along the way. On one occasion, while attempting to land on Lake

Roosevelt, high winds made the maneuvering extremely difficult. Joe was there for Penny in the right-side seat but decided to coach her instead of taking over as the plane bounced them around the cockpit. A good decision as it turned out, because Penny proved to be more than capable of handling the low-flying aircraft.

"Penny, remember as you land on water – in high wind or if you have engine trouble – keep your speed up as you angle the nose down to level. And stand on the rudder if that's what it takes. Make sure of your heading, straight in with landing gear up into the sponsons. You're in control, or there is no control."

"Got it, Dad."

"Ti amo, baby." Joe loved his little girl and was amazed at her piloting skills.

Penny's parents always worried that she was taking on too much. Her various business enterprises had been mounting up: store, restaurant, post office and now, expanding her flying service. Joe tended to agree, just to a lesser extent than his wife. He knew that Penny would ask for help if she needed it. So far, she was settling into a new life nicely, in a beautiful part of the world, making her own way. Plus, she had friends like me and my sister Jess who became like family over the years.

Since Penny's father decided to move closer, she asked him to become her chief mechanic. Joe had years of experience with aircraft engines and avionics because of his time in the Air Force. He was more than willing to honor her request. When Joe relocated, he settled on a small rancher right on the Pend Oreille River, five miles from Sandpoint, close to Penny and her plane.

Penny considered her dad a business confidant, there for her when she needed him. He also volunteered with the Pend Oreille Water Rescue Unit, whose chief, Chet Davis, happened to be an old friend and my sailing buddy.

Joe was happy to report the good news about being able to meet her deadline this week. And as he handed her the keys to the plane this morning, she asked if he wanted to go to coffee. Normally, he would have said yes, but not today.

"Raincheck? I'm going home to bed."

§

BOSTON, MASSACHUSETTS

The Boston Coffee House is a central location for all kinds of business people, college students, and tourists to meet. The building, in which the House, its shortened name, is now located, served as Boston's first post office, dating back to colonial times. Visitors enjoy the ornate ceiling and roughed-out plaster walls that reflect decades of history. Lorretta Petrulo considered this quaint place *her* House. She didn't have to stand in line like the others. Her drink was brought to her: a decaf salted-caramel breve latte.

"Thank you, Robbie," she said to the waiter as she carefully held the white china mug. She blew on the soft white foam and carefully studied the room, watching for him as she took her first sip.

Lorretta was cupping her hands around the drink when Michael Castillino entered through a side hallway. My God, he is a handsome hunk, she thought as Michael removed his dark glasses, noticed her, and smiled in her direction. After ordering, he made his way to the table with dark roast drip coffee in a signature BCH mug, decorated with colonial landmark drawings.

"So, how are things, Mikey?"

Lorretta remained seated as she crossed her legs, removed her gum, and smiled at the man. He looked at her and smiled once again as he sat, his weight slipping a bit of Lorretta's latte onto its saucer.

"Things are good, Lorretta. Careful, I don't want to spill this on you," he offered as he gently placed his cup on the table to the side of her. He liked to sit so he could watch the front door at all times. It was a habit. Their conversation meandered for a few minutes before she put her hand on his knee, and with a sweet smile revealing perfect teeth, turned to look straight into his deep brown eyes, and quietly uttered:

"If you EVER touch one of my employees again, I'll take it personally. And you don't want that, big boy."

Michael put his cup to his lips, slowly sipped, then scanned the room as he gently set the cup down, still not looking at her. Lorretta watched his movements, removed her hand from his knee, and sat up straight. Michael continued to look around, and without looking directly at her, replied:

"Better that small-time little prick than the entire warehouse crew, Lorretta." Michael said this as he continued to keep watch on the room.

"Is that a threat?"

Michael finally turned and fixed his gaze on her; they locked eyes.

"No, Lorretta. I'm sharing my options. I had one more, but a fire would have endangered my property, as well as yours."

"No, Michael. You don't get to play the tough guy card with me, remember? We scratch each other's back, drink scotch on occasion, and flirt when no one's around. So, no, mister big shot. My nephew is on an extended vacation, no thanks to you and your overzealous brother. He won't be returning to his job, in case you have any concerns. I apologize for his actions and promise to take a personal interest in your shipments. You can rest assured that your future business with me will be safe. Let the past go, amante."

She flashed a beautiful smile, then added, "If you have any questions about shipping or hauling or life in general, let ME know. Okay, Mikey?"

Michael kept staring into his coffee, jaw clenching and

unclenching. Only one person in the world had ever dared to call him by that name. After a few seconds, his face suddenly relaxed, and he looked up smiling bigger than ever.

"Got it, Lorretta. And by the way, you look . . . nice."

She pushed her chair back and stood to leave. Michael started to rise, but a perfectly manicured hand touched his shoulder. He sat but kept his eyes on her. Lorretta winked.

"Good boy."

She walked, slowly moving her hips back and forth to the door as half the people in the place watched. Her tight black skirt appeared to be signaling left and right as she made her way through the door that had been opened for her by a sheepish-looking, wide-eyed, accountant-type gentleman in a tan suit.

She is the sexiest truck fleet owner I've ever known, Michael thought as his smile slowly faded. Lorretta Petrulo is a devious creature, he reminded himself.

Then he replaced his dark glasses and left out the back way in which he'd entered. Michael felt more comfortable walking down dark hallways and into back alleys. He'd left his car in a loading zone. Anyone doing business back here knew not to touch it. His thoughts were on the lady he'd just had coffee with. Lorretta was hard to forget, easy on the eyes, and tough to do business with if you feared her.

Devious was the term that Lorretta's high school advisor used in telling her parents about a bathroom incident. It involved two girls who were found in the girls' restroom, duct-taped like mummies to each other. Both students had made fun of Lorretta's handmade outfit earlier in the day. Their taunts, and the laughter that ensued, didn't sit well with Lorretta. After all, her mother stayed up late hand-sewing most of her clothes in order to save money. More importantly though, she loved Lorretta, and sewing for her little girl brought them closer.

What made the bathroom incident worse was the fact that

the girls weren't discovered until after school had been closed for several hours. The youth were located after their parents reported them missing. The advisor, who was used to managing lesser issues like food fights in the cafeteria, could not imagine anything like this happening at Saint Mary's Catholic.

She called the school principal and, together, they met at the Petrulo home later the next day. Lorretta, her mother and father, the advisor, and the school principal sat around the dining room table as the advisor described the condition of the girls: dehydrated, scared, and in pain from laying in their own pee and in one position nearly all night. When the advisor relayed how difficult it was to remove the duct tape, Lorretta suppressed a laugh by coughing into her napkin.

"She used nearly a whole roll of the stuff," the principal sighed.

"They will obviously be in need of psychological therapy for years to come," the advisor offered as tears began to well up.

Lorretta's mother was taken by surprise. She could not imagine her little girl doing such a thing. Her father didn't say a word; he remained calm as the advisor suggested various disciplinary options. Mrs. Petrulo would be the one to carry out the sanctions they all agreed to, which included an appointment with a therapist for Lorretta. Mr. Petrulo, who had the most discerning look on his face, didn't seem upset when he suggested:

"Let this be a lesson for all concerned, not just our daughter. You would be wise to think carefully before you pass along judgment only for Lorretta."

He said this in a slow, deliberate tone, raising his right hand and extending the index finger to make his point. To everyone in the room, it felt more like a warning, rather than a suggestion. Lorretta was pleased to see both the advisor and principal sitting quietly with their mouths agape as her father stood. Both the student advisor and the principal caught his icy stare as Carlo carefully pushed in his chair before exiting the room.

It was at that moment, Lorretta realized a special connection had formed between her and her father. Mr. Petrulo had become more powerful and well-respected in the community. He had various business arrangements and some very special "associates" that visited the house often. She never really paid that much attention to what he did for a living. Up until now, it didn't matter. She made a point to find out who these people were and how they interacted with her and her father.

Other misdeeds followed. And so, the decision was made to send Lorretta to boarding school for her senior year. That turned out to be one of the first stepping stones embedded in a long road that led to a relentless life of crime. At the new school, she managed to organize a drug ring that specialized in peddling prescriptions stolen from houses that she and her girlfriends voluntarily cleaned or visited socially.

Lorretta made enough money from that enterprise to put herself through two years of college. She also bought her first car, a Ford van. It just made sense at the time. She learned and earned enough to leave school and enter her father's business with his complete blessing, though it upset her mother. Tough, Lorretta thought.

It turned out that as a take-charge person, Lorretta was very good at being bad, a quality that only grew in the real world.

§

Penny's seaplane roared overhead with a full complement of excited passengers. She was headed north towards Bonners Ferry, then east to the Montana border, and back around the lake to Harbor Beach. She told me the whole trip takes less than an hour, most of it at low altitude.

We have flown north over a similar route together before. Penny allowed me to take the controls once we were airborne, switching from pilot to instructor. She enjoys sharing the sky with clouds, birds, and special friends. Her bird is loud and flies low and slow, which creates a more exciting experience for the passengers. It also entertains the witnesses below who eventually become customers.

As Penny flew out of sight, I docked Fore Sail on the pier outside of Penny's store. After locking the hatches and securing the lines, I headed for the post office, located in a corner area of Penny's store.

On my walk I saw her coming out of the store before she noticed me: Lannie Culbertson, owner of Harbor Beach Barber & Tavern.

Lannie's high energy showed as she flashed an engaging smile. She was wearing sturdy leather sandals, cut-off jeans and a psychedelic Grateful Dead t-shirt. She was running, with her salt and pepper ponytail swinging freely behind as she came flying off the steps and looked up.

"Ricky, I'm throwing down the gauntlet. We're going to win that regatta cup back next year!" She laughed and hugged me, then asked: "When are you leaving, dear?"

"Friday."

"Friday? Come by for a haircut and a beer soon. You need it."

"The beer?"

"No, smart ass, the haircut," she blurted out as she released her hold and side-stepped me, waving hello to a couple as she went.

HBT is right on the water with a dark-stained wooden deck hanging out some sixty feet over the water. It is literally the oldest hangout on the lake. Guests are seated at four-tops with bright blue tablecloths over dark wooden tables, and four community tables that seat ten to twelve each run down the middle of the deck.

Multi-colored lights crisscross through a wisteria vine that clutches tightly to a pergola, built to withstand heavy weather, over the entire deck. Overseeing the whole experience is the neon Hamms Beer sign showcased in the peak of an upstairs window overlooking the deck. That dancing bear can be seen by boaters coming from a mile away.

Inside there's an old wooden bar with a brass foot rail right out of a western movie. Behind the bar, to the left of the vintage cash register, sits a two-way radio. Lannie monitors all air traffic in the area, mostly Penny's takeoffs and landings, along with some U.S. Forest Service surveillance and general aviation that flies from the local airport in Sandpoint. There is no control tower in the area, so it's incumbent upon the pilots to announce their movement over a general aviation frequency, which Lannie monitors.

The stools, along the bar, are topped with old tractor seats, painted in various colors. My favorite color is green, of which there are three. Lannie says they are reserved for big asses. I love that woman.

The interior centerpiece is a huge fireplace made out of river rock, with a Ross Hall, black and white, photograph of the lake frozen over in winter late at night with a full moon.

Lannie, a former hair designer from Portland, Oregon, cuts hair, daytime only, for both men and women, mostly by appointment. She sees men on Monday and Friday, then ladies each Tuesday and Thursday. Wednesday is her day off, and the weekends are too busy for hairstyling. Customers enjoy relaxing in her vintage black leather barber chair, complete with ivory accents, which sits off to the side of the bar. She'll simultaneously visit with customers, cut hair, and supervise the serving of drinks and food. It's always amazing to me how she spins, cuts, dodges and weaves, all without spilling a drop or wounding a patron.

"Men are lousy multi-taskers. They're better at other things, when they're up for it," Lannie told me one time with a wink.

She caught me journaling one night in the bar when she said

that. And I wasn't sure if she was referring to my writing or sex. No, that's not true. She was talking about sex.

Ted, my therapist, believes journaling is good for the soul and helps people get in touch with their inner selves. This trip is my latest attempt to write every day, after promising Ted, for months, that the journal will become part of my daily routine. I suppose if I ever get writer's block, that means I'm dead, so I keep writing. My journal has slowly become a more familiar part of me.

3. "Take a Deep Breath, the View Will Take It Away."

I was up with the sun on my last full day on Pend Oreille. The morning was, as usual, beautiful, which made it difficult to leave. So peaceful. The sky opened from a dark to a soft blue. I had yoga on my mind. Monday, Wednesday or Thursday were intended to be yoga on the dock days. Good intentions locked horns with bad behavior, resulting in fewer days of meditation and relaxing poses than I had originally planned.

Yoga came into my life because a client suggested I be more flexible. At the time, I thought she was talking about my personality. I didn't realize that she meant my body as well. I do now. Especially today, I envy yoga teachers. Life seems to slow down around them. I wish they could bottle that aura of stillness so that some of us could swallow a pill or take a whiff of the vapors and eliminate a major portion of the bending, twisting, and rolling required. Namaste to you too.

After yoga, I read Brenda's work summary. She emailed a very comprehensive report that I retrieved earlier this morning at Penny's store, on my way up the lake to the Starbucks in Sandpoint. Some people think the Northwest is so remote, but not Starbucks. I'm sure they're planning to put a location on the moon someday. With the report in hand, I now have what's needed to prepare for tomorrow afternoon's meeting in San Jose with the Blaine senior management team.

Blaine Manufacturing employs some of the most creative minds in Silicon Valley, or anywhere as far as I'm concerned. They believe in our company mission because they came up with it: To produce innovative products at a fair price. We don't need anal perfection; Steve Jobs I'm not. Our products are unique, as they serve to protect valuable pieces of equipment. Our collective company's expectations run as high as Penny's seaplane on a Saturday afternoon charter. And that goes for all of us, starting with me.

I finished reviewing Brenda's email checklist and moved onto an envelope of important documents that required an ink signature and overseas mailing, which I'll mail in Spokane on my way to the airport. Among the paperwork, I found an envelope from the mother of a friend. I was taken aback as I read her Thank You note. It referred to her son, Mike, a good friend.

One of Blaine's most innovative production developments came from Mike's creative genius. He had a science background, and because of a freak accident in his lab, he developed a thin coating process for all kinds of surfaces. He gave us the first opportunity to do something with the process, and sold it to Blaine a few years ago. Eventually, he sold us the patent when Mike couldn't strike a deal with a large furniture manufacturer. The application didn't work as well for wood-grained furniture, but it has for us.

Unfortunately, Mike fell on hard times, and volunteered for the Army as a last resort. He felt more discipline was needed in his life. He deployed to Iraq where he died serving his country.

My dad used to say: "You make plans and then God enters the picture and everything changes."

Part of my patent deal with Mike was compensation in the form of a royalty, based on sales, forever. Instead of going to Mike, royalties now go to his parents. While they're grateful for the income, they don't completely understand what Mike did to improve Blaine's instrument covers. I know his father questioned my involvement in any business deal with his son, but Mike's mother, whose note I just read, was always understanding and very sweet.

I think about Mike once in a while, especially when I have to make the tough decisions regarding product expansion. I mentioned that in my note back to Mike's mother and father.

My flight tomorrow is in the afternoon, and I'm ready for it. I'll travel back to Silicon Valley and dive headfirst into a fast-moving stream of consciousness. It's time to leave, and the anticipation is slowly creating butterflies in the abdominal area.

After the Blaine meeting, I'll drive to Los Angeles, Venice Beach, for the weekend. I need to check on my condo and spend some quality time with beach-loving surfer friends.

The first step, however, is a ninety-minute drive from paradise here in Idaho to the airport in neighboring Washington. That's part of the allure of this place; it's not like the anthill I'm headed to.

But, for now, I'm headed for my haircut. It's Thursday, meaning Ladies' Day, but Lannie let it slide. Then lunch and a beer afterward. Being around Lannie is invigorating and even more pleasing when beer is involved.

Slowly and methodically, my thoughts are shifting from escape and into business mode. Later, I'll pull all the reports from my key people, review those, and create questions. My team is a potent mixture of proprietary wisdom and loyalty, and I appreciate their points-of-view.

My co-captain is Jose Taragano, the executive team's right arm. Jose is officially COO, but I think of him as my "hitman." He's six-feet three-inches tall and weighs in at around two hundred and thirty pounds. Jose is a good-looking Spanish/Italian, married, with one boy, and one on the way. Jose takes no crap from anyone, except you know who: Me and possibly his lovely wife, Tanya. Jose and Brenda correspond daily, even more when I'm away.

Brenda's resume keeps expanding in the right direction. We have worked closely together for a few years now. She replaced two people who couldn't keep up even if they wore track shoes. Petite, five-foot-five, blonde hair, blue eyes, self-assured with a smile that just feels good to all who witness it.

Brenda's family homesteaded in the Midwest, Iowa. Her father and mother farm over ten thousand acres of corn. She has two siblings, both younger, and according to her, plenty of relatives. She loves her family but felt a need to get away from the farm life to create a better sense of self. That statement she made, in a later conversation, resonated with me. She chose a more metropolitan locale on the west coast. Brenda lived with her aunt while she looked for work and within a week, she found herself on the selling side of a perfume counter at Nordstrom in San Francisco, near Union Square.

Although Brenda appreciated the opportunity to work downtown in a large city, she always continued to look for a job that more closely resembled what she majored in at college – Human Resources, with a minor in Economics. Her job search eventually led to Blaine Manufacturing.

We literally ran into one another one day when I was coming out of our parking garage elevator. Walking out of an elevator while reading a phone message was never a good idea. We bumped, or more correctly, I bumped into her.

"Excuse me. Is this Blaine Manufacturing?"

"Yes, and it's my fault, sorry," I answered distractedly, looking over her head at my car. I was running late.

She could tell I was in a hurry, and graciously stood out of the way as I ran off apologizing, again, for bumping her. Her interview obviously went well, and two weeks later, she and I met in a conference room for an employee orientation meeting. She was on her third day at Blaine and sat quietly with six others as I entered the room.

Jose had just finished explaining his position with the company, then turned to introduce me.

"Everyone, please welcome our president and chief executive officer, Rick Blaine."

The room was full of impressive new employees. Each one looked me straight in the eye as we shook hands. When I came to Brenda, she said:

"Nice running into you, again, Mr. Blaine."

Immediately, her comment hit me. I remember thinking at the time: This lady is impressive. She added:

"By the way, you drive a very cool car. My uncle has a seventies model 911 Porsche. It's his pride and joy.

Weeks later, while reading through our employee reports, I learned more about Ms. Brenda Johnson. She quickly gained a reputation for solving problems and offering up new ideas such as improving our Employee Handbook. One thing led to another – mainly my need for a better working relationship with those working with me in the executive office – and she interviewed to be my assistant.

Interviews were scheduled in my office, and after meeting two sent over by a headhunter, Brenda walked in. Brenda's business knowledge was extremely impressive, plus she had an incredible awareness of Hollywood movies. Especially film noir.

"Great poster. *Casablanca*, one of my favorites. We did a case study of it in college. I have a copy of the screenplay somewhere in the basement at home in Iowa."

That did it. I mean, she came highly recommended for the job, AND she was an old Hollywood film buff. I admire take-charge people. Ms. Johnson and my grand uncle would have gotten along just fine.

"Welcome to the Executive Offices, Brenda."

Men have impulsive behavior, and women, intuition. I get it. But being impulsive has been a family trait for as long as I can remember. I may have used it for most of our hires, except for one.

Eve, CMO, is chief marketing officer. She is a person on a mission. No one gets in her way, only out of it. Point of fact: She hung a well-used highway sign, riddled with a few bullet holes, above her door in the hallway. (Where she obtained the sign is anyone's guess, but no one is asking.) The bright red on white metal piece reads: "Wrong Way." I felt the sign was counterproductive at first, but now I find it refreshing. Eve does not like to waste time. Everything she touches has a deadline connected to it. And she has no time for small talk. Everyone, including me, has to do their homework before meeting with Eve. I love it.

I'm in her office, or she's in mine constantly, because of all our social networking and related advertising. Eve feels it is necessary to maintain top awareness in our markets, which means we are constantly promoting the benefits of our protective products and analyzing the results. Eve is so good at what she does, it's scary.

Everything Blaine Manufacturing does has my name all over it, so I have to be kept up to date on what I've said, or done. That may sound odd at first, but it's true. Eve and I have to be on the same track, as she makes it all happen, according to plan, even when I'm on hiatus.

Last time I returned from hiatus, Eve had some very choice words for me behind closed doors:

"Where in the hell have you been, Rick?"

I thank God for her every day. She keeps Blaine out in front of the media, and me on my toes.

Rounding out our management team are Victor and Jodie, co-national sales directors. Victor makes calls on Industrial and Manufacturing, Jodie focuses on Sports and Fashion. Ashley is the Customer Service manager that every company would love to hire; she gives service a good name. Frank Connors is the Vice President in charge of Production. I like to call him Major, because he runs that department like a military unit. He sports the appropriate Marine crew cut. I mean, if you're going to be a leader, you should look like one as well as act like one. Jose and Major connect to make products fly off the conveyor belts, on time in order to meet customer demand. When we first started here in Silicon Valley, our product line was smaller and therefore easier to supply. Today, nearly a decade later, we've added to our production capabilities in order to keep up with demand.

Our company is growing, and everyone in our employ means a great deal to me. We employ nearly five hundred people, which is moderate compared to other firms in our arena. Blaine is on a positive track. Our turnover is low. Part of the reason: Our wages are higher than the industry average. We can't afford turnover; we can afford happy employees. I'm a fortunate son who enjoys rewarding success.

The transition into my work mode has taken hold as I finish with my questions for the team. I have to; friends will be stopping by soon to see me off. I opened a bottle of Maryhill red, with a few on standby. It's time to celebrate.

I raise a glass of my favorite red blend to salute the lake. Today it's like a Monet painting out the kitchen window, perfectly framed. Fore Sail is sealed tight, docked next to our boathouse that's anchored by rusty iron pillars, which allow the dock to move up and down with the water level, spring to late summer. Up and down, down and up, in a constant rhythm.

I'm ready; it's time to go. C'est la vie.

4. "All Good Things Must Come to an End, Unless You're Too Busy."

Driving from the lake to Spokane's airport goes quickly in comparison to San Francisco and L.A. commutes. Ninety minutes of just sitting in a car, glaring at my exit ramp only a stone's throw away, can be the cause for a revolution. Then again, sitting in my Porsche, listening to my playlist will turn a bad attitude around, quick.

My mind is picking up speed. Thoughts of tying the perfect slipknot around a cleat give way to landing a new account, or reviewing the latest sales figures, which indicate we're up 8% overall year-to-date. Nice, congratulations to all. But we can, and will, do better. In addition to the good news about sales increases, the team is going to hear a few ideas for saving time and money, by streamlining our production on the iPhone covers. Innovation can also be a good reason for celebration.

One idea came to me when I was on an early morning walk with Butch before leaving Idaho behind.

There we were on one of our usual cedar-lined paths when Butch suddenly went on alert. He stopped dead in his tracks and began to whine. I froze, thinking it was either a bear or Sasquatch. Neither appeared until, finally, something even more sinister emerged. The scent hit me like a ton of bricks, a heavy aroma from THE largest skunk I'd ever seen. This guy should be in the skunk hall of fame. The nose-shuddering animal was in shock as well. Note to self: Do not shock a skunk, especially one this big. Almost immediately, he was bottoms-up, ready to spray again.

I'm not sure why, but Major's new polymer float line, in our number two production facility, came to mind. That sounds crazy, and if I'd shared that thought with Butch, or anyone who would listen at that moment, they probably would have bit or hit me. But the black and white coat on this aromatic creature, in a zig-zag pattern, triggered a thought in my head that released a sensory reaction. Yes!

We have to alter the valve on the float to allow for a random mix with the colors. That will be left to the engineers to figure out. The smell disappeared for a few seconds as the idea gained traction in my mind.

Butch's bark snapped me back to reality. He chased the skunk, but that soiled stagnant smell remained. We met back at the cabin, Butch for a tomato juice scrub, and me a shower. While showering, I made another mental note to prepare a zig-zag proposal for today's meeting. Major will be there, hopefully in a receptive mood.

§

The flight from Spokane to San Francisco left right on time. Settle back, relax, and breathe deep. I got comfortable and piped the Revivalists in through my headphones.

Upon arrival, my first stop was long-term parking. One of my most trusted assistants left my car there yesterday, where there's more security. After removing the canvas cover off my vintage ride with a high-gloss, army green exterior, I stood back for a second and admired this 1979 Porsche 911 beauty. I stowed my gear and got in. Once I had the engine purring, which is such a sweet sound, and green aviators in place, I was off. Within minutes I was competing for space on the airport exit ramp, leading to the freeway. This road contest is played all over the world on a daily basis. But nowhere is it more exciting than here in SF, home of the Giants and 49ers, and no signal lane changing limos like the one I nearly hit that day while going through the gears. I imagined a seamless barrier stretched across the freeway like a clear film as I drove. It was waiting for me to pass through it. The large wrap represents the divide between where I came from and where I'm headed. And once the car passed through it, smack, I was back in the race. Easy, Rick, became my mantra. Talking to myself somehow helped.

Traffic behaved that day, and thirty minutes later the car angled into my personal parking space in Silicon Valley under Blaine's bright green logo. Passing through the front door of our headquarters, Billy, our Chief of Security, greeted me as he always did:

"Hey, mister Rick. You look too relaxed to be here. Go back! It's still not too late."

He let out a gut-busting laugh at his own joke.

I like Billy. He enjoys his job and keeps us all grounded. There are days when I would trade lives with him in an instant. Once at a Dodger home game, he came up to me with his wife and three kids, all dressed in their Dodger gear. Billy's the real deal with a beautiful family.

Before I could push the elevator button, the doors opened and out popped Bob Kulors from our sales department.

Bob, as only his six-foot three-inch frame would allow, turned right around, jumped back in, and said with a long face, "Hey, stranger. How ya doin'?"

Bob always acts like he feels sorry for everyone, me included, for some reason. All I could think of was how Bob reminded me of Eeyore in the Christopher Robin series.

"Fine, Bob, thanks for asking," I replied and patted him on the shoulder.

We continued up to the 8th floor together, and Bob went on and on and ON about how he and his team were bonding and beginning to kick "serious butt in our new target market, the New England region." I told him that I'd just reviewed the latest figures, then congratulated him. Bob is seriously good at his job. My hope is that he will one day learn to enjoy success. Bob shared his misgivings about being one of the presenters at our annual meeting coming up in July. He's perplexed, of course. I asked Eve to work with him on his approach. She suggested he smile when the good news concerning new sales developments is delivered. That and a triple shot breve latte should help. It does for me.

It was focus time. I had a meeting to facilitate. That's a part of my life I honestly enjoy. One thing about getting away is knowing to appreciate certain times when you return. This is one of them. Even if I wanted to run out to the corner coffee place for a triple shot, it had to wait. I had people ready to go. Then came the butterflies; adrenaline pumped, reminding me that I had a legacy to maintain. Okay, walking a little faster toward my office, I couldn't help but smile. I stopped in a small alcove for a quick body check and I noticed my socks didn't match. Great.

Brenda looked up as I walked into my office area. We exchanged smiles as she pushed away from her desk and pulled out her trusty folder. It had the appearance of a neatly organized overstuffed pillow. She greeted me and added the fact that we were set; everyone was in attendance and prepared.

Brenda – all business. Game time.

Brenda cleared her throat and fell in step with me as one of her assistants joined us. No stopping to check my office. I'd already answered all my emails, voice messages and texts. Time to work the room and greet everyone. This was my crowd. I love these guys.

The meeting began promptly at three thirty-five.

All department heads were in attendance, Brenda strategically positioned to my right, her assistant sitting behind us against the wall, cell phones off. Perfect. Both ceiling fans set to medium-high – storm warning, not hurricane force.

We dove right into it, with Major highlighting some of the new production improvements and ending with Bob's outstanding sales report. He even smiled, a little. The agenda was completed by a quarter after five, and to my amazement, questions and answers lasted until six. Impressive.

Everyone was ready for the weekend. All except Eve, who had a few marketing interns training for a couple of hours tomorrow and needed to prepare. But that was Eve.

I congratulated Eve on her continued success with college interns.

"How do you do it?"

"What, the interns?"

"Yes. What's your secret?"

"The Stones."

"Really."

"Hey, I learned from one of the best that. You can't always get what you want, but if you try, sometimes, you get what you need."

Ah, the Stones, I thought as Eve walked toward her office around the corner. That response was totally unexpected, especially from Eve.

That feeling of satisfaction, again the Stones, came over me as I reviewed our meeting.

The "zig-zag" realignment of the color application was a big hit with the production people, especially Frank Connors, our production manager. He's the oldest person in our company at sixty years of age, and somewhat of a father figure to many of us. Major worked with my dad in the seat cover business, unofficially celebrated around here as the first Blaine product.

"I think you've got something here, Rick. Can I ask how you came about this particular color revamp?" Major asked after I presented the skunk idea.

It was times like these when I could be accused of embellishing before getting to the point. But Ted, my therapist, has worked with me on "getting to the point sooner." So, I let the room savor Major's question for a few seconds, then took a breath, and quickly blurted out:

"I had a confrontation with a wild creature and my life flashed before my eyes."

Frank looked as if he had just swallowed a fly. People shifted in their seats, and Jose, who knew the zig-zag story, fought the urge to laugh. Major recovered quickly, told me he'd have a review team assembled by Monday afternoon, and an action plan on my desk by the end of the week. Nice recovery, Major.

In the back of my mind, as the meeting wound down, my thoughts went to important visitors, traveling here from London, looking for a new business relationship. This was going to be a very important meeting as I considered doing business overseas for the first time. I had been working on some preliminary plans for several months. Hey, at least they were coming our way this time.

I said my goodbyes and headed back to the garage and toward another home, further south on I-5. It had been about a month since I last saw the place, and the condo was calling to me. Normally, when I wasn't in a hurry, I'd take the 101 to Venice Beach. That roadway was as familiar as some of the bays on Lake Pend Oreille. I had to remember to change my socks.

§

Venice Beach has been a very special place for the three years I've lived there. The area is a great change of pace for healthy living, even if I'm only there part-time and mostly on the weekends. The community knows no reality, has no rules, and most likely never will. My attitude changes the minute I change out of my work clothes and open the first beer.

I have a small sign posted on my deck that reflects what I consider the unofficial VB covenant. It reads: NO REALITIES BEYOND THIS POINT.

Before I knew it, Malibu flew past, followed closely by Santa Monica. Highway 1 gave way and became Lincoln Blvd. I turned right, rolled down the windows and let the ocean breeze hit me. Eventually, the beach came into view and led me to the condo.

The condo is located near the beach and just three blocks from our ad agency, full of long-haired creatives who know how to charge for every nanosecond of their time. That's why I got the condo here in the first place.

Once, when Eve and I were here on business, I spotted this complex under construction and put money down before it was completed. The view is incredible, sunup to sundown. Once the sun sets, however, there's an added feature no outsider, including the realtor, could have anticipated. Beach fires dotting the landscape really add to the beauty. A very cool and relaxing illumination.

We had a great fire on the beach with my neighbors the night I arrived. Not that it was pre-planned; it never needs to be. Not in the land of no reality.

5. "Don't Knock the Pounding."

VENICE BEACH, CALIFORNIA

BAM! BAM! BAM!

The constant banging on my front door contributed to the moderate throbbing at my temples. The pounding and throbbing combined to pull my eyelids open as my alarm clock came into focus. The display read 5:05 a.m. I shouted to the door and told whoever felt the need to pound that they needed to go away. I also reminded them of the time.

Half awake, I could faintly make out a familiar voice. It also sounded pathetic as one word came through loud and clear:

"Dude."

Is that who I think it is? Resisting, but knowing I should, I slid my feet across the sheets and hit the floor. In an involuntary trance-like step formation that didn't even feel like me, I moved downstairs, headed for the front door like Apollo 13 headed back to earth. Barefoot and wearing only my boxers, I was ready for action.

BAM! BAM!

"I'm coming. Take a breath."

Yep. I checked the peephole and saw a bloodshot eyeball pull back to reveal my neighbor, Artie. He helped organize the beach barbecue last night. Through the door in a muffled but very deliberate tone, Artie conveyed his most urgent concern:

"Hey, man, sorry to disturb, but have you seen my flip flops?"

"Seriously, Artie?"

My eyes closed for an instant, trying not to hate every fiber of my shirtless, unshaven neighbor. Artie had that surfer air about him that causes me to never question where he's coming from, only how he ever made it this far in life.

That said, it's his free-loving, happy-go-lucky spirit that intrigues me. For that reason alone, the bolt flipped and the door opened, almost as if done by a ghost of myself, fueled by the fumes of last night's tequila shots. I was squinting; the sun was up. Terrific.

"Honestly, Artie. I haven't a clue."

"Really, dude?"

The look on his face changed from hope to anguish in a flash. I half-invited him in and managed, as if on remote control, to brew what I'd referred to as Rescue Coffee. It only required three tries to find the dark bold pre-cupped blend while Artie checked my deck for his flip flops. I went out onto the deck and served us up two steaming cups without any further issue.

"Looks like you lost your shirt too."

There Artie stood, smiling with perfect teeth, bronzed head to toe, blonde hair further bleached by the sun, early forty-something and built to near zero body fat on a six-foot frame. What a waste.

"I'm also missing Jillian, but I'm sure she's okay," he shouted as he leaned over the deck railing, nearly causing himself to fall. Instead, he rotated on his belly, feet up, and caught himself at the last minute.

"Take it down, Artie. I'm right here, wondering why I'm not still in bed."

"Sorry, man," he whispered.

Jillian is Artie's love interest. Most people would think she's a fashion model at first glance. She's a gorgeous take-charge lady, who proves that coming together with Artie is the epitome of opposites attracting.

Artie cleared his throat and rotated his head from side to side, wildly blinking his eyes as if experiencing some form of electroshock therapy. Preparing his explanation of what happened last night after I left took him a while.

Finally, he said, "Ummm, this coffee smells so good, man."

"Artie."

"Ya, oh, hey, my flip-flops (takes a sip) and a . . . Jillian!"

He took another sip while my brain attempted to rationalize why Artie would prioritize his flip flops before any mention of Jillian's disappearance. Then it dawned on me; those aren't just any flip flops. In the world of flip-flopping footwear, Artie's are the pinnacle, with each flop masterfully handcrafted by him to resemble his favorite surfboard. He wears them proudly. When I see him stride along the beach, he reminds me of a tall Asian samurai gone beach boy. In addition to the oddity of his creation, his flops create a certain swagger that I believe will affect his ability to walk, without a cane, well into the future.

"It was late, man. Jillian handed me her caffeine drink and told me to get a life, then walked off. That's when I noticed it."

"What?"

"I could feel the sand between my toes. My feet . . . my feet were cold, and, well, flopless. The beach fire died and there wasn't much light. Dude, I was in panic mode. Looking around, checking with a few people, didn't help. THEN it really hit me, Jillian was gone."

As Artie strained to remember the beach shenanigans from last night, my mind conjured a picture of him in his flip-flops. Hand-carved varnished dark monkey wood with brown leather straps, white pinstripes leading to scrolling R and L indications, rubber tread, and contoured to match his feet. He noticed my smile; we both chuckled, and not for the same reason.

"What?" Artie asked, scooting closer to the table.

"Oh, nothing," I responded, trying to take this whole ridiculous situation seriously. "Go on."

Artie looked as though he was trying to recall his name as he continued.

"So, I went on the search."

"What time did you start looking for Jillian, and your flip flops?"

"A few hours ago, before sunrise. Dude, I haven't been to bed."

It was obvious then why Artie looked like a zombie.

He half-smiled, and with a most forlorn look, caught me completely off guard as he said, "Those caffeine energy drinks are amazing, man."

Okay. I couldn't think of anything remotely reasonable to say but could tell that Artie was asking for my help in his search for footwear and his girl (in that order).

Artie's strategy, if that's possible, was simple: You find one and you find them both.

My schedule was clear, so I decided to help my barefoot, hopeless, unshaven friend.

My beach clothes, shorts and checkered Vans created the sleuthing look I was going for. And after grabbing a few granola bars, we were off on the hunt.

My need to discover what exactly took place last night kicked in. The questions started flowing as we walked along the serpentine Venice Beach sidewalk, lined by palm trees and shops. A few tourists, attempting to inline skate away from the beach sand, unknowingly accompanied us on our journey.

A few thong-bearing ladies gracefully sped past on in-line skates, which I considered part of the lovely swaying environment. Artie never noticed. Head down, one barefoot in front of the other, we marched on. Men on a mission.

Artie, focused and intent, looked extremely serious, especially for Artie.

"Okay, let's review," I said. "When did you first notice that Jillian was missing?"

His overly caffeinated answer was perfect:

"When I could feel the sand getting colder on my feet."

It made Artie Sense, which is not always clear right away, but if you let his comment float on the breeze for a while, it begins to take shape. We moved on, walking from the concrete sidewalk to the beach near the location where we gathered with friends last night.

Artie grabbed my arm.

"Dude, hold up."

He recognized one of the guys that works with Jillian and attended the barbecue last night.

"He'll know something," Artie shouted as he took off running.

When I caught up with Artie, he was asking questions:

"Hey, Stuart, did you see Jillian leave the beach party last night?"

"Well, if it isn't the old surfer boy."

Artie dismissed Stuart's sarcasm, which was a good thing. I didn't like this Stuart guy the minute he opened his mouth.

"Was she with anyone?"

Even I could tell from the look on the guy's face that he knew something, but he hesitated for some annoying reason. What a jerk. Artie's anxiousness increased as he yelled more questions. Jillian's disappearance started to feel a little more serious at that point. Artie's face strained. Stuart smiled and told Artie to settle down, that Jillian was a big girl. Wrong move, Stu, I thought.

"Where the hell is she, man?"

Artie's patience played out; he was tired, and frankly I was starting to get a little upset myself.

"The last time I saw her, she was visibly angry – at you –

and headed down to the Pier Restaurant. Who can blame her?" Stuart mumbled with a slight smile.

Then it happened. Artie swung Stuart around and put him in a chokehold.

"Okay, Stuart. Do I have to choke it out of ya?"

"Ughhh, ret go, ret, pass . . . out. Stot, stotppph."

Artie had him on the ground in an instant. He was spitting and yelling at the same time. Try not to murder our only witness, Artie. Come on, Stuart. I decided to intervene.

"Okay, boys. Break it up. Stuart, what's going on?"

Artie was turning red in the face, matching Stuart's contorted features. He was half Artie's size and ready to bolt. Artie, in one motion picked Stu boy up, plopped him down and stood over him like an eagle ready to share his prey with the rest of the nest.

Stuart, suddenly realizing there was no room for sarcasm, relented. He looked up at me, then half spit as he sputtered:

"Jillian was pissed because Artie kept flirting with the date I brought to the beach barbecue last night."

After a few minutes of discussion, we discovered Jillian took off with Artie's prized flip flops in a rage. And she wasn't alone when she left the beach fire around one a.m.

Stuart leaned forward, spit again, and finally, showing some concern, grunted out:

"She's a friend, and if she's still missing, I'd like to join you two. Sorry for being a smartass."

Artie slapped Stuart on the back, fully intending to bring peace to the situation, but in reality it caused Stuart to nearly throw up on the sand. After taking a few minutes to gather ourselves and convince Stuart we were now friends united, we headed out in three different directions. Each of us had a cell phone and a plan to go for sixty minutes, texting updates every fifteen minutes. It wasn't like Jillian to disappear, and according to Artie:

"I must have really upset her, dude."

My hand automatically reached out to this poor creature's shoulder.

"No shit, Sherlock."

Jillian, among other attributes, was a pilates nut with a black belt in karate. And at five feet, eight inches, she was more than capable of taking care of herself. She's a confident lady with auburn shoulder-length hair, green eyes, tan, and slender with a muscular build. She and Artie make a handsome couple.

Jillian made it clear to everyone that she and Artie were not serious. Jillian, more than anyone, knew that surfing came first with Artie. Surfing was his sport that eventually became a business. Winning a few competitions, each on his own handmade boards, helped him to finally open his surf shop eight years ago. People who knew the sport of surfing, and those just entering, gravitated to his place. It was a bit tucked away, and for that reason, his sign is almost as big as his store. The hand-painted sign is clearly visible, yellow and blue, and reads: WAVES by Artie.

Stuart said she left the fire with two guys he didn't know and a girl friend of hers who was visiting from out of town. Artie headed off to the Pier Restaurant. I covered the sidewalk and beach while Stuart crossed at the light and walked the Boulevard. Artie and I headed west, Stuart east, each hoping to find some trace of the lost.

6. "Hey, What Just Happened?"

Artie, Stu and I were thrust into action on the Venice Beach scene as amateur detectives. We became better acquainted as our sleuthing came together. Visualize: The three stooges sleepwalk over hot sand and stone walls.

The three of us did manage to stay in touch, even though Artie is phone challenged and kept dropping his in the sand. After an hour and a half, Stuart sent a final text. He found no trace of Jillian and had to run some errands but would help later if we needed. I thanked him and promised an update later.

My part of the search continued along the beach bordered by a serpentine concrete walkway, which was full of weird and entertaining distractions. Dodging the inline skaters and the lime scooter people turned out to be an art in itself.

"Hey, buddy, got a light?"

A man had set up a temporary vendor booth offering what he claimed were homemade candles. I shook my head and kept going. I noticed he had trouble keeping the creations shaded and consequently from melting in the hot sun. Evidently, business was slow. A young couple stole the show. They had a good crowd gathered around them. The woman danced while the guy played a flute. The scene could have been right out of the sixties, and people were eating it up.

After a few minutes, I decided to head down toward the water and into a cooling breeze. About a quarter of a mile later, Artie called to say that a friend spotted Jillian on the pier just ahead. I joined Artie, and we made our way past a lifeguard tower and on to the pier. Thirty minutes later, we found Jillian, sitting alone at an umbrella table, drinking tea. Even though she had on dark sunglasses, it was easy to see that she was still not happy with Artie.

"You've got my flip flops, thank God."

Jillian carefully removed her sunglasses, looked at me and said, "Hi, Rick." Then slowly turning toward Artie, she said, "Is that it? You were only concerned about your damn flip flops?"

Jillian let him have several pieces of what was on her mind in front of everyone within earshot. Never in recorded history have so many words penetrated the atmosphere with such velocity in under sixty seconds. Artie spun around as if hit by hurricane winds, then knelt down and half crawled around her table, begging for forgiveness. Actually, the scene was pretty cool to some bystanders who thought he was proposing marriage, especially when the tears started to flow. Later I found out that he had gathered copious splinters, causing pain in one kneecap while making his way to Jillian. That hope emanating from the crowd quickly diminished when she squirted her water bottle all over him.

As it turned out, Jillian remained upset over last night, because Artie did his famous "pogo" dance with some stranger, a young lady who just happened to be walking along the beach. According to Jillian: The bitch was more than half-naked and looking for a good time.

Artie did his best to explain that he would never look beyond Jillian for a good time, but to no avail. I remembered Jillian explaining to me that Artie was just a fling. I began to wonder.

Normally, Artie's "pogo" dance was kept private for his closest friends. No one, I repeat, no one, could jump repeatedly on sand, spinning and twisting wildly like our dear, fun-loving friend, Artie. It didn't take much encouragement for him to perform the pogo dance, because that's what it was, a performance, especially after a few beers with chasers. The dance culminated in Artie jumping over the largest fire on the beach. It was fun to watch, but hard to emulate. Whenever I witnessed his special dance, I hoped we wouldn't have to take him to the ER. I didn't want to leave.

Suddenly, Jillian grabbed Artie by the hair, pulling him forward. She whispered something in his ear, which made his eyes light up. He sprang to his feet and went for ice cream cones, as requested by Jillian. Once he returned and delivered the coned treats, smiles emerged, including from the old man standing next to me.

"That guy is an odd duck," the old man stated as he shook his head full of orange hair and walked away in a white polka dot and purple suit, holding a large assortment of balloons on tightly woven strings attached to an oversized glove.

All was forgiven. Jillian delivered Artie's flip flops right into his gut, like a quarterback to a running back. As soon as he could stand up again, he retaliated with a kiss on Jillian's forehead. Artie once again proved that it's better to be happy than smart. I try to be careful when judging Artie. After all, he is a friend. And as I thought about friendship, I couldn't help but question their relationship for a second time that day. Especially after all the drama we just went through.

There were still some answers left hanging that bothered me.

Who accompanied Jillian all night?

Could it be the mystery woman she brought to the party?

I called Stuart and gave him the good news about Jillian. He was relieved and apologized, once again, for his behavior. As he finished with his apology, I caught sight of Artie and Jillian arm-in-arm, Artie with his flip flops now safely strapped to his feet.

As they walked past, I shouted to Jillian:

"Didn't you have some people with you last night?"

She looked at me, winked, and made the "call you" signal with her hand up to her ear. I took that as a good sign.

I'm confident we'll be warming ourselves by another beach fire again soon. That thought gave me a warm feeling, one that only friends can ignite. The people we choose to be around. Being with family by a campfire is different. This is a ritual, rite of rejuvenation and irresponsibility we just can't lose, with one exception: fewer tequila shots next time.

Jillian came running back after me, looking like a crazy lady. I thought something was wrong:

"Don't tell me you lost Artie," I joked.

"No, funny guy."

I waited for her to catch her breath. She leaned forward and put one hand on my shoulder and said:

"I forgot to tell you that Libby had a good time last night and would like to meet up while she's in town."

My brain was running below its normal power level. Libby was a name I could not recall.

"Who?" I asked, squinting, trying to remember this person.

"My friend who's in town, Libby. Remember, she was at the 'Q' last night?"

"Nope, sorry I don't. Oh, wait a minute. You mean the cute brunette who was demonstrating salsa dancing?"

"Yes, that's her." Jillian went on to remind me that we really weren't introduced, but Libby saw me leave as they came up the beach singing and dancing.

"Hey, I was tired," I said, "but yeah, if you guys want to come over later, I'll be around."

Jillian offered to check with Libby and call me to set it up. The barbecue or "Q" resulted in an especially good time last night. Maybe a little too good, but good all the same.

§

This last escape exposed a much larger elephant running wall to wall in the living room of my life.

Sure, I was going places, attaining higher levels of professional achievement, but so what? My last trip to Lake Pend Oreille started me seriously thinking about finding someone special. So . . . why not take someone with me! There, that's it. Add a new goal: Find that Soulmate!

Time to reprioritize and ask myself: What needs to happen in order for me to share my life with someone special? My opportunities, in no particular order: work, exercise, sports, shopping, hanging with friends, driving (driving?), reading (even at Starbucks), and travel (including interstellar) need my immediate attention. In the past, I've waited for other people, like Jillian, to introduce me to new people. My mind has been distracted by business. Jess, Brenda, even Ted mentioned dating habits on my last visit. Ted asked me last time we met:

"So, Rick, how's your love life? Or do you want to bore me with more updates on Blaine Manufacturing?"

That did hit a nerve, but I had nothing to report.

No one is worse than Mom. She still thinks I keep in touch with girls from high school, which I don't, except Julie Schumaker, a girl I dated sophomore year. I don't actually keep in touch with her; in fact, it's just the opposite. She sends a Christmas card to Mom every year and asks to say hi to me. Julie's a border patrol agent in North Dakota last I heard. Julie was fun, but I have no desire to date someone who reminds me of a character in the movie *Fargo*. Up until recently, everyone's been concerned about my love life except me.

That changes now.

Heading back to my condo, I dodged a few rollerbladers as I crossed from the oxbow concrete sidewalk along Venice

Boulevard and headed up the hill. The view of the boulevard was nice this time of day; it flowed like a steady mountain stream when populated by healthy, fun-loving people.

The Herb Garden Grocery, one of my favorite places to shop, was right around the corner. The place makes me feel healthier the instant I enter. The scent of fresh-brewed coffee and made-from-scratch take out each provide hypnotic aromas that make shopping more pleasurable. I tend to buy more than necessary, which I did this time, mostly because of guests arriving tonight, but also because I just feel better buying healthy.

The day was picking up. A fresh breeze accompanied me home and then, after putting groceries away, I went right to my desk to work on my "re-priorities" before exercising.

It's amazing how quickly a personal agenda comes together when you finally decide to have one. I surprised myself. Occasionally, I've been known to decompress on weekends and keep somewhat to myself. I have now created a new Friday evening to Monday morning rule: Be more open to schedule changes and meeting new people.

And I close the journal.

7. "Things Change, So What Else Is New?"

There are a few people that totally understand why I arrange my life the way I do. Artie and Jillian are two that top that shortlist. They watch my place when I'm not around during the week. They take great pleasure in introducing me to new people they believe share my mutual interests. Jillian understands that my work comes first. However, I get the feeling she's out to change that. Since leaving her military career recently, Jillian is out to reprioritize things in my life as well. She called earlier to say they'd be by around six with Libby.

I pushed myself to do some quick tidying up, and opened windows to make sure the ocean breeze worked its magic. I even lit a few scented candles, just in case.

The second knocking on my door today went much better than Artie's earlier at five this morning. Speaking of my dear friend, I could tell he had been smoking something very pungent and formerly illegal in all states, especially California. As a result, the surfer dude ended up taking a nap before dinner. Poor guy was up all night; sleep tight, Arthur.

As Artie stretched out on my bed, I poured some beers into chilled glasses, then escorted the ladies to the best part of my condo: the deck outside. Jillian made some hummus, then fixed a full plate of fresh shrimp, which paired well with their huckleberry-flavored beer. Ladies who drink beer deserve special care and attention in my book.

The deck is larger than the average because I purchased the lot next door too. Construction of it required a special permit and too much money, but it was worth every cent. It's a redwood deck with a matching pergola overhead, accented by tiny lights, a built-in hot tub for eight, an in-ground pool, with ornamental seating built all around. The new design allowed for an expanded view that overlooks the ocean from a one-hundred-and-eighty-degrees. From here, you can see tourists, surfers, boats, and Ju-Ju, the one-man band, all of which combine to captivate and entertain for hours.

Watching the horizon where the water meets the sky is almost overwhelming, especially on a day free of smog and rain like this one. Sharing Venice Beach at its best is fun, and the amusements were not lost on Libby. She seemed to be enjoying herself, asking one question after another. She asked about my deck cooler.

On the corner of the deck was an old mooring buoy that I cut in half and converted into an ice chest. Because of its round bottom, it sits in a specially designed metal frame, white on the bottom with blue accent letters that spell out: COOL. Coronas, huckleberry-flavored beer (for the ladies, not my favorite), and Perrier water chilled while we cast our lines in the visitation pool. After the first round, we quickly moved away from huckleberry-flavored brew. They both preferred Corona stuffed with lime wedges. Jillian watched as Libby and I returned smiles, as she played the part of the matchmaker, proud of her ability to bring strangers together.

If you watch people who matchmake, you'll notice a sense of pride that causes them to smile more than usual, which then gives way to raised eyebrows and pursed lips, revealing a tense look. It's human nature in action and fun to watch. Both reactions can lead to an increase in alcohol intake, which I attempted to monitor. Inwardly, I felt for Jillian and her hope that the newbies got along. It's like having parents watching you on your first date using the family car, with them in the back seat.

Ted, my therapist, says that this friendly attempt at connection or matchmaking is a matchmaker's idea of nurturing, allowing them an opportunity to toss their friends a life ring. Well then toss away, because I don't mind it, not anymore. Especially as I looked at Libby trying to pay attention to what Jillian was saying. Libby turned her head, smiled, and looked at me with the most distracting blue eyes.

"I have to go check on my beautiful boyfriend, Artimus."

"Artimus?" I countered with a chuckle. "I thought his name was Arthur."

"Oh, God, don't tell him I told you. He'd just die."

Jillian turned at the sliding glass door, checking on us one more time before she left her charges.

I gave her a toast salute with my glass of beer, feeling very comfortable being left alone with Libby. As Jillian left, I took another Corona from the buoy cooler, then stretched out in the lounge chair next to Libby's.

I asked, "Are you from California?"

"No, the Pacific Northwest, originally."

That's a coincidence.

The more we talked, the more her confidence became apparent. Libby was a curious, well-educated lady with a Master's in Oceanology. Really. She loved to travel, was a good conversationalist, preferred beer to wine, had a nice smile, beautiful eyes, plus she enjoyed beer? She also planned to get a job at the Ocean Pacific Institute not far from here.

Turns out, OPI is famous for cleaning up major areas of the California coast, and she'd be part of a new team assigned to study the effects of global warming and the rising tidal effect along the west coast. Interesting. She sported an attractive smile, with light brown hair and eyes that were as engaging as her personality.

"No tan yet; I'm working on that," Libby whispered as she turned toward me and winked.

"Tan? Oh, yes, tan. Well, you're in the perfect place to make that happen."

Okay, Rick, try not to sound too stupid.

I asked her about a professor I knew from the institute. She answered without hesitation that she hadn't interviewed yet, but would look him up when the time came. Never mind.

Suddenly, Artie appeared through the slider like Kramer on Seinfeld, barefoot and ready for a beer.

Thank God.

Jillian made an incredible seafood salad. We laughed and joked about what had happened to Artie's flip flops. I was desperately trying to remember anything I might have said to Libby by the beach fire when Artie blurted:

"Where are my flippers?"

"Honestly, Artie. You are a child," Jillian laughed with an emphasis on the word "are."

"We need to help Rick clean up," she added.

"Absolutely not," I insisted.

Cleaning up was my game, but Libby asked if she could stay and help. A much better idea for sure.

Jillian and Artie said goodbye with Jillian giving me the "you're on your own, big boy" look.

We spent time in the kitchen loading the dishwasher, wrapping up food, side-stepping each other and flirting like crazy. She talked, and I listened as she continued asking questions about my work and background. At the time, the flirting outranked the questioning, and after we finished, I suggested we go for a walk. She was dressed in light-blue tight-fitting jeans with a white gauze blouse, and red and black flip flops with nail polish to match the red. Very cool, I thought, as she turned to face me.

"Saturday is the one day in the week that should last twice as long as the other days, don't ya think?"

My smile took over. I suggested we check out the beach and head to one of my favorite destinations farther down the boulevard.

"Is it very far?" she asked.

"Not to worry – we have bikes!"

My neighbor's bikes were hung up in his garage, which I had access to when he was out-of-town, so we were off. Libby carried beach towels in her basket and my backpack held a few brews, a wallet, suntan lotion, flare gun (only because I forgot to take it out), my phone, and another pair of shorts. It was about 7:30 and we decided to watch the sunset and take our time along the walkway, dodging walkers, other bikers, and rollerbladers. We were on a date. Cool.

Fifteen minutes later, we arrived at our destination, locked the bikes, and made our way down toward the surf. We spread out beach towels and laid down with my backpack as a headrest. Libby started us laughing by making a comment about the king-sized bed we'd just planted on the sand. She then told me about her hometown of Spokane, Washington, which I was somewhat familiar with, having driven through on the freeway from North Idaho. Libby thought she knew the lake I had just spent two weeks on, and found it amusing that I would pick that particular place as a sanctuary away from all of this California craziness. Are you kidding? Did she really know the place?

The buzz from the alcohol began to vibrate in my arms and face. I decided to take some water instead.

"Hey, Pend Oreille is an area where no one would think to look for me," I said, feeling a little defensive about my escape route. My right finger found its way to my lips and I whispered: "Promise not to tell."

Libby looked at me with a serious face, then changed quickly and laughed. We both were laughing and I said the word promise again.

My laughter caused me to spit right in her face. The look on mine must have been one of fear and bewilderment, because she burst out laughing again as she grabbed my shoulders. Being defensive wasn't where I wanted to go tonight, but I could tell that Libby enjoyed throwing me off my game. Why? Forget it, I told myself. Who cares? We were having too much fun to get serious.

The temperature dropped as the sun slowly set, and the ocean breeze went from warm and comfortable to chilling and cool. Libby inched her way toward me, shivering. Her body heat felt good. Isn't nature wonderful in the way it works together with a guy's thoughts? Suddenly, I had a brilliant idea:

"Let's head back to my place and see if the cooler needs restocking."

"Can I ride on your handlebars, Rick?"

"You can. But first we have to ride back to my place. We have two bikes."

Libby laughed so hard at my remark I thought she'd choke. A towel came flying my way, then the backpack. We both had a buzz on and it felt great. Libby became more familiar to me as we spent time together. Not like last night when she blended into the shadows. I stood, trying to balance without being noticed. Feeling awkward had more to do with Libby than the beers. That's what I told myself, at least.

She pulled her hood up and we started back, retracing our steps to the bikes. Then we cruised a mile or so to the condo. When we arrived, she hopped off the bike, hit the kickstand, smiled, and gave me a big kiss good-bye.

"I need to get up early tomorrow and meet some friends coming into town for the day," she said with that perfect smile.

I walked her back to Jillian's, where she had parked her rental car.

"You don't have to, Rick."

"Are you kidding? After what happened to Jillian last night? I am definitely not taking any chances."

She smiled and wrapped her arm around mine. Her car was parked on a side street next to Jillian's condo. We traded phone numbers, then hugged. Libby rolled the window down as she drove off and shouted:

"Don't lose your shoes on the way home."

I immediately reached down and took off one of my shoes and waved goodbye with it. While in my buzzed state of mind, Ted suddenly came to mind. I had to schedule time with him right away. There was a new woman in my life.

How exciting for Ted!

8. "Careful What You Say, It May Come Around and Smack You Upside the Head."

U.S. I-95 NORTH OF BOSTON – LAST WEEK

Michael Castillino was not happy. Three of his largest east coast distributors reported meeting with a west coast electronic accessories manufacturer with some very unique, high-volume items. The meeting went well, until they were faced with a conflict in the payment arrangements. The manufacturer was not willing to pay an additional "slotting fee," which was critical to the Castillino empire revenue equation. That fee was part of Castillino's untraceable and illegal revenue stream that suppliers were expected to pay. That is if they had any hope of gaining distribution in the eastern region of the United States.

"Carmine, who are these people and who do they work for?"

He was on the phone with his man, Carmine Scarelli, who handled all his business contacts in the northeast. Carmine reported talking to the west coast representatives for Blaine Manufacturing, the largest manufacturer of covers, pads and accessories for electronic equipment in the United States.

"It would be to our extreme advantage to have these guys on board, Michael. But they have their heads up their west coast asses so far that I can't see any way they're going to compromise on their approach. Unfortunately, Blaine Manufacturing produces exclusive high-volume items that our customers are looking for."

Michael waited a minute, his teeth grinding back and forth like waves on an ocean. He was contemplating.

"Michael?"

"Okay, okay, Carmie. I got it. This, of course, is bullshit. Here's what you do."

Carmine received very explicit, non-negotiable orders from Michael. It was understood if he, Carmine, couldn't convince the Blaine reps to change their minds, there would be someone else working with Michael to correct this matter. And that he, Carmine, could lose more than his position if he didn't come through with a workable solution. As Carmine listened to Michael go from a calm explanation into a fever-pitched rant, sweat began to form on his face and hands.

Carmine, the man who knew the Castillinos better than most, would lose sleep for the next week. His wife, normally his rock, suggested he find another job. They both knew that in doing so, Carmine, and his wife and daughters, would also have to relocate and change their names in order to escape the Castillino family. He had to think of something and fast.

§

EMBARCADERO SQUARE, SAN FRANCISCO

"You look like shit," Ted said as I walked into his office on that Monday night at 7 p.m.

It was the only time he could squeeze me in, and I could tell from his face that it had been a long day.

The rain, slapping against Ted's office windows in continuous waves, probably added to his haggard look. A heavy torrential downpour created deep puddles along city curbs, making it difficult to cross streets while trying to keep your shoes and socks dry.

"Feel like I just survived a drowning," I replied as I stripped off my shoes and socks in the doorway.

Ted stared at me. He looked as he normally does with long silver locks down to his shoulders, dark blue khaki pants, brown leather moccasins, and a faded Steely Dan concert t-shirt. His John Lennon glasses made him look like some anachronism out of the love-child sixties. As I passed him and proceeded to his all-too-comfortable brown leather couch, he made his way to an equally faded denim bean bag chair located in the middle of the room.

"Sorry about the shitty comment, Rick. It's been one of those days, oh captain of industry. Please, sit. You dry out while I begin our session with a few questions."

"Mind if I imbibe?" he asked, reaching for his lighter. I nodded my approval and my therapeutic guru took a long drag off his "do-si-do" pre-rolled doobie. I watched and enjoyed the secondary drifts. He smoked cannabis only at night and rarely in front of clients. Evidently, Ted considered me to be someone other than a client. That or the fact he just needed to get high. I didn't care; I needed to talk.

Ted works with me twice a month, providing a firm-sounding board and dialogue that often stings with truth but, eventually, offers wisdom that comforts. My original intent in attending therapy was to find out why I wasn't enjoying my life. It wasn't that I didn't enjoy the benefits of being successful; I did. I just wasn't happy.

When we first met, Ted had me fill out a form that asked probing questions. Supposedly, the answers gave him insight into my very being.

"It may sound like a bunch of crap, just do your best," he had noted as I worked on filling out the form.

Amazing direction from a man who came so highly recommended. I was immediately hooked. People say that therapists themselves suffer from a variety of mental issues. And that they are in this business because it helps them work through their own problems. Makes you wonder, until you meet someone like Ted.

My company was doing better than ever, and I wanted to know what could be done, emotionally, to kick my ass into an appreciable gear. On top of that, people close to me were concerned about my lifestyle and finding that special someone.

"Soulmate, do each of us really have one?" I asked Ted.

"Oh, so you are going to be asking the questions tonight?"

Ted then rolled himself carefully out of his bean bag, stood, and walked to the coffee maker around a small corner. I heard him pour a cup before reappearing. After walking my way, he stopped mid-office and took a sip, then offered:

"Rick, you first have to believe you have a soul, and they, whoever they are, have a soul. Once you are on that plane, you are ready to dive below the surface and evaluate people by how they make you feel. It's a worthwhile exercise – believe me. What you discover in the process becomes what we investigate here. The trick is to be able to see into the realm where souls exist."

"Yes, I was raised to believe in souls," I uttered as Ted suddenly took on the appearance of a rather poorly dressed Dalai Lama.

Ted slowly, carefully, withdrew the cup from his lips and replaced it with the marijuana joint. After one more drag, he slipped the doobie from his mouth as if pulling the pin from a hand grenade, holding the smoke before blowing. Simultaneously, he moved slowly toward a large picture window. Was it me, or was Ted really walking that slow?

The rain beating against the window took on a rhythmic cadence, wap, wap, wap, just as Ted released air from his smoke-filled lungs. The smoke hung over us like an alien spaceship about to land, as Ted pulled the shade down in an attempt to quiet the room. He turned, and with a look of quiet wisdom on his face, asked:

"Do you know how airline pilots refer to the people on board their aircraft?"

Hoping like crazy that Ted wouldn't sprout wings and begin to fly around his slowly rotating ceiling fan, I replied:

"Not sure what you mean, Ted."

Ted gathered himself and slowly descended, floated really, as he re-entered the bean bag chair. Upon landing, he offered:

"Each person on the plane is recognized as a soul. We have two hundred souls on board, the pilot or co-pilot will report."

We looked at each other like both of us had a third eye. Ted added:

"Aretha Franklin was the queen of . . . soul."

"That's different, Ted."

"Is it, Mr. Blaine?"

"Rick, are you ready to discuss soulmates?"

"Yes, Ted, of course. And airplane pilots and Aretha Franklin."

His breathing was heavy, eyes watery. After a slight pause, he carefully explained that there's reasonable enough evidence to prove we connect in many ways with people we love, souls being the most spiritually conductive part of us. The room suddenly felt like church; Ted was conducting a homily. He stood by the window, still as a statue, and looked up.

"Rick, how's your love life?" He turned my way, revealing a marginal grin.

This was Ted's space and he proved it by managing to carefully sit back down without a sound. His last question still lingered in the ether. It became my turn to say something, hopefully, true and compelling.

"I'm still searching, but I'm open to anyone who doesn't carry a gun, or use too much perfume."

Ted smiled, turned, and appeared to levitate once again from the bean bag chair, this time targeting his sofa. Once he settled in, there we were, head to head, sofa to sofa, both looking up at the ceiling like two stargazers watching for the return of Haley's comet. A few minutes went by. The room was full of silence – still nothing from Ted. I enjoyed our time together but questioned whether payment should include quiet time, so I offered a new thought, trying to move my lips, which felt numb for secondary reasons.

"I've met someone."

Ted exhaled and whispered, "Did you find her or did she find you?"

My overview of what happened at the barbecue beach fire and the next day ran like an old newsreel in my head. He laid there silent as I recapped our search for Jillian, and how she introduced me to Libby.

"I find it curious, Rick, that you didn't remember her the first time you met at the beach fire."

Surprised by his comment, I retraced, once again, the moments at the beach barbecue on Friday. I still couldn't remember first meeting Libby.

"Sounds to me like she found you," Ted continued. "Which is not necessarily a bad thing."

He was right. Ted's tone suddenly turned parental.

"Be careful. You are a prize catch, Rick. Make sure you're ready to be caught. If not, just keep searching. For now, I'm pleased to see you open to a stronger relationship. Good progress, Rick."

His comment, and the remaining fifteen minutes of conversation, were the most productive words Ted had shared in eight months of regular appointments. It's taken that long because, to use a sailing analogy, I was below deck taking a nap aboard my life's boat. No more wondering about Ted's effectiveness. He's the man. I felt renewed.

The pelting rain continued as I left Ted's office and headed to my car. The comforting hum of the Porsche's engine sounded even sweeter as I made my way through traffic. Life suddenly felt better. Driving through downtown San Francisco in fiercely pelting rain was like being washed clean. A sense of being "reborn" came over me as the car escaped into rain.

The Embarcadero District quickly disappeared in the rearview as I headed out over the Golden Gate Bridge and onto the Tiburon Peninsula. By the time I entered my apartment, it was nine-thirty. The night was devoid of any color. I was tired, having driven home by instinct, thanks to Ted's habitual cleansing.

§

Tiburon is a great place to live if you can afford it. Since it's close to work, the location makes drive time a non-issue for me, and the peninsula provides solitude with a beautiful view of San Francisco, especially at night. It's very different from Venice Beach. No one really cares to know one another in Tiburon, unless it helps them climb another rung on the social ladder. I'm not into that; consequently, strangers and neighbors are on an equal plane. Mr. Murphy is an exception, an elderly gentleman who resides in the apartment right below mine in our four-plex. He has a better view of the Golden Gate, which makes him happy.

He and his brother Dan arrived from Ireland just before the Second World War with no relatives or friends to greet them. From what he's shared in passing, he and his brother ended up owning half of Fisherman's Wharf at one time. That included warehouses, apartment buildings, radio stations, an amusement park, and several restaurants, including a chain of steakhouses. I believe his first name could be Midas. Midas with a closer view of his Golden Gate. I'm not sure how old or how much Mr. Murphy is worth. My hope is that he's happy, since that's all that really matters.

As for my living conditions: I work in San Jose, live in my apartment in Tiburon, near Sausalito, during the week, and drive to Los Angeles on most weekends, no problem. A big part of my adventure in life is to be driven, especially when I'm on my own, late at night on I-5, or Highway 101, headed south. The same feeling applies in the skies above.

§

VENICE BEACH, CALIFORNIA

Libby watched through the window shades of Jillian's apartment as Jillian and Artie walked hand-in-hand across the beach, heading, she guessed, to his surf shop. The three of them had been on a social rampage since Libby's arrival two days ago. It was good to have some down time. She committed everything he told her to memory. Nothing was written down for others to find. Libby had a good mind. She was a smart, fast learner. That's what they had told her. After all, she had to review information that they had gathered on the Pacific Northwest, places she had never been to, but had to be engaging enough to be able to convince Rick Blaine, the target, that their meeting was a chance encounter.

Closing her eyes, she quietly arranged her to-do list. She was on a mission and needed to keep her priorities straight, now that she had made it this far.

She wasn't used to being around gentlemen. She thought of Rick as cute. Well, more than cute – handsome and fun. She liked her men at least six feet tall, which he was. He also had dark hair, a slender but muscular build, and kind eyes. Her thoughts were focused on last night at the beach and how she and Rick enjoyed each other's company. Guys were so predictable. Yes, with Rick, there was a spark, but unfortunately for Libby, that spark could never develop into a flame. She knew that, even if Rick didn't.

Her phone vibrated. The display read: Michael. Calling right on time.

"Hi," she whispered, as if receiving the call in a library.

"Are you alone?"

"Yes, just a little nervous, sorry."

"Talk to me, cousin," he replied sternly.

"I met the target last night. We hung out together."

"So, what's he like?"

"Nice."

"What did you find out?"

"He's the man. No other details to report yet. We just met for God's sake!"

"Hey, I told you to move on this. I got too many people looking for answers. Now get to work!"

"Michael, I may need more time . . . ."

He hung up as Libby turned to look out at the beach. Michael Castillino made his point, but he was back east, and she was looking at sunshine and thinking about other possibilities. She would try, for now, to handle this investigation her way.

9. "Cheerio, Old Chap."

The British are coming, the British are here, finally. I literally ran past the guard at the front desk and took the stairs, two at a time, instead of waiting for an elevator. Traffic had been at its worst today of all days. As I entered my office, I could hear Brenda with the Lampersons in my office.

I met Winston Lamperson III and his son, Benjamin, at a European Trade Fair in Paris a year ago. Little did I know how much these two gentlemen would change my life and the future of our company.

For the past decade, the French government produced an extraordinary exhibition of Internet Technologies' latest and greatest inventions and accessories. In recent years, a team of executives from Blaine attended the event and reported back on what they learned. Keeping up on the latest technology was important for Blaine; having the event in Paris made it more enjoyable.

Last year was different, mostly because of Ted, my therapist. He suggested that I rearrange my schedule and accompany the team to Paris. Visiting Paris sounded like a waste of time then, but that changed when I remembered a friend from college lives there. He's in the diplomatic corps, and this trip would give me a chance to catch up with him. Plus, the Exhibition was taking on more prominence, so it gave Blaine Manufacturing an opportunity for greater media exposure. I agreed to lead the Blaine team, consisting of Eve, Victor and Jodie, plus a writer from Forbes who was doing a story on business overseas. What we learned from the people we met, especially the vendors, made it all worthwhile.

Our small contingent worked intently through the various booths, each one set up to show off the latest in IT software and gadgets. Two days went by quickly. While our days were spent diligently attending the show, we reserved our nights for exploring various bars and entertainment venues. Paris eventually won me over and became one of my favorite cities to visit.

Our last day was spent at a food fair connected to the exhibition. We split up. It was early, and I hadn't had anything to eat. Since most people were sleeping in, the place wasn't that busy. As I rounded a large table full of breakfast items I couldn't pronounce, I decided to scoop up some duck eggs and toast. I had just filled my plate when I heard the first loud cough, followed by gagging and choking sounds. I turned to see where they were coming from.

I discovered a very stately looking gentleman on the ground with his hands at his throat. Evidently, he'd been right behind me, sampling some of the unpronounceable French cuisine as he walked. The combination of walking, talking, and sampling caused him to choke. A portion of French Something lodged in his throat and sent the poor fellow to the floor.

A young man held the choking man who was beginning to turn blue.

"Father, father . . . Winston."

The younger man looked right at me and didn't need to ask. I reflexively turned the choking man over and wrapped my arms around his waist, then began yanking. I had never actually performed the Heimlich maneuver, but had a good idea of what needed to happen. One problem: Winston was a big man.

"Loosen his tie," I ordered the young stranger.

It wasn't easy since we were both on the ground. I managed to get behind him, found a grip on his mid-abdomen, and pulled and yanked, once, twice, then it happened. I heard a gurgling sound, and with the third thrust the impediment popped out. The young man and the people standing around watching were visibly relieved, no one more than me. I had one or two yanks left in the tank.

Sudden relief came over me. It was as if I'd just won a wrestling match. I knelt behind the poor guy, hands on my knees.

"I believe you can stop now," the old man said in a whisper.

As the crowd began to disperse, Winston, an older gentleman with a very red face now, appeared to be embarrassed yet composed. Who wouldn't be embarrassed? He sat up, took a deep breath, smiled at his son, then at me, and said:

"What a shame, it was a delicious cherry-glazed crepe." Wiping his mouth with a towel from his son, he slowly began to rise.

Benjamin, Winston's son, and I helped him up off the floor. After a series of "Thank You's," we said our goodbyes, traded business cards, and I went back to my eggs.

The crepe incident happened in less than five minutes, and we've been friends ever since.

After breakfast that fateful morning, I was leaving the area and ran into the Lampersons at a table nearby. They invited me to sit for a few minutes. Winston and Benjamin were principals in a company that, among many services, furnished market data to companies attempting to find their audience and improve market share. Ben, which he preferred, created a unique internet software program, and his father's money and input helped to develop it. Winston had a deep understanding of the international intelligence business that he developed over the last thirty years. He and his son joined forces five years ago, in order to merge some ideas Ben brought to his father regarding international business, his major in college. Their new association proved to be very lucrative.

Since then, Eve and Jodie have retained the Lampersons' services for nearly a year now. They've been very impressed with the fact that Lamperson International Services not only provides great service, but also possesses a very impressive client list. The Lampersons recently presented ideas on how Blaine could sell products internationally. Up until now, those ideas had been put on hold.

This meeting's theme, consequently, had an international flavor. Winston and Ben were in San Francisco for the first time on business, primarily to see our operation.

"Quite right, old boy. I've traveled through, stopping once to sample offerings in Napa Valley. I'm afraid to admit, but I've never been to your Silicon Valley. I have to say: It's not as tasty," Winston offered as he laughed heartily.

They both appeared to be enjoying themselves, especially the limo ride to our offices that we had arranged for them this morning. Their U.S. tour also included stops in Seattle and Minneapolis, drumming up more business for Lamperson International Services.

I enjoy their friendship and find them to be "spirited chaps" for sure. Winston is a shrewd businessman. He has a talent for finding the missing link, those critical details that give businesses an edge. After a tour of Blaine full of military banter between Major and Winston, both having served their countries proudly, Ben was introduced to our creatives downstairs.

Eve, Jodie, Joe and I had a productive meeting with the Lampersons in my office, then we all headed to Fisherman's Wharf for lunch. Brenda made the reservation at Tommy's Joynt. I had suggested the Crepes Cafe, totally in jest. Brenda was having none of it.

"Rick, if you're going to the Wharf, have Wharf food. Something they can't get anywhere else."

Brenda was right, of course. We walked along the Wharf and caught a cable car at their request, stopping for Irish coffees along the way. We arranged a limo for the Lampersons to take them to their hotel. After they were off, Eve drove me back to the office. Checking for messages along the way, I discovered a voicemail from Libby. Since it was personal, I waited to listen until I was back at the office.

We arrived around four. Eve went off to another meeting with staff and I caught up with Brenda at the elevator.

"You have someone waiting in your private conference room. Said she was a friend from Los Angeles, in San Francisco for the day."

Brenda had a long to-do list for me and I was able to maneuver through most of them comfortably, until I saw Libby standing at my door, waiting with a pair of my sunglasses in her hand.

"Hi, I believe these are yours." She winked and handed me my glasses.

There must have been a look of bewilderment on my face, because she quickly added, "I drove off with them the other night. They were in my jacket."

I turned toward Brenda, who was walking away, and asked that she hold my calls.

"You have an amazing view," Libby stated as she turned her head, scanning my office as if looking for something.

"Hey, it's good to see you!" We held each other in a long hug, then sat down.

"What's up?" I asked as my head shook, still not believing Libby was here in my office.

"You look great." I continued trying to find words to say while checking my phone calendar.

Libby looked beyond great; she was radiant. I wondered if

we'd made an appointment or if there was a reservation that should have been secured. Damn if I forgot.

"Brenda didn't tell me . . ."

"No, no," Libby offered quickly. "I was up here visiting people for the day and thought I'd drop over and see what Blaine Manufacturing was all about. It was an on the spur of the moment kind of thing."

The relief felt good, as did her smile.

"No problem. I like impulsive behavior," I said unconvincingly. We both laughed at the same time.

Does anyone else notice how familiar surroundings, like an office space you've seen for the last four years, suddenly change when someone special literally walks into your life unexpectedly?

The room temperature must be set higher than usual. Put sunglasses on or quit looking at her with your mouth open.

Libby asked if I had time for a drink after work. My "Yes" was almost too quick. I texted Brenda, asking to cancel my racquetball time at the club. I had one call to return, then Libby and I were off to a favorite getaway of mine in South Beach. We ended the evening at my apartment in Tiburon, around midnight, and Libby fixed breakfast in the morning. The whole evening was perfect.

We spent so much time together over the next few days, I felt like I was on a rollercoaster, a thousand feet in the air, at night, performing loop de loops. We went nonstop, visiting wineries, sightseeing, going out to dinner, a symphony benefit concert, and a play. Libby was having fun, and so was I.

"So, Rick, do you like what you do? At Blaine, I mean."

"I like what I'm doing right now more," I playfully offered as we kissed.

This behavior was not like me. Spending time away from my busy Blaine schedule, when I'm here not escaping, plus doing all of this with one lady, what was happening? Odd looks were coming from my associates, but the oddest was the one looking back at me in the mirror. Even Major gave me the old evil eye when I came to work looking like I hadn't slept.

Then Jillian called.

"Hey, mister, why haven't you been here with us on the beach lately? Venice just isn't the same without our Rock Star Ricky."

I told her about Libby and how we had been bonding since Artie lost his flip flops. When I stopped talking, there was silence on the phone.

"Libby is up there with you?" Jillian finally said. "I thought she was on her way home to pack up. At least that's what she told me. I must have misunderstood."

After a few more minutes on the phone, Jillian hung up. Then Libby came up the stairs with our to-go dinner. We were going to spend her last night in California together at my Tiburon apartment before she left in the morning. Her plan was to move to San Francisco within the month, but playing the "goodbye for now" game was fun and very satisfying. Libby was amazing, bright, intelligent, full of energy, and plenty of questions, about life in general and business in particular. A curious combination that appeared to be sealing our bond.

I was having a great time and enjoying the ride.

10. "Back to Business and up to No Good."

I'd been missing work and feeling guilty about my absence, so I arrived to work at six a.m. this morning, an hour earlier than normal.

Monday morning has always been the best business day of the week for me since I can remember. It's a clean slate on the weekday blackboard. Even though my schedule for the week was filling, each day presented all kinds of promise that can be converted into business. That's how my father felt. It's in the blood.

My desk had two small piles of work-related matters that took about an hour to manage. Watching out the window, I took a few minutes to stretch to instrumental music as people arrived several floors below. It was good to see people filtering in this early, at 7:30. I'm determined to get back on track, as I normally do, only this time seemed more urgent. I needed to energize my team.

Brenda's daily agenda was full of new items. Among the "must make" phone calls was a request from one of my favorite people, my older sister, Jess. We have a special connection. She filled in the gaps when Mom and Dad weren't around, like when I needed some help tying my shoes, wiping my nose, or completing homework. Oddly enough, she'd perform the same tasks later in life when I'd had either too much to drink or got into a fight. Her phone messages always bordered on the dramatic like Mom's:

"Hey, Rick. Nothing too earth-shaking, just need to talk. Be sure to check with Brenda first though. Bye, little brother."

Really? Jess wanted me to contact her, but wanted me to specifically check with Brenda first? What's going on? Oh, and then it will be okay to return Mr. Cook's call at Apple?

"Brenda!"

They had "quite a chat," as my British colleague, Winston, would put it. Brenda took it upon herself to call my sister with concerns about Libby. Evidently, Brenda overheard a phone conversation Libby had in Capri, the coffee shop around the corner from our offices. Brenda wanted to get Jess's thoughts regarding Libby's strange behavior before coming to me.

I happened to be checking emails when Brenda walked into my office and closed the door. She looked good with her blonde hair up in a tight bun, dark-framed glasses, wearing a tailored dark blue business suit. I shifted in my chair and motioned for Brenda to sit.

Brenda sat down and quietly stated:

"I hope you trust what I'm about to say."

I shut my laptop, turned away from her and looked out at the rolling Santa Cruz mountains. Once I took a deep breath to clear my head, I went over and pulled up a chair next to her. Brenda had my full attention.

A small part of Brenda's job description has been to assume responsibility for parts of my life that require more attention than I'm willing to give them. It's happened before, but not in this way. Parking ticket violations are one thing; new flames are an entirely different beast.

"What is it, Brenda?"

She smiled, and without hesitation, looked directly in my eyes.

"I think someone is trying to fool you and cause trouble," she added a little nervously.

I must have looked shocked because she came back with:

"We think Libby isn't who she appears to be."

"We?" I asked, feeling a little defensive.

"Yes. Jess and I feel there's something going on that you aren't aware of and could be overlooking."

Brenda held her gaze and didn't waver.

I admitted to enjoying our new relationship, but didn't feel as though it was anyone else's business. Since I began to feel a little uneasy about our conversation, I stood and walked to the window again, then turned back and tried to smile.

"Look, I know you mean well, but…"

"Stop, please," Brenda asserted with more directness than I thought possible.

"I overheard Libby talking to a man on her cell phone the other day, and I believe they are planning something concerning us. Blaine Manufacturing, I mean."

Planning something? This is serious if it's true, I thought. I sat back down across from her.

"I'm listening."

Brenda suddenly moved into a more aggressive posture. This side of her, confident and to the point, is what sets Brenda apart and makes her such a key person. Brenda got up, poured herself some coffee and sat back down. She took a deep breath and continued:

"You know my friend Janet, from Google?"

"Yes."

"We met for coffee on Tuesday."

Brenda explained that she and Janet were catching up at Capri when Libby came in talking on her phone. She sat close enough for Brenda to hear every word. Libby was talking to a person named Michael, and from what Brenda could tell, my name came up three times in the conversation. Brenda had trouble deciphering the entire discussion, but from what she overheard, Michael was very interested in Blaine Manufacturing's new plans for penetrating the New England market.

"Not only that: Libby's voice changed during the conversation to a 'Jersey Girl' type accent."

What? Brenda now had my full attention. Who was this Michael? Competition? The questions in my head were mounting when my cell phone rang.

It was Libby. I showed her the display screen, shrugged my shoulders and whispered:

"Well, this is ironic. Do you mind?"

Brenda motioned for me to take the call. She started to leave, but I held the phone away and whispered for her to wait. Libby was very bright and bubbly for a Monday morning. Her enthusiasm was normally contagious, but not now. She wanted to make sure I was in the office, because she had a surprise coming my way, and added that she missed me already.

When the call was over, I turned to Brenda:

"Hey, I appreciate the fact that you and Jess are looking out for me. I'm confused right now and a little angry, to be honest. I need a moment."

"I understand. Here, these documents need your signature."

We finished the paperwork in time for her to greet someone who made it all the way up to my office area without being announced first, and came in asking to see me.

I heard Brenda tell a man that I was busy, then ask, "Do you have an appointment, Mr.?"

A man with a deep voice answered, "Dobson. I just need a quick minute."

Brenda checked with me, and I, distractedly, said to let him in. When Mr. Dobson approached, I could feel what was about to happen, and then it did. Bam, in my hand.

"You, sir, have been served," Dobson declared, exiting as quickly as he entered.

I looked down at the papers with my name on them and those of Miss Liberty T. Scarelli.

Brenda asked what Mr. Dobson wanted. Unknowingly, I began crushing up the papers I'd just been handed, looked at her, and whispered:

"I've just been served."

The short paragraph that I had just read declared that Ms. Scarelli was accusing me of rape, and that I was to appear at a hearing, "As noted," set a week from today. Rape, the most despicable of all crimes in my book. What the . . . .

"Brenda . . . " is all I could think of saying as she stood there reading through the document.

"We have to do something," Brenda gasped.

This can't be happening.

"Call a meeting of the executive group, then contact Ralph Phillips."

Ralph Phillips is our corporate attorney. I consider Ralph to be one of my lifelines. He's not only very good counsel but extremely well connected in the greater San Francisco area. His offices are in downtown San Francisco, close to Ted's. Some days, when I'm meeting with Ralph at his office, I'll make an appointment to meet with Ted right after. For all kinds of reasons, that one-two punch really helps to keep me on track.

My mind was replaying the last few weeks. Places, names, conversations. I couldn't stop thinking about Libby and how we met and wait . . . I needed to talk to Jillian.

11. "Hail, Hail, The Gang's All Here."

Brenda set the meeting in my office instead of the conference room. There they sat: Jose, Eve, and Jodie. Major had multiple production jobs going and couldn't make the meeting. Brenda told her assistant to hold all calls, except Ralph Phillips's who would join us on a conference call. She found someone to take her place in a pre-scheduled HR meeting, then joined us.

I paced slowly toward the oversized *Casablanca* movie poster. I suddenly felt as helpless as the strangers stranded in that movie.

"Thank you for rearranging your time. There's some startling news to share, and I'll need you to be discreet. No one can know about this matter until our legal counsel says so. Is that clear?"

They nodded, yes, in unison, looked at each other, then at me. Brenda handed out copies of the papers I'd been served and began outlining a communication plan. My emotions were a blend of anger, nerves, and embarrassment. My mind raced. I decided to sit back and listen and let the room do the talking.

After some quiet reading of the facts, there were a few unnerving moments of staring at one another, note-taking and coughing.

"Who is this woman?"

"How's this situation going to affect Blaine?"

"Rick would never."

"When did this supposedly happen?"

"We have to get to the bottom of this, now."

Their conversation became a debate, not about my innocence, that was understood. Instead, talk centered around next steps, which eventually grew into a resolution. Everyone knew the accusation couldn't be true, so the previously empty whiteboard filled rapidly with a communication plan. Ralph Phillips said that the plan's talking points had to achieve one goal: Protecting Blaine's reputation.

"Making that happen won't be easy," Ralph stated. "Rick is single, rich and has been seen with this woman."

The group, after talking into the late evening, unanimously agreed that a press release should come from Eve and Mr. Phillips instead of me. And, the response to the accusation should coincide with the media exposure that was sure to erupt.

Everyone impressed me by not questioning my innocence. All agreed that I had to be careful questioning Jillian. Brenda was adamant that I remain calm and in complete control of myself and not seem anxious or upset, which would be difficult. My emotions were moving quickly away from surprise and into anger.

Excusing myself, I left the meeting to make a call.

For some reason, I didn't have Jillian's phone number. So, I resorted to Artie's. Unfortunately, I got the hippie surfer's voicemail:

"Dude, you missed me, haha. I'll get back to you when I come up for air. Later."

Jillian sometimes used Artie's cell phone, so I left a message asking Artie to call me ASAP.

After our meeting, I pulled myself together and managed to get back to work for a few hours even though it was late.

Meanwhile, Eve and Jodie were drafting an "accusation action summary" that would defend me and reinforce our company's image. This situation couldn't have come at a more devastating time. Business was good, and the company's financials were better than ever. Our second quarter set a record for sales, and production was gearing up for additional business anticipated in our fourth quarter. Negative publicity is never good, and this type of accusation could definitely slow us down, or at worst, put us in a tailspin. We had to get ahead of the situation.

Right in the middle of mindlessly reviewing a production report, my phone rang. It was Artie. He was on an amusement ride with his cousin on the Santa Monica Pier. The reception was poor, but I wasn't about to let him go without finding a contact number for Jillian.

"Ya, dude, her cell . . . on . . . her . . . 56 . . . 467 do wha. Did y . . . it that?"

"No, Artie, give it to me one more time. Maybe you should call when you get off the damn ride!"

It took Artie three more tries before I was able to confirm Jillian's number. He left the ride and my phone call laughing like a little kid. Knowing him, he could've been making the whole phone interruption thing up just to get a rise from me.

I immediately called Jillian. We set a time to meet the next day. The pretense for my call was setting up a surprise for Artie and needing her advice. She gladly accepted. I knew then that Libby had not shared anything about the charge with her.

Just as I prepared to leave, Major knocked on my office door.

"Got a minute, Rick?"

His team was running at full speed, and I thought we'd be talking new lines and product conversions, but to my surprise, he began with:

"Rick, I heard what happened and I want you to know that . . . I know people. People who can make bad situations go away, no questions asked."

He held my gaze, looking a lot like Clint Eastwood daring me to make his day. Did I just hear what I heard? We were standing facing one another. I clasped my hands together and said slowly:

"Major, I appreciate what you're saying, I think. Just so you know, Ralph is on it, so let's concentrate on business for now, okay?"

He gave me a quick military salute and a wicked wink. He then switched into production mode and proceeded with the update. Once we concluded our meeting, I thought about how it had been a welcome distraction to hear good news about the increased volume of product we'd be producing in the near future.

As I left the office, Major became my shadow. He escorted me to my car like a secret service agent, including the dark glasses, even though the sun had set two hours earlier. He may have even been armed, though I didn't ask.

Things at Blaine were looking up, regardless of the fact that Libby rattled me with her false accusation. I felt dirty and somewhat stupid. It was hard to shake.

I called Jess. This situation would put her Big Sister knowledge to the test. I respect my sister's practical outlook and resolve and told her so as I aimed the Porsche south on the fastest route to Venice Beach.

After talking with Jess for nearly an hour, it was clear to me that she would do whatever I needed in order to help make this situation go away. My plan was to lay low in the Northwest until the media turmoil subsided. Because of that, I asked her to leave her family for a few days; she would become my best means of transportation when I arrived in the Northwest. How my team and I would get there was another matter. She also made reference to the fact that Brenda was the main reason our family keeps up-to-date on what's happening with me. I noticed a little sisterly nudge or suggestion that I pay more attention to those around me. In Jess's words:

"You never know until you ask who's got your back, Rick."

I got that. My mind is always thinking ahead; it has always been hard for me to be in the moment like Jess just suggested. I've never really thought of Brenda as someone who cares for me beyond our business relationship. If that's what Jess meant. First of all, I would never think of Brenda in that way. We've shared a few light-hearted moments in the past, but nothing more than that. I respect Brenda as a colleague and nothing more. Period.

Life is full of challenges. Some that need to be dealt with immediately. Working from a plan in business helps you make better decisions, but what about everyday life? Who has a backup plan when you break up with someone? Or worse yet, what happens when you end up on the wrong end of a false rape accusation?

You see it all the time: "This is the kind of thing that happens to someone else, not me." But this rape charge came out of nowhere. Hard to plan for that. Surprises are the shits, unless it's your birthday or Christmas.

So, according to my new life plan, my next action was to meet with Jillian and find out what the hell was going on.

12. "Okay, Let's Get to the Bottom of This."

Jillian met me at Stack Mans Eatery. The restaurant is ensconced in an all-metal building with a double-thick metal roof, formerly a warehouse near a rather fragrant commercial boat launch. There must have been hundreds of seagulls roaming the sky, waiting for that perfect moment when fish scraps are tossed overboard from loading docks nearby.

The place is an out-of-the-way café. Locals can't get enough of their specialty breakfast menu and roasted coffee blends. Even though I was hungry, my main interest did not concern food nor drink.

Our conversation began slowly like the rain that was beginning to beat on the roof in an even rhythm.

"Jillian, thanks for meeting with me."

"Hey, sure. So what's this about Artie?"

"I lied, which is ironic. This is not about Artie. Actually, I'm more interested in Libby."

That comment caused her smile to vanish. She looked at the door, the floor, then back at me as if she were planning to escape. We'd just ordered omelettes with coffee and were waiting. Jillian's eyes circumnavigated the room, all the while avoiding mine. I must have had that "need answers now" look on my face. For a second, I had visions of me tackling her as she bolted for the door.

Jillian was obviously nervous, and after a few more painful seconds, she looked up and said, "Okay, what is it you want to know?"

She was forcing that perfect smile back onto her face, but it wasn't working. She more closely resembled one of Picasso's misshapen cubist paintings.

"How well do you know her, Jillian?"

While I waited for an answer, our orders came. My phone rang as if on cue. It was Winston Lamperson. I had to take it. I excused myself and walked outside.

"Winston, what can I do for you?"

"It's not what you can do for me old chap, it's what we can do for you."

Evidently, Brenda talked to Ben earlier in the day about setting a meeting with Jodie and Victor regarding various target market identifiers when Ben let it be known that their company also provided very sophisticated background checks. Brenda knew the Lampersons were competent and felt compelled to ask more about that particular service. She gave Ben the inside scoop, trusting him to keep the "Libby" issue a secret. And before she knew it, Winston was on the line asking to talk with me.

"We will find out as much as possible, not just name, rank, and serial number, if you know what I mean. Undercover, of course. No one needs to know. INTERPOL will never find out."

Though he was joking about INTERPOL, he knew the seriousness of this matter and that it was of the utmost importance.

"As much as you can find on her would be great, thanks."

"Your Brenda let us know. I hope you don't mind."

"Of course not, Winston. I didn't realize…"

"Few people do, Rick. We like it that way. With your approval, we'll really drill down on this Libby person."

"Anything you can find will be appreciated. Thanks."

"I believe Brenda, who by the way has an uncanny sense

about things. She's the one to thank right now, Rick. We'll be in touch."

And then he was off like Sherlock Holmes in hot pursuit.

A heavy aroma of garlic overtook me as I re-entered Stack Mans and sat across from Jillian. She'd barely touched her food. With eyes fixed on her plate, she whispered:

"I have something to share about Libby and I don't think you're going to like it."

I kept quiet as I took my first bite. Jillian began to open up.

"Liberty and I met on the east coast, in jail, a few years ago, before I moved out here. She'd been convicted for her part in some drug scheme. I was in for disorderly conduct. We hit it off and watched out for each other for the three months I was there. I learned that she and her brother had fallen in with some mob types. He introduced her into the drug business, starting out as a mule. Libby is smart and full of ideas, and she's a felon. We caught up here in Venice Beach a few weeks ago. She had been scoping out you and Blaine Manufacturing and wanted an introduction. I should have known she was up to something when she offered me money, which I refused. Rick, will you ever forgive me?"

I was at a loss for words, so I just stared at her. The rain now pelted the metal roof as if someone was dropping marbles in a syncopated rhythm. Somehow the beat matched the pounding at my temples.

"Well, are you going to hit me or something?"

I dropped my stare down to my plate along with my fork and knife. The utensils made a semi-loud sound, but the people around us were occupied with their own dramas, so we just continued with ours.

Still looking down, I whispered, "She's accused me of raping her, Jillian."

Jillian stopped mid-bite and put her fork down, then wiped her mouth. Her eyes began to well up.

For the next few minutes, Jillian shared how Libby had come to her with a proposition, asking to meet Rick Blaine. All Jillian knew at the time was that Libby wanted an introduction, and that she, Libby, would take it from there.

"She can be very convincing, Rick. I thought she was on the level, and I wanted her to meet a great guy. I had no idea that it would come to this."

Throughout our conversation, Jillian was never privy to the slanderous details that Libby listed in the serving documents. There was no purpose in sharing the lies. I needed the truth. In the end, I felt as though she told me everything and didn't know anything about the false accusation. Libby had been lying to Jillian too. Her reasons for showing up unannounced were made up, but why? All Jillian had in regard to contact information for Libby was a phone number.

"How would you feel about getting back in touch with Libby?" I asked Jillian.

A more familiar smile spread across her face. My instinct told me to trust her enthusiasm. It's interesting how someone you thought you knew could suddenly change into someone so totally unrecognizable. As we finished breakfast, she shared as much as she knew about Libby.

The rain began to subside as we left Stack Mans. Jillian gave me a warm hug and promised to call the second she connected with Libby. I had one more question:

"Disorderly conduct?" I asked with a half-smile.

"It was a bar fight. I was defending a girlfriend's honor and broke a guy's arm in the process. Not my proudest moment. Best not to bring it up again, alright?"

"Of course," I said, trying to hold the smile and to keep from laughing.

The more I learned about her brief time with Libby, the more there was to know about Jillian. She is one personable and dangerous lady. Then it dawned on me why she and Artie were an item. Opposites attracting made more sense than ever before.

Time to take action. I needed to review the plan my group created. They recorded the key points, so I could memorize them as I headed back to San Francisco, switching onto the coastal Highway 101 from I-5. The meandering drive gave me time to think.

A coastal fog greeted me about halfway there. I don't mind the fog; it keeps me on my toes as it moves back and forth across the landscape, making the ocean appear as an apparition. It's like an ever-changing picture framed in my windshield. Huge cypress and cedar trees seemingly float on smokey-grey clouds continuously rolling past, in and out.

That's it! A new color combination: Misty fog-grey and lime green. Yes. We have to have it! I made a mental note to check on our projected new color combinations for next year.

My phone vibrated. Brenda called. I let it go to message.

13. "Justice Meets Patience."

I stayed in Tiburon, studying and making some revisions to the plan. Monday morning, 7:30 a.m., and my office felt unusually cold. Could it be the heavy rain clouds obstructing the picture-perfect view? Maybe. It could also have something to do with the fact that I was being wrongly accused of a terrible crime.

Our attorney left some interesting news on my voicemail. The attorney that filed the documents for Libby was located in New Jersey which, according to Ralph, was important to note. When I mentioned it to Winston, he told me that Ralph's concern was "spot on," and he would have Ben look into it immediately.

Brenda started a file on Libby that included the action plan, an update from Ben, Ralph's suggestions, and the team's review of the situation. I spent the next hour going over the material. I didn't like being on the defensive. Offense is what moves you forward.

My plate was full, and I couldn't be more thankful for the supportive people in my life.

After a few hours, my head hurt.

"Brenda, I'll be downstairs," I called out.

My mind required a cleansing. I exited via the stairwell and down two flights to our "imagination" area where I pay people to look out the window and dream.

Part of making things happen comes from knowing when

to help yourself. Bring on the distraction. Our Imagineers are incredible thinkers who will take the smallest idea and make it pop into reality. They enjoy the challenge of creating something new. They also like to joke around; the room is full of stand-up comics. I'm not joking. They refuse to take life too seriously, and at the time, that was a space that needed filling.

Frankly, I'd rather raise a little hell or, in this case, come up with a unique idea that would take the foreign competition months to figure out. The patented high-tech equipment covers we produce can easily be copied in look but not quality. After all, a cover is a cover, right? Not exactly. And certainly not if Blaine is to continue blazing new trails.

Recently, our "imagination team" came up with the addition of smell to go along with feel. We now incorporate, for a few more dollars, an assortment of cover skins that range from coarse to fine. We added fragrance two months ago, and those products moved us into the sales stratosphere, especially with women. You combine each of those with our color pallet, and we are in a league of our own. Who would have thought that a cowhide cover could have a salted caramel scent? Somehow, it works, and helps to keep Blaine on the leading edge.

At least that's what our web page says, and I believe we will stay there as long as we have Eddie Newland, head Imagineer, who came to us from Apple. Eddie, as his story goes, upset Steve Jobs one day and was fired the next. As Eddie was emptying out his desk, Jobs sent for him. The end result was that Eddie was rehired before he could leave the campus. From that day on, Eddie never felt completely comfortable around the unstable and brilliant Mr. Jobs. Eventually, Eddie found us after buying one of our products for his phone, then presented me with a terrific idea. It was a light-weight metal laptop frame that protected the device and doubled as a desk stand. He had the patent on the frame, but we would develop the cover. That project moved forward the following year and proved to be very successful. That was three years ago. As Eddie put it, "I'm looking for a new Jobs."

The next hour was spent with Eddie and a few of his people just looking out the window and envisioning what the next smell, color or texture combo might be. It was as refreshing as one of Artie's famous margaritas. When I mentioned the fog mixed with the light green tree color, you would have thought God himself had just spoken to the apostles. Eddie launched out of his chair like he'd been shot from a cannon.

"That's it, guys," he said.

"Mr. B, I'm going to ask you to leave now. We have work to do."

I wasn't sure if Eddie was serious about the idea. It didn't matter. I loved these young men and women.

The fact that my new idea sent me packing kept me laughing as I bypassed the elevators, then bounded up the back stairway to my office where Eve had been waiting to discuss some website upgrades.

"What's so funny, may I ask?" Eve said as I came around the corner.

I couldn't contain myself and related to Eve and Brenda what had just happened on the floor below. We had another good laugh together as Eve brought me up-to-speed on a new product marketing idea which would only work if we upgraded the website to the tune of a few hundred thousand dollars.

Brenda sat up, trying to get my attention as I walked Eve out of my office. Brenda let me know that Ralph would be calling. He had some new information, and she thought it would be best if I took the call here rather than in my car.

It was about six, and the office was empty as Eve had said her goodbyes. Once she was gone, that left just Brenda and me in my office for when Ralph called.

"I have some good news and some not. Here comes the not.

We believe Libby is connected to a New Jersey-based group of unsavory characters," Ralph said in his deep, gravelly voice.

"We know she has a troubled past, which includes dealing drugs for the mob and an extortion conviction on her record."

Ralph was silent as I shared what Jillian told me over coffee the other day. I could hear paper shuffling over the phone as he wrote, taking notes as I recalled her jailhouse conversation.

Then came a random question:

"Is it true, Rick, that Blaine Manufacturing is entering the New England area?"

"Yes."

"It's just a guess, but there may be some connection between that and this false accusation. It's a long shot, but one of my guys who knows this crowd came up with the idea. I think it has merit. Otherwise, I would've kept it to myself."

Ralph didn't know for certain, but he wouldn't discount the fact that the mob had all kinds of businesses they used as "fronts," which Blaine could be interfering with, unknowingly, during the new product distribution launch. He was going to have a private investigator check into it and get back to me with more details, hopefully by the end of the week. Ralph was good about putting deadlines on details. I thanked him and then asked:

"So, what's the good news, Ralph?"

"Oh, yes. Well, there really isn't any good news, Rick, but I hope to have some for you soon."

"That's why we pay you the big bucks, Ralph. I'll look forward to hearing what your detective uncovers."

In the meantime, I met with Jodie and Victor to find out the status of our sales launch in New England. I asked Jodie to put a temporary hold on plans, which created some understandable frustration for them both. This was the first time we had ever held back on entering a new market, which felt counterproductive to them.

§

TIBURON PENINSULA, CALIFORNIA, 3 A.M.

The black van rolled to a stop, headlights off. The sound of slow-moving rubber tires on gravel faded as two men dressed in black took their time checking the pier for any movement. The tide was in; they needed that. The pier was empty too. Perfect timing.

Her body was in the back, carefully rolled up in plastic. The young lady had put up one hell of a fight. One shoeless foot protruded out from under the cover, exposing carefully painted toenails that now seemed so unnecessary to the men who hurried through the last stages of their murderous task.

The boss ordered the kill a few hours earlier after finding out more about Mr. Blaine. He then set up the rendezvous that eventually ended her life. There could be no mistake; the target had to be made to squirm like a rat skewered on a stick. And this sudden change of plan, coming from her psychopathic boss, was intended to shock everyone who did business with the target. The irony, of course, is that this unfortunate occurrence would also increase loyalty within the Castillino family. Michael would undoubtedly be congratulating himself on creating such a clever scheme.

The two henchmen were very good at their criminal craft. These jobs were proof of their undying loyalty. They'd be generously rewarded by their superiors. This simple hit came to them with great urgency and a request: Kill and allow the body to be discovered. No elaborate measures were required to make the body go away. That would be counterproductive.

They carried her to the water's edge where she rolled slowly into the cold bay. The men then covered their tracks as usual, stowed the cover in the back of the van and drove away. The driver noted that this part of the job lasted just twelve minutes.

"Nice view of the bridge and the city," one of them said as they drove off, turning onto the main street with the headlights back on.

14. "This Can't Be Happening"

Traffic was surprisingly light that morning as I drove to the office, half-listening to the news on the car radio. Out of the blue, I heard, "The body of a young female has been found floating off the Saint Francis Yacht Club pier in Sausalito."

Today's sunrise came with a bang. I fumbled for my dark glasses. Nothing better than a California bluebird day, alright, but that sun was right in my eyes. No clouds in sight, and the commute seemed a little less congested across the Golden Gate Bridge. I felt unusually empowered as the news went in one ear and out the other, almost. Did the announcer say Sausalito?

A few days later, authorities confirmed the body floating in the bay was that of Ms. Liberty T. Scarelli. It seemed as though my life went automatically into overdrive. People who knew of my relationship with Libby sent texts and emails asking if I had heard the news. Yes. I had heard about Libby's fate. The empowerment I'd been feeling suddenly vanished. What happened? Who would do such a thing? Questions rained down around me, pelting every fiber with pricks of emotion.

My desire to switch into escape mode loomed like a dark cloud overhead when Ralph called. He wanted to set a time to meet. Brenda made the arrangements after I handed her the phone. I was trying to prioritize my options. All I knew was that Brenda had to be in this equation.

We assembled in Ralph's office near Union Square in

downtown San Francisco. Brenda dropped me off first, at Ralph's request. Two of his associates met me in the lobby, walking me immediately to the service elevator, then to Ralph's office. After parking the car, Brenda joined me in Ralph's private waiting room in preparation for the meeting. His secretary served us fresh-brewed coffee while we waited.

"Let's hope Ralph has some good news this time," Brenda said with a look that made me feel as though there was some hope headed my way.

"I've never felt so blindsided in my life," I said.

A few minutes later, Ralph opened his private side-office door and ushered us both quickly inside. He was not alone.

"Come in, sit down, and meet Bear." Ralph gestured toward a tan leather couch as I looked over Bear. He explained that Bear was a Private Investigator who worked closely with Ralph and his team. Ralph knew I needed the best, and Bear had outstanding credentials.

"He can be trusted. This is the man for the job, Rick."

As Ralph pointed toward the man, he slowly emerged, unfolded really, standing well over six feet tall, out of a corner of the room like a pop-up in the middle of a kid's book. He stuck a big meaty hand out for us to shake and said:

"My real name is Bobby Hansen, Mr. Blaine, Miss Brenda. I'm here to help."

His hand felt like a big pillow, and at his height and weight, he cut an impressive figure.

Once everyone was seated, Ralph asked Bear to say a few words about the latest developments in Libby's death.

"Well, she wasn't treated like a lady. I can tell you that," he said. "Whoever ended her life made it look personal. All cut up and stripped down, if you know what I mean."

Brenda and I looked at one another as Ralph offered more.

"We need to know who murdered Libby. We can't depend

on the police – they will be asking to interview you soon. I feel like with the Lampersons investigating the east coast operation, and Bear watching out for you here, we have our best chance. Tell them your theory, Bear."

The big man was back to sitting in the corner, off to one side, which I found oddly comforting.

"I think you're in for even more trouble, Mr. Blaine," Bear muttered.

He removed a toothpick from the corner of his mouth, then went on to explain how the people he'd been tracking on the east coast appeared to have made a visit to San Francisco at the time of Libby's murder.

"Oh, Rick," Brenda suddenly blurted out. "These are just conspiracy theories!"

Bear shot back quickly:

"Think about it. Mister Rick here, Blaine's number one man, is the perfect mark. He's enraged by the rape accusation and wants it to go away. He's rich, single, and has motive. Plus, you, sir, live very close to where her body was found."

His overview made sense. Everything Bear said was true, except for the part about me possibly committing murder. We went over my best options, and Bear noted he would be "widening his investigation," which meant two things according to Ralph:

• Bear would be on a retainer and

• He was going to disappear for a few days but would keep in contact with Ralph.

It would be one day, possibly two, before any report would be coming our way. I couldn't wait that long, but what was I to do? In the meantime, Brenda would be the main contact between Ralph's office and me. Ralph would be working on legal matters that would extend the time for a hearing on the rape accusation, which now changed into God knows what, especially if I was being considered as a murder suspect.

We left after two hours of questions and answers that resulted in strict instructions. All the details boiled down to me keeping my mouth shut and staying out of sight.

Jillian was on my mind. She knew the real Libby, and that could lead to big trouble. Instead of laying low, I wanted to catch up with Jillian right away. She had to be on the bad guys' radar. My instinct was to handle Jillian myself, and not involve Bear or Ralph. They had enough to do for now. Besides, Jillian and Artie were special friends, and this whole damn affair with Libby was really my fault.

Brenda caught an Uber ride back to the office as I headed for my car. I exited the downtown parking garage in second gear and almost ran over a kid, jumping the curb on inline skates. My mind was reeling, especially after Ralph alluded to the people back east as "the mob." I called Artie and asked him to find Jillian and stay with her until I got there. It was becoming evident to me that whoever killed Libby was counting on me taking the rap. What a devious and clever plan. We had to find out who was behind it.

While I drove back to my apartment in Tiburon, I replayed the questions Libby had asked regarding what I did for a living and who was in charge of what at Blaine. I remembered thinking at the time that she was either very interested or the nosiest individual I'd ever met.

So, this is what it's like to be set up, I thought. And it's all about business, really? Of course. We make protective phone covers, and the mob protects themselves by covering things up. My head was spinning.

Our New England launch was in the last phase of our continental business development plan, and that action created all this mess? No way. I had to take charge. I decided to head south and leave the rest up to Bear, Ralph, and Winston.

§

HIGHWAY 101, CALIFORNIA COAST

The coastal drive normally relaxes and distracts me enough so that I only focus on my driving. The sun heading for the water on my right provides a good indication of the time without looking at my watch. The ribbon of road slipping underneath the car creates an undulating motion that works in syncopation to the turning of the wheel and shifting of the gears. Hard to explain the feeling, better to experience it instead.

Yes, that was a very different day from all the rest. I felt like something else was driving me to be on that road at that moment. What was it? After more miles, I decided the answer had to be chasing me. And so I kept driving, turning, shifting, wondering and hoping. Nothing, not even the blue sky and rocky cliffs fighting back the angry surf could soothe me.

I remember the sun's glare becoming more of a driving distraction as it fell further toward the ocean. The Porsche seemed to be driving itself when I suddenly realized that I hadn't eaten. It was close to six-thirty, and the last thing I ate was a bagel at ten that morning. Up ahead, an exit beckoned me. It was one that I normally flew past. A few restaurant signs were posted just beyond as I downshifted and pulled off.

A surprising number of fast-food places came first and looked tempting, but I felt like trying to take a few minutes to eat. I took a quick breath, relaxed in the driver's seat, slowed and allowed a moment to decide. A hunch led me to take a chance on a place called The Settlers Inn. The Inn had a fair number of cars parked out front. A good sign. And a very cool BMW parked at the same time I pulled in. That did it, I decided. I was going to stop and take a few minutes to collect myself.

The place reminded me of a ski lodge, with a big fire and home-cooked smells. In the restroom, I splashed water on my face and washed up. After being seated, I managed to relax some.

The meatloaf special with all the trimmings sounded good. It was the kind of meal you could savor for hours, but I knew not to delay for too long. Forty-five minutes later, I was at the counter paying and tipping my waitress, Joyce, who had the most reassuring and motherly voice:

"Son, be careful out there tonight. Weather report calls for fog if you're headed south."

As I left the Inn, a cool breeze came up, causing my take-out coffee to steam through the tiny sip hole. Here I am, contributing to the fog.

The temperature had dropped a few degrees in the time it took me to eat. A shiver ran up my spine. Along with it came a sense of urgency. My heart rate increased, and as I took the next step, my feet weren't moving like before. I found it hard to walk without purposely placing one foot in front of the other. Slowly, and with some newfound deliberation, I made my way to the car. I reminded myself to breathe deeply and find some calm. The evening chill blended with a sick feeling, and everything around me moved strangely, as if in a bad dream.

I must have eaten too much or too fast. With the coffee in one hand, I fumbled with the keys until the driver's door finally opened. I pivoted and hit the driver's seat a little harder than normal. The leather seat molded around me, and for about a minute I sat there, feeling the hug, trying to get my bearings. Start the car, Rick.

The engine fired, snapping me back into a more familiar state of mind, and I was off. It wasn't until I turned right toward the on-ramp that I realized the BMW was leaving at the same time. Those cool blue headlights, had I seen them before? I noticed a phone message as I placed it in the dash holder. It was from Jose:

"Hey, Rick. This may be nothing, but I thought you should know that Bob Khulors just called to say that the people back east had suddenly changed their tone. They now sound more threatening than business-friendly. Let me know if you want to change your mind about that situation as soon as possible. Stay safe, wherever you are."

A red flag went up as I pulled over to double-check the message. The BMW did the same. A man got out and opened the trunk. It was a sleek black sporty BMW 630i with at least two people inside. I sent Jose a text telling him to talk to Ralph, then took off again. The on-ramp flew past as I sped through the gears. It was just over four hundred miles to Venice Beach, and I wanted to arrive safe and sound and without company.

The car and my mind were racing to find syncopation again. Pumping adrenaline helped to warm me up as I went through some options.

First, I needed to lose the BMW boys who were about a quarter of a mile back. If this was a coincidence, fine, it would make the drive go faster. I knew this road – every bend, straightaway, rise and fall. I figured that if these were strangers to the area, they wouldn't know the road as well, especially in fog now beginning to materialize.

My thoughts went to a mountain tunnel about forty miles ahead, a road map flashing in my mind. On the other side of that tunnel, there was an ocean viewpoint on the right. This time of night, and with the fog, few people would stop to appreciate the view. If the BMW crew was after me, I didn't want them to think I was on to them just yet. Neurotic? Sure, add it to my list for Ted to work on.

I checked for headlights behind, then carefully scanned the road ahead as the fog thickened. I shifted from fourth to third around the corners, checking to see if the road had any slippage, then went up to fifth gear along the straightaways.

As I reached for my coffee, the BMW's headlights appeared in the rearview mirror like tiny blue cotton balls. That black cat was ready to pounce. I still had some straightaway for another mile or two, so I took the Porsche up to one hundred and twenty in seconds. I knew this part of the road had just been resurfaced and would drive like a dream. Being ahead of the BMW put me in a favorable position, and the straightaway allowed me to take off like a rocket. Advantage: me. It was obvious now that whoever was driving wasn't used to this highway or making turns at high rates of speed, especially at night with an ocean fog moving back and forth over the roadway. Slow down, kitty. Speed kills.

I called Bear, who had given me his cell number in case of emergency. He answered.

"Where are you, Rick?"

I gave him my location and situation, trying not to sound desperate. My hope was that he'd give me some options.

"Well, if it were me, I'd ditch 'em by going dark and hiding somewhere on the side of the road."

"Just what I was thinking," I told him.

The tunnel plan was on. Bear said that he would try to catch up. As it happened, he was on the same stretch of road, driving in the opposite direction from the south about ninety miles from the tunnel. He knew the location where I planned to ditch the Porsche and said to keep in contact.

"Be aware, Rick, don't call 911 for help. There's a warrant out for your arrest. Nothing that Ralph can't handle. We'll stash the Porsche at the viewpoint and leave it behind. That is, if I can make it there in time. On my way. Be safe."

Alright, I thought. No, this was good. I was tired of being on the defensive.

The BMW was about a half-mile behind and had to know by now that the game was on. Having Bear approaching from the other direction gave me a boost of confidence. My main focus now was on timing. What would I do if they didn't take the bait and pulled off when I did for some reason? No room for error, I thought. This will work.

A new, invigorating, escape mode came over me. Failure was an option that I refused to recognize because, for the first time, I realized that I had the mob, or some form of them, and the cops after me at the same time. At least that's what was now going through my mind as I took a wide and forgiving curve at eighty-five miles per hour, knowing the Porsche could slide out at any second. I had to take a chance that the California Highway Patrol was on duty somewhere else.

With approximately twenty miles to go before the tunnel, I called Jillian again. She answered.

"Rick, when will you be here?"

I explained that I had a stop to make first and would call her when I was close. She told me that she was with Artie as we discussed. I asked her to stay put and not to go near my place. Before hanging up, I told her about the warrant and told her to let me know if the police came around, asking questions.

"Oh, God. Okay, thanks, Rick. Be careful."

The tunnel would be coming up soon. With adrenaline pumping, my focus on the road ahead increased. I tipped my shoulders down, chin up, and breathed deeply, in through the nose and out. I sped up and took the Porsche to the max, leaving my new friends working hard to keep up. Fog normally makes driving more challenging, but I decided to take a chance and see if it could work to my advantage as I sliced through it at a much higher speed than my following friends. So far, so good. The Porsche was made for quick responsive driving, so long as the driver remained alert. Pink Floyd was belting out "Eclipse," one of my favorites, and now seemed so apropos.

All that you touch, and all that you see, all that you taste, all that you feel...

Where's the tunnel? Come on, come on. Then, there, there, no, yes, that's it. Closer than I expected. It looked smaller for some reason, wait, that's just one part of it. I downshifted too soon and the back of the car lurched sideways, then steadied. I decided on no brake lights. An eighteen-wheeler entered about a hundred yards ahead going the same direction.

Slow, slower, and then it hit me, a wave of fog that completely eliminated the tunnel. I froze, staying the course and trusting my position, hands welded to the steering wheel like a racecar driver steering through a smoke-filled accident. I slowed to fifty, looking for anything to get my bearings. Suddenly, a road sign popped up in front of the car, straight ahead. My reaction caused the Porsche to swerve, then the car slid to the left onto gravel. I responded by turning right, overcorrected, pumping the brakes once. The car spun like a top. I yelled, "NO!"

Everything went black and stopped.

Miraculously, the Porsche had only glanced off one of the tunnel walls. The car sustained some damage, but to what degree? The motor sputtered, then stopped. There was no airbag to deploy since it was a vintage 911. I felt like I'd just taken a punch to the face. My head throbbed as pain shot from my left foot up my leg. The dashboard lights were on, and Pink Floyd kept playing. Meanwhile, I checked around inside for damage and turned the ignition key, hoping the engine would catch, and I could somehow get through the tunnel.

While attempting to restart the car, the fog from behind took on an increasingly bright blue glow. They must have slowed down, I thought. The fog continued to dance back and forth, revealing shapes of trees near the road, then, like a magician, making those same images disappear in an instant. Was my head playing tricks on me, or was this lightshow really happening? The headlight glow appeared brighter as the engine reluctantly caught, choked, and caught again. The car began moving. The engine managed to gain power and a little speed as I carefully worked the accelerator, the tires crunching over debris in the roadway.

"Rick, keep watching for them," I whispered as the song faintly echoed inside the car.

And everyone you fight, and all that is now, and all that is gone, and all that's to come.

I turned the headlights off and used the dome light to follow the centerline. How far to the end of the tunnel?

It had to be close, even though the car crept along at ten miles per hour. I started to smile, then noticed that my pants were wet. Had I pissed my pants? No, no. The coffee cup was missing – it must have spilled in the accident. I laughed and reminded myself to always keep the lid tight from now on. A drink of coffee would have been nice, just not on my pants. Oh, God, my head hurt.

I pushed against the gas pedal, hoping the car would respond. It did, sort of. Gently, the car increased speed as the fog dissipated and the roadside overlook appeared on the right, just past the tunnel exit.

"Come on, come on, baby. Just a little further."

It felt like the drummer for Pink Floyd was now sitting on my shoulders, wailing away on my head. Concentrate, concentrate.

Ditch the car and find a hiding place until Bear arrives. The fog lifted for an instant, and I saw the parking lot with a restroom facility about fifty feet from the mountain tunnel. A big location sign with a large arrow pinpointed the "You Are Here" spot, and various landmarks for one hundred and eighty degrees. Fascinating. I'll stop back sometime and check it out.

"I've got this," I said to myself while maneuvering the ailing Porsche into the opening between the sign and the restroom. The Porsche shuddered as it came to a stop. My car was badly damaged; I felt bad leaving it behind. A few low-hanging tree limbs and the fog would hopefully camouflage the car until I could get someone to come and haul it back to San Francisco. No time to think about that. Move.

I slowly swiveled both legs out the door. Standing was a challenge. My left knee must have hit the dash. The pain was almost unbearable. I managed to find a few branches that had fallen to the ground and put them down across the back of the car, adding to the camouflage. Moving required more effort than I'd ever needed.

My phone and backpack were in my hands before I knew it. I took off limping.

15. "Roadside Assistance"

From my vantage point at the corner of the tunnel, I could watch the glow from the BMW headlights play back and forth. They grew brighter as I half-crouched near the tunnel's east opening. My mind was on "ready to run" mode.

The Porsche's green bumper sat upside down on the asphalt, the largest of the fragments; a fact made even more evident when one of the men came around the front of the BMW and brought out a flashlight. There the bumper lay, defeated, as the man looked up and smiled. He had to know that if I was still running, I wouldn't be going very fast. The question was: Where's the Porsche?

"Find the car, find the driver," the man yelled over to his buddy as he watched for oncoming traffic. The second man shouted back to his partner to make a phone call.

The tunnel suddenly darkened as the BMW backed up and parked off to the side, just outside the entrance to the tunnel. Both men used their feet to clear the road of debris. Evidently, they didn't want to chance getting a flat tire. It took them a few minutes, which gave me time to take off. I made it to the side of the road and hid behind a large cedar tree. They started the BMW and carefully made their way through the tunnel. I could hear them mumbling; they must have rolled the windows down.

"He wants him alive," one of them said.

Alive. That was reassuring.

My call to Bear was quick. He didn't seem to register that I'd been in an accident. Bear seemed like someone who operated on the "Shit Happens Rule" anyway. He asked for my exact location and told me he was twenty minutes out, then instructed me to hang tight. So, it became time to wait, listen, and breathe.

I couldn't see the Porsche from across the highway. The additional branches across the back of the car really helped to hide it. Even though I planned to dump the Porsche for now, crashing this vintage ride made the pain feel even worse.

My left leg needed to move, so I climbed farther up the side of the hill opposite the overlook. Any movement had to be coordinated carefully so I wouldn't give my position away. Just then, a semi-truck slowed as it entered the tunnel. Perfect. Go. The rain-soaked slope was fairly steep, and each thrust forward hurt. The ground gave way with each step, which slowed my progress and caused me to walk with my knees. Breathe, exhale, breathe, exhale.

As I pushed through branches and bushes, the smell of the cedar nearly overwhelmed me. There was a spot next to a fallen tree where my field of vision widened enough for me to see traffic coming from the south. My back was to the hill, which became almost too comfortable as I reclined. The view was practically one hundred and eighty degrees from the south to my left, and turning through the fog-covered highway in front of me to the right where the south tunnel entrance sat like an upside-down horseshoe. Visibility was intermittent, about an eighth of a mile at best. I moved my head back and forth, watching for Bear, and then over to the right to look for the bad guys. It was like watching a television monitor with bad reception.

"I've heard of hunting for bears, but never waiting for one to come to the rescue," I chuckled to myself as I began shivering.

The jacket I'd grabbed from my backpack was not warm

enough here on the ground as the temperature continued to drop.

My thoughts were quick and random, levity included, evidently, as I waited for Bear. Heavy fog and complete silence surrounded me. The lights from a car brightened the end of the tunnel. The BMW burst through with high beams on and continued down the highway. They missed the Porsche – the camouflage worked!

My cold, dirty fingers fumbled with my phone before I finally hit the numbers on the pad. Shaking caused the phone to drop in the process. My hands were trying to work in concert with my fingers. It felt like I'd never done this before. Somehow, I managed to make the call. Bear was ten minutes out, in dense fog, doing his best to maintain his speed. Then it dawned on me; my briefcase was in the car. Instinct tried to convince me to leave it, but it contained critical information from Ralph. Damn me.

Nothing ventured, nothing gained. That saying became my mantra for the next few minutes.

Should the BMW keep heading south, I'd have plenty of time to get to the case and back. Unless they hit a long stretch and could see far enough to determine they'd been tricked. I had to take a chance. I took a deep breath and made my way down the hill and through a small dip next to the roadbed, only stumbling once. No traffic in either direction, so I made the crossing both feeling and probably looking like a crab.

The briefcase was in the trunk. I had the key and slid it into the lock. It appeared to be jammed. As I was fooling with the lock, I heard a car moving very slowly along the other side of the highway. The BMW eventually revealed itself as I hurried with the lock. After the third try, it gave, and I quickly removed the briefcase, along with the tire iron. Backpack, briefcase, tire iron. I felt ready, closed the lid and looked right into the eyes of a man holding a gun. I froze.

His voice came out in a confident whisper:

"Mr. Blaine, don't move. The fog makes it hard to see – I'd

hate to shoot you for no good reason. Now, slowly turn around."

I did as instructed, partially because it was a challenge physically to go much faster. He walked behind me, gun in his right hand. The man shoved me and demanded I move toward the BMW.

He pulled back some of the low-hanging branches, and I walked carefully out from the car's hiding place into the open and toward the highway. The man appeared to be about my size; he was dressed in black with a black knit cap. I glanced back over my shoulder at the man. There was no weapon in sight, though he'd put his right hand in his jacket pocket. Ah, it was cold. I was still shivering, although being held at gunpoint will get the blood pumping. He pointed with his left hand and kept telling me to move faster.

My thoughts went to the tire iron. No way was I going anywhere with this guy. And where the hell was Bear?

"Okay, walk slow, across the highway."

Our foggy march continued as we walked in unison onto the pavement. The man directing my every move had a heavy Jersey accent, which started to become more pronounced the more he talked.

"Walk slowly, Mr. Blaine. We wouldn't want you to get hit by no car now would we? Oh, and it's a shame about your ride there. What did it use to be, a Porsche? Them parts should be worth something though. Too bad you can't stay to pick them up." He offered a quick, monkey-like laugh.

Rage began to build inside me as the weight of the tire iron, suddenly felt light as a feather.

The misty fog settled uniformly across the roadway, making it damp and slippery. I could sense that behind me, the man with the gun was having trouble maintaining his balance. When I glanced back, I could see he was wearing leather slip-ons. Not the usual outdoor type of apparel. He switched the gun to his left hand, waving his right in an effort to maintain balance. His balancing act made me nervous. I thought he might shoot me by accident.

The tire iron was conveniently stuffed up my right coat sleeve and out of sight. The move reminded me of times I would hide Butch's throwing stick behind my back before tossing it off the dock. Concentrate. I can do this. Drop the tire iron into my hand and swing at the guy's head in the same motion.

As I carefully choreographed my spin move in my head, another car pulled up on the other side, and a man got out. A car door opened, then closed, and the driver asked if the guy in the BMW needed help. Even though the fog prevented me from seeing him, I knew the voice belonged to Bear.

The gunman tailing me continued to shuffle his feet like one of the three stooges. He was busy, trying to watch what was going on across the highway as he slipped and slid.

"You need ice skates," I said.

"And you need to shut it. Keep wa . . . walking."

3,2,1. The crowbar came down my sleeve to my hand a little faster than Butch's stick. I grabbed the bent end and swung in one motion. The blow sent the shuffler to the ground. I jumped on top of him. There we were, in the middle of the highway, him groaning and me contemplating my next move.

The groaning man faced the asphalt and was in the process of doing a push up when I hit him again.

"Stay down, fool," a line from a movie that came out of me almost automatically. It felt so good to say that I said it again.

Tossing the tire iron, I ran, slipping and sliding my way toward Bear, who now had whoever he'd been talking to in a chokehold. After laying the passed-out stranger on the side of the road, he grabbed me, and we ran for the Jeep. A shot rang out from behind me as Bear returned fire, causing dancing boy to scramble to the side of the road and tumble into the ditch as we reached the Jeep. The shooter cried out as he fell. I had to roll up and in as Bear started the ignition, then locked the doors. We were off, heading south on the wrong side of the highway, racing to Los Angeles in dense fog. Bear swerved to his left as a big rig came shooting past, blasting its horn, heading for the tunnel. We didn't see it, but we heard the horn blast again from the rig. We looked at one another and shrugged. My guess was that "dancing boy" just missed becoming roadkill.

I didn't feel so good and tried not to show it. We were both breathing hard, and I shared my concern that the Jeep would be no match for a high-performance BMW.

Bear just smiled.

"They have four flat tires and will need roadside assistance, thanks to this little baby."

Bear revealed a large hunting knife that hung in his jacket. His big grin showed one gold incisor. And that's the last thing I remember, his gold tooth, before I passed out.

16. "Escaping Is Definitely More Enjoyable When People Are Not Trying to Kill You."

Bear ended up parking his Jeep three blocks from Artie's Surf Shop, behind a gas station's concrete wall. The giant detective made the decision to park and stay the night in the Jeep since I was out like a light. Once the sun rose, it became more than Bear could manage, reclining in the Jeep trying to sleep. I thought I heard my name. Yes, I did.

"Rise and shine, Rick."

It could have been the word "Shine" that pulled me out of a deep sleep. That and the deep timbre of Bear's voice. When we exited the Jeep, my aches and pains were evident but tolerable. We walked along a small hedge bordering the beach as the sun continued to rise. The coastal fog drifted out to sea. I gave directions as Bear walked ahead, glancing back and forth, watching for anything that moved. As we approached the path leading to the backside of Artie's workshop, Bear went into a crouch and held a fist in the air. I stopped. Someone was in the bushes up ahead. Bear reached for his gun at the small of his back and, slowly turning, whispered:

"There's a guy up ahead taking a leak."

I asked: "Surfer dude with long blond hair?"

"Yep," Bear replied, replacing his gun after I told him it had to be Artie.

Both Jillian and Artie were relieved to see us.

"You okay, Rick? You're walking funny," Jillian said as we approached the hut.

"I crashed the Porsche last night. I'm a little shaken up. Give me a minute."

Both Artie and Jillian shifted their focus to Bear as I sat down. Bear had a way of making first impressions with his action figure-like appearance. He did stand out in a crowd with his military look: Boots, gun belt, camouflage pants and knitted cap, and an army-green t-shirt that revealed his oversized biceps.

"This is Bobby Hansen, a private detective working with me. He goes by the name Bear."

After the introductions, Bear sat across from Artie in the workshop. The normally good-sized work area became smaller with the addition of such a large man. The workbench in the center of the room looked like a coffee table with Bear sitting next to it. The room had a slight marijuana odor in addition to paint and varnish. We sat around the workbench like patrons waiting to be served a meal. Jillian came forward from a small room in the back and served some freshly brewed coffee as Artie moved one of his newest creations off the workbench.

Surfboards hung in various stages of work production along one wall. They held Bear's attention as Artie returned to his seat. The two of them, Artie and Bear, sat on old kitchen stools, engaged in a staredown. Neither said a word to each other as Jillian and I stood and walked off to the side of the room and casually began talking.

Artie was obviously taken by Bear's physical appearance. Looking Bear straight in the eye, Artie asked:

"You ever surfed?"

Bear, looking as though he was not at all impressed with Artie's appearance, replied:

"Never felt the need to."

Jillian did her best to distract me after learning what had just happened on the highway.

"These are some of Artie's newest boards. One of them is for the head of Fox Searchlight."

Artie's way-too-cool surfboard designs were definitely unique. The guy may be crazy, but damn he was good at crafting his boards. I made a mental note to talk to the Imagination Team about new color combos based on Artie's surfboard artistry. Before snapping back to reality, I took a few photos on my phone.

"Rick, are you in the market for a new surfboard?"

Jillian gave me a wide-eyed look.

"Sorry. Never stop working, I guess."

Focus, Rick.

Jillian told me that she became even more nervous after talking to me on the phone. She put Artie on alert, which meant he stopped surfing, drinking, and smoking even a minor amount of pot. Still, Jillian had reason to be extra cautious. Even though she and Artie could defend themselves physically, she knew Libby had mob connections. That cast a whole new light on our danger.

Jillian suggested we use Artie's surf store workshop as a hideout for now. The relatively small and well-hidden hut was located directly behind his store. No one would know to look for us there. We needed time to decide our next steps, now. The more I thought about escaping, the better my head felt. A reasonable escape plan started to take shape. Planes, trains and automobiles were out of the question because of the warrant for my arrest. A hot air balloon was not out of the question but highly unlikely.

We were confident that the plan would come together. We, me and whoever, most likely Jillian, just needed to be ready to go at a moment's notice.

Artie thought about calling on some surfer friends as reinforcements, but Jillian talked him out of it. The fewer people involved at this point, the better. The surf was up, and Artie knew he had at least ten surfing buddies close by the shop who'd be willing to help. Meanwhile, Artie passed the time stripping and waxing rental surfboards.

§

HALFWAY BETWEEN LOS ANGELES AND SAN FRANCISCO ON THE PACIFIC COAST HIGHWAY

Michael Castillino did not expect what he found on the highway. His men had made bad decisions in the pursuit of their target.

He led a group of six men involved in the hunt. They were traveling behind the BMW as reinforcements and clean up. The operation was supposed to be simple: find and detain the target for "questioning." Or, if he resisted, run him off the road and make it look like an accident. Mr. Blaine's rescue had thrown a wrench into the works, and the battle, according to Michael, had now become a war.

They picked up the two stranded goons, one of which had been grazed by a shot from Bear's gun, and then narrowly escaped being run over by a semi. All eight were headed for Venice Beach. The six men were tasked with finding the target and reporting their progress to their counterparts back east. Change of plan: They wanted Rick Blaine dead, along with anyone who accompanied him.

Rick and Jillian continued their planning conversation while Bear and Artie got to know each other.

"You design all these surfboards yourself?" Bear asked in a slow, soft tone.

"Oh, ya, yes," Artie said. "They're all my creations, man."

There was something about Artie that Bear found interesting. He wasn't used to hanging out with surfers, but he found Artie's child-like innocence to be refreshing. It could be he'd just spent the most uncomfortable night of sleep in his life and was hallucinating. No, he decided it was that Artie seemed like he didn't have a care in the world, except for anything related to surfing, and Bear sort of admired that.

"Like I said, I've never surfed."

Artie looked Bear over quickly. A smile slowly appeared.

"Hey, man, the Pacific Ocean will hold you. Let's go!"

"You sure about that?" Bear laughed as he held out his big paw to shake Artie's hand. "I'll stick around and see about taking you up on a lesson or two. But first, these two have got to go," referring to Jillian and me. We both overheard Bear's statement, which caused us both to look at him and then at each other.

Bear explained that he saw no good reason to stick around here in Artie's hut like sitting ducks. The mob and the cops were on the hunt. The plan had come together as far as Bear was concerned, whether we liked it or not. Bear had talked with Ralph last night, and they both decided that the two of us, Jillian and me, had to escape, pronto. We agreed.

"How?" I asked.

"I came up with an idea yesterday, and Ralph just texted me with his approval. Listen up," Bear said.

We couldn't risk using commercial transportation or even a private jet. Between the authorities and mobsters, our travel options were limited. Jillian didn't own a car, and my Porsche was not in the best of condition. Traveling on the highway would be difficult anyway, or so we thought.

Bear broke off the brief silence by raising both hands above the bench, elbows down, palms facing one another, then calmly said:

"I have a friend in the trucking business who's always looking for long-haul drivers. I remember you saying that you drove a truck for your father. True, Rick? Ever drive a big rig?"

Evidently, Bear had made a call to a friend in the commercial transportation business who said he could make arrangements for me to drive north to the Seattle area.

I grinned and responded like I did when Dad let me drive his truck alone for the first time: "I've always wanted to drive a big rig pulling a trailer. I guess now's as good a time as any."

Taking that as a yes, Bear smiled and immediately made the arrangements with the owner of Alvarez Trucking. Both Jillian and I had our backpacks ready. All we needed was transportation.

The twenty-mile drive to meet Mr. Alvarez took longer than I expected because Bear had to make sure we weren't being followed. Passing from the sandy beaches and million-dollar condos into the more urban and industrial area of Los Angeles was an eye-opener for both of us. These were locations you either lived or worked in, or you stayed away. Every business had bars on the windows. Pawnshops, run-down strip malls, mostly one- and two-story structures lined the road, each one tagged with graffiti that only made sense to the gang or individual who created it. We met Manny Alvarez in a grocery store parking lot that came out of nowhere like a desert oasis. The parking lot had just been paved and lined for parking. At one corner, along the side of the store, sat a long-haul rig with a trailer. It looked new, with an all-white paint job and blue trim. After making the introductions, Bear said his goodbyes, and within a few minutes Jillian, Manny, and I were heading north out of the hood in a Kenworth T680 – trailer in tow. Mr. Alvarez preferred we call him Manny, so we did. He pointed out various features of the truck, and we smoothly exited one busy arterial after another, heading for I-5.

"This rig will do seventy-eight miles per hour top speed because of a twelve-point-nine-liter engine," Manny pointed out as we drove.

He appeared to be friendly enough. He stood about six feet tall, had black hair, dark penetrating eyes, and a big-toothed smile.

And when it came to driving, Manny Alvarez was all business.

"You lose track of what you're doing and you or others may die faster than you can shift from one gear to another.

He spoke to both of us about the controls as he eased the big rig through traffic. I sat in the right seat like a little kid fulfilling a fantasy as Jillian looked on. She had toured the back area of the truck and checked out the eight-foot-wide area behind the cab prior to leaving.

We were like concert-goers watching the conductor of a symphony orchestra as Manny shifted through the gears, now heading for the freeway on-ramp. I tried to imagine myself at the controls as Manny paid close attention to the checklist of "driving priorities" attached by clipboard to the dash. Adjusting the side mirrors and seat height became our first important maneuver.

Manny said:

"With forty feet of tractor and trailer and over twenty thousand pounds of weight, moving at sixty-five miles per hour, it's a challenge to stay in control for anyone, especially a newcomer. You'll learn to look back as well as ahead. By the way, I trust you only because Bear trusts you, understand?"

"Yes," and after saying the word, yes, I felt a new weight in my currently crazy world fall directly on my shoulders.

Even though the trip would only last a few days, Manny pulled into a truck stop in order to show us how to fuel and service the truck efficiently. He also showed me the engine and the hydraulic connections for breaking. I had no idea how complicated this style of driving had become. I must have made a good impression because once Manny convinced himself that I could be trusted with the rig, we headed north on I-5. Our first stop was the San Francisco area. Manny demonstrated how to monitor the oil pressure, check all the gauges, and, most importantly, drive efficiently. He was impressed by how well Jillian and I both responded, taking it all in and asking the right questions. I hung on his every word and considered this experience a six-hundred-plus-mile test drive.

According to the documents, we were delivering a load of building supplies to a distributor in Vancouver, Washington. After that stop, we would drive empty up to Seattle and drop off the tractor and trailer. An Alaska option was out; the U.S. border patrol would be on high alert, watching for fugitives like me. Driving north, staying ahead of the chase, became our only option. My confidence level rose as Jillian and I talked things over.

I assured myself that we were doing the right thing by making this escape together. The drive would go better with someone to ride shotgun and help me in making decisions. I could also use the company. Truck stops and weigh stations were going to become our new hangouts for the next few days. Drive-through restaurants were not an option:

"Your rig is too tall," reminded Manny, again with a big grin.

I called Jess and shared our new plan while trying to sound upbeat. She listened as I explained how far off the radar we needed to be. It didn't take much convincing, and when the conversation ended, Jess agreed to meet us in Seattle in two days.

"Just be careful and keep in touch. I like the plan, little brother."

Once we connected with her in Seattle, she would then drive us to eastern Washington, and eventually on to North Idaho and Lake Pend Oreille. A rental car was not an option. Our plan was to remain at the lake in North Idaho, undetected, while the legal process progressed under Ralph's supervision. My mind was churning with all the steps that needed to go right. But for now, driving along the freeway, I needed to focus on this first stage of our plan.

Line up your options and keep them prioritized, Rick.

The men in the BMW were more of a concern than the rape accusation. Protecting my friends and making sure

Blaine Manufacturing was in good hands were also important considerations. Prioritizing my problems and their related actions didn't make me feel any safer, just better organized.

We removed the SIM cards from our cell phones and bought two burner phones. Untraceable, as Ralph had suggested. The attorney was not keen on me disappearing in the big rig, and preferred to have me safely guarded closer to San Francisco or on a private plane off to somewhere far, far away. Neither of those options felt as plausible, especially now, sitting in the Kenworth.

There were undoubtedly other options left to consider, but for now, driving the rig north felt right. As for Ralph, he missed the moment in the fog when the Porsche was nearly totaled. Having Bear on the case, out there somewhere attempting to find the thugs chasing us, gave me some relief. Finding bad guys and dispatching them was something Bear was born to do, Ralph assured me, and I had witnessed that first hand. The false accusation and Libby's death were part of my motivation, and after our altercation on the coast highway, Bear demonstrated that he was definitely motivated to help.

Bear and Brenda were the only ones who had our burner phone numbers. The fewer contacts, the better.

Jillian appeared to be comfortable with our escape plan. Leaving Artie and fleeing town in a big rig wasn't ideal, but given the circumstances, it made sense in a weird way, according to her. What she found interesting was my enthusiasm for driving a long-haul truck. This whole experience seemed to be a necessary distraction, at least for now. Jillian was thankful that the time period we allowed for the escape was two days, which she mentioned in her last call to Artie before removing her SIM card.

Artie wished us well and told her that some strangers had been snooping around the beach asking questions. He played dumb, which he was very good at, and gave the men a Mexican storyline that seemed to make sense. It was an idea that Jillian had concocted, and both Artie and I agreed, could send the bad guys in the wrong direction for the time being. All we needed was enough time to get to North Idaho.

Before he left, Manny showed me a small overhead compartment with a loaded handgun, safety off, ammunition, and a spotter's scope.

"Let's take it outside. I'll feel better leaving it if you assure me you know how to use it."

We were standing in the motel parking lot. Manny put his hand on my shoulder and asked me to walk with him to the driver's side of the rig, away from traffic and out of sight near a bordering hedge. He reached into his back waistband and pulled out the Glock nine-millimeter after looking around to make sure no one was watching.

"Rick, I want to make sure you and Jillian have some protection, just in case," he said as he laid the gun carefully into my hands as if he was awarding me a prize.

"Thanks, Manny."

Both Jillian and I knew how to operate the gun, which we demonstrated without firing it. Jillian was ex-military and not only knew how to shoot the gun; she could also disassemble it if she had to. Major, our production chief, insisted on taking me to the shooting range last year and put me through a basic training course of his own. Manny suggested that Jillian be in charge of the gun, leaving me more time to focus on driving. We both agreed.

"Too many crazies out there, Rick. I'm glad to know that you and Jillian are familiar with the gun . . . this little baby will level the playing field, quickly."

Manny left in an Uber, and I returned to the front of the rig. I managed to open and enter the Kenworth driver-side door on the third try without banging my knee, which was still a little sore. Jillian, who had gone for a short sprint around the lot, slipped in on the passenger side and, with a huff, declared: "This baby ought to come with a climbing rope and hiking boots."

We laughed, because crying didn't seem productive.

Jillian spotted the gun lying on the seat and suggested:

"We should probably stow that here in the dashboard storage box, right?"

"You're in charge."

I showed her where the ammunition and scope were in the overhead compartment. She loaded the magazine but kept the safety in the "on" position. The gun was registered under the company's name, and we, as temporary agents, had the right to use it for protection.

My hands felt empowered as I gripped the steering wheel. I felt comfortable. The engine fired up, and, after checking for traffic, we were off. Sitting in the driver seat this high, moving through traffic, felt good. My mind was already headed north to Concord and onto Fairfield before turning north on Highway 505 bound for the Pilot Truck Stop in Dunnigan.

But that would happen tomorrow. Just like that, Jillian and I were on our own.

Jillian fit right in as co-pilot. It's amazing how people who know each other as casual friends can suddenly change roles and still be friends. As co-pilot, part of her job would be to pay for fuel inside the truck stops as I capped off the fuel tanks. She also checked the map with me and helped prepare documents for weigh stations. Google Maps were out of the question since we didn't have that capability on our temporary phones.

We eventually found the overnight parking area Manny suggested and shut down the tractor. We agreed to make the best of our sleeping conditions, which meant that I slept forward in the cab.

Life on the road was beginning to take on a new meaning, and we were both in for a long-haul adventure.

17. "On the Road Again."

The following morning's sun was bright and radiated nothing but hope as we headed out early on our journey north.

Driving required so much attention that I lost track of time. The learning curve for driving a big rig is steep and unforgiving, especially if you forget something important like oil pressure maintenance, causing the engine to overheat. The biggest challenge, which Manny mentioned more than once, was trying to keep the cab from shaking and bouncing in first gear. Jillian's patience, which I tested that morning, proved to be her greatest virtue. She told me that monitoring my learning curve from the passenger seat gave her a new respect for all long-haul truck drivers.

Starting the engine and warming the tractor properly proved vital for a smooth drive. Once the engine idled properly and the gauges checked out, I'd inspect the hydraulic hose fittings for any sign of leaks, then lights to make sure braking and signaling worked. Lastly, the load straps had to maintain proper tension. After the last pull on the straps, I'd head back to the front, checking tire tread depth as I walked. We were in good shape and ready to pull out. When I got back in the cab and turned toward Jillian, all she did was smile and say:

"Good morning. I feel like I've just been to the gym. Truck prep is great exercise."

"Good morning. Sun's up. Let's do this!"

"Hey, since we have no choice, the gun's loaded, and we're all gassed up, go for it."

"Diesel," I replied.

"What?"

"We fuel up with diesel, not gas," I smiled.

"Don't press your luck, Ricky. I have a loaded gun," Jillian chuckled.

The rolling hills in the countryside showcased field after field of various crops, mostly grapevines, carefully planted in various stages of growth. It amazed me how the further north we drove, the better I felt. An anxious relief for sure.

Dunnigan, a town of about twelve hundred, disappeared quickly in the rear-view mirror as Jillian kept herself busy in the right seat, monitoring the two-way radio and checking maps. She also made time to acquaint herself with the cab's interior storage compartments. The traffic lightened up as the hum from the tires became a dependable confirmation that we were not only on our way but that we'd be alright.

Without looking up, Jillian declared, "This truck cab has more storage space than my condo."

The Kenworth was relatively new and well-appointed. It even had a hint of new car, or in this case, new truck smell. I could see how the right person could make long-haul driving a career.

"Well, captain, how's life at the wheel of a big rig?"

I smiled and gripped the steering wheel a little tighter:

"Honestly? Even though we are on the run, I'm having the time of my life."

Both of us understood that we had the added responsibility of keeping the mood light.

Jillian unfolded the road map that Manny provided. Our main route, clearly highlighted in yellow, flowed straight north to Seattle, then east to North Idaho. There were a few "alternate routes," just in case, highlighted in green. My hope was that we could stay on the yellow route the whole way. As my uncle Fred used to say: "I hope you get your hope."

Neither of us had used an actual map in a while. But, it was nice having a larger picture of what we faced. In addition to the yellow and green, we had blue and red markings. Off to the side in the margins, marked in blue, were suggested roadside stops with names of store owners and mechanics. The red marker showed the "must do" stops for fuel and load checks at weigh stations. The word "mandatory" was double-underlined next to each station stop. Proprietary information that felt like on-the-job training.

Moving along the highway at this height took some time to get used to. Up ahead, I saw a deer with two fawns off to the right. I geared down and watched them as they considered crossing the highway. Jillian sat up in her seat. We slowed to forty, thirty, and there they went. Mom ventured across first with the little ones close behind. I geared up as a car passed us. We were on a two-lane stretch instead of constantly driving I-5 the whole way. I think Manny also wanted to take it slower at first.

Driving the Kenworth required my undivided attention. I knew, however, that as the day wore on, I had to watch for whoever might be after us. For now, Jillian was on watch as we navigated north.

The interior of the cab was sweet. We were sitting in a surprisingly comfortable, air-conditioned and well-appointed atmosphere. The color scheme was mostly black with grey and white accents. The dash lighting was blue, green and white; very cool at night. In addition, the view out of the huge windshield was spectacular.

We were on a long stretch, attempting to relax into our new routine.

"Jillian, tell me about yourself, before Artie and Venice Beach."

She hesitated for just an instant as if trying to put all the pieces of her past together before answering.

"Are we playing twenty questions, or do you really want to know?"

I just looked at her and smiled.

"Okay. Let's see, I grew up in Tucson, Arizona. My father was stationed at Davis-Monthan Air Force Base. He worked as an electrical contractor for the government. My mother was a nurse, an RN."

She went on to explain how in sixth grade her mother unexpectedly passed away from a brain aneurysm. Jillian had no other siblings, and with her father's occupation requiring him to be on the road most of the time, the decision was made to send Jillian to live with her aunt and two cousins in Albuquerque, New Mexico. That move was both life-changing and mind-altering. Although her aunt was very nurturing, she spent long hours working at the hospital. Her father kept in touch when he could, despite being deployed overseas. Younger Jillian, who had been used to spending time alone, now found herself in the middle of a very busy life.

Her aunt was a single mom and very independent. She was also an exercise nut.

"My Aunt Delores became my idol. I wanted to be just like her. She looked a lot like my mom, but she was the complete opposite: outgoing, adventurous, a risk-taker, which is just what I needed in my life. Hell, every kid should have had the life I had with Delores."

Delores moved further north to Santa Fe when Jillian turned fourteen. Jillian and her two older girl cousins enjoyed the more "artful" experience that surrounded Santa Fe. Her aunt taught art classes in her home and yoga in the yard. Watching the students and eventually becoming one herself delighted Jillian. She evolved into a more independent and confident free spirit.

"I enrolled in nurses' training during college, fell in and out of love with a boy, and then left school. I quit after two years and joined the Army. I served four years as a medic and just completed my six years of duty. So a proficiency in self-defense, bandages, needles, and firearms are all on my current resume. Hopefully, the right healthcare business will need somebody with my skills soon. For now, I'm content filling in at a community health clinic when they need me."

Jillian sat back in her seat and listened to the soft jazz that had been playing in the background. She looked content and completely satisfied to be in this place at this time.

I appreciated all that she felt like sharing. I knew she had a story to tell that went far beyond her time in jail.

We were on a very long stretch of road. In fact, the road appeared to be pulled by some invisible force causing the sides of the road to come toward the rig as the ribbon of highway curved up and around the low hills that disappeared into infinity. Orange road signs indicated work ahead, so I geared down as we came up behind some traffic. We sat for a few minutes before the line ahead of us moved.

The impulse to shift gears up to driving speed did not come naturally. The first time I accomplished it without grinding the gears was, as I imagined, equal to learning to fly a plane. Eventually, shifting became a workout, especially in heavy traffic where the Kenworth must have been invisible to some drivers. Incredible.

Ahh, the open road. I understood why they call it a "freeway." My right arm was given a reprieve as a friendship slowly developed between me and long stretches of asphalt and concrete. Between learning to drive and watching for suspicious characters, my senses were on full alert. Jillian, meanwhile, proved herself invaluable. What I didn't think of, she did, like managing provisions.

The truck was equipped with a small refrigerator, so we shopped for a variety of food at the Pilot truck stop back in Dunnigan, which involved improving my current diet.

"Rick, we can't just eat carbs the whole way. There has to be some protein and veggies in the mix."

Jillian was right, of course. So, she did the meal planning. The truck stop offered what we needed. Our travel plan was to stop only when we needed to refuel, shop right to eat right, stay on the alert, be positive, and drive, drive, drive. She, fortunately, took charge of fixing our meals, which led to bouncing between the driving area and the back cab. She called this new activity her culinary workout. Jillian happened to be in the back, cleaning up after lunch, when I called her forward. My phone was ringing.

"Hello?" Jillian said, answering it. "Oh, hi. Just a minute."

She handed it over to me:

"It's Brenda."

Even though we were on the run, there were matters of business to attend to at Blaine. Once the call ended, I looked at Jillian and said:

"Business."

"No problem. Life goes on," she answered with a smile.

"Brenda mentioned an incident involving Artie."

"Artie? Anything wrong?" Jillian looked concerned.

"Artie had a rough time last night," I stated flatly. "The guys asking about us weren't satisfied with his answers and didn't appreciate being sent on a Mexican wild goose chase. So, they strapped him to a chair and got his attention, but not before he was able to send an urgent text to Bear. Bear knew about the visitors' original confrontation with Artie, so he stationed himself close by, just in case they returned. Bear thought the bad guys were probably pissed off but wouldn't kill Artie. He was just too goofy for them to care."

Bear made it to the rescue in time to cause some physical

damage of his own. In the end, the attackers managed to get away while Bear took Artie to the emergency room, mainly for stitches and a rib wrap. Artie would be staying with one of his friends down the beach for a while.

"Good, then he's all right?"

"He was shaken, not stirred," I replied.

She looked relieved as we shared a laugh. Reluctantly, though, Artie admitted to Bear that he might have let it slip that we were "trucking up north," as he put it. We both looked at each other and decided to keep rolling after our stop in Redding instead of resting for an hour.

We took exit 673 and found the Redding truck stop, no problem. I refueled as Jillian went inside and paid. We both performed our tasks with an eye out for any car resembling the BMW that tracked me down the coast highway. Bear had also suggested watching out for larger sedans, which the mob was known to use.

The mandatory instructions Manny left were becoming less burdensome and more rudimentary as the day unfolded. Thankfully, we were splitting duty and improving our performance with each stop, putting our lives in perpetual motion once we parked for fuel. I likened our fast pace to a NASCAR pit crew and jokingly suggested that we time ourselves during each stop along the way. Jillian rolled her eyes and smiled, which to me suggested she appreciated the humor.

"I'll take that as a NO on the NASCAR idea."

Hey, if you can't laugh, even in our predicament, you'd go crazy. We were anxious to be on our way to North Idaho and the safety of remote seclusion.

Bear had gone silent for some reason. His text message hadn't come through as expected. Hourly updates were part of his plan, at least for now. When they didn't come, it caused a little more anxiety. Think positive: no news is good news.

Clouds rolled in, hiding the sun. After a few minutes, rain started pelting the cab, carried by a strong crosswind. It took me a few moments to find the wiper switch, hidden in plain sight among the dozen toggles and buttons within reach. As it turned out, the switch was above my head. Go figure.

The wind direction changed, and the rain continued to beat steadily against the cab. We were headed straight into a strong headwind, which required changing gears as the engine began to groan. The windshield, which was nearly the length of my picture window in Tiburon, cleared completely, thanks to the oversized wipers the size of two baseball bats running back and forth at full tilt. We were cruising easily into the wind as we crossed over the California/Oregon border. There was so much water coming at us; we might as well have been a fishing trawler on an open ocean.

Good visibility is always important, but especially then as we were trying to locate the next weigh station about two miles ahead. The landscape was a blur, and it wasn't, and then it was, until:

"There!" Jillian shouted all of a sudden.

A long line of trucks waited in the downpour a quarter mile ahead. I barely had time to get the truck and trailer off the freeway and onto the exit ramp.

As we waited, Jillian checked for radio stations and some jazz or comfortable R&B. She was scanning the stations as a news alert came on: ". . . rain with snow in the higher elevations is expected for tonight in northern California and southwestern Oregon from Redding to Eugene. Travelers are advised to be on the alert for slick road conditions and specifically hydroplaning. Drivers are cautioned to reduce speeds and not to use their cruise control."

Jillian stayed with the station and asked if I needed anything as we pulled up in line.

"Ya, how about those cargo papers in the pouch Manny left over there in the corner?" I pointed to the area in the cab right behind Jillian.

As she reached for the papers, a loud bang hit the cab driver-side door, and she screamed. I went for the gun and looked down to see a man standing on the running board shouting.

"Hey, buddy, we're starting another line. Move your rig over to the right, over there."

The man pointed to another small hut where a neon OPEN sign now flashed. My face went from terror to relief as Jillian returned the gun to its location under the dash. The man, wearing a yellow slicker with an Oregon Department of Transportation logo on it, jumped off and began yelling at other drivers as he pointed once again at me then at the hut. I waved back and proceeded to turn, but then the engine light went on and the engine died. All eyes, including those of the guy in a yellow slicker, were on me.

"Hey, rookie, move the damn truck!" the man yelled in desperation as I fumbled to restart the engine. "You've got to move this rig now! We have a backup beginning to build out onto the highway, fella."

My smile strained as I went through the starting routine one more time. Seconds felt like hours. Finally, the engine fired up and sent smoke billowing everywhere. Jillian, in the meantime, was rifling through the owner's manual to see if there were any "restart" instructions mixed in with the paperwork. Nailed it!

The rig began to move. We were in too low a gear, bouncing and jumping like two kids in daycare misbehaving. I steered the rig clear of one line and managed to become the first in the line.

Jillian whispered as she settled into her seat:

"You can stop smiling now."

My facial muscles relaxed as I reached for our papers. The documents were all in order, and the attendant was very helpful as she suggested we checked the road report channel for the next couple hours. Jillian tuned to the frequency, and we were off, glad to be on our way into Oregon, loaded with building materials and concerns about some of the higher elevations where snow was forecasted. Chains, we must have them.

We high-fived as we passed a road sign that read: Welcome to Oregon.

18. *"What We Fear Takes Over If You Let It."*

Despite some miscues, the rig continued to roll along, and my attitude remained positive. My pride, however, took a few hits. Humor helped, but it didn't do a thing for my neck and shoulder pain. That thought made me laugh, which caused Jillian to look up from the map she studied. I rolled my shoulders back and stretched as I sat back in the seat.

Jillian circled an area on the map, looked up and said:

"Is it my imagination, or is this – what is it you call it, rig? – riding smoother?"

A comment like that can sure make neck and shoulder pain disappear, even though my whole body ached. Jillian held my gaze as I answered: "You know what? I could get used to doing this full-time if my day job goes away. I may have to reconsider my employment options."

The idea of me driving a big tractor cab for a living made us both laugh out loud. It felt good. I was kidding, of course. There are training programs that teach people how to drive long haul. Driving heavy pieces of equipment for hours on end in all weather conditions was not for everyone. And judging from what my body went through in just a few hours, I didn't think I'd last in this profession.

The rain let up a little as it changed direction. Highway

traffic was sparse as we drove farther into Oregon. Towns were noticeably few and far between. Our routine included listening to the hum of the road surface as we crested the top of a hill near Crater Lake. We were literally humming along.

Jillian spotted the car first in the ditch, off to the side of the road. A young girl waving a white towel appeared to be in distress. The Cascades and dark clouds were hiding the sun. Darkness enveloped us as I activated the rig's flashing lights and slowed to a crawl, causing the exhaust stacks to rumble. Jillian rolled down her window. We could see that a car had swerved off the highway and ended up about twenty feet into the roadside ditch. The car's back-left wheel was up, off the ground, about a foot in the air.

Since there was no traffic in either direction and we were moving slowly, I decided to move the rig over to the shoulder of the highway and stop. I had to be careful. The rig was heavy, and the shoulder of the road, gravel mostly, had been softened by the rain.

I shifted into neutral and set the brake as Jillian leaned her head out the passenger-side window.

"Are you alright?" she yelled as the rain returned.

"Thank God, you stopped. I'm okay, but I need help," she said.

Jillian turned toward me with that "we've got to do something" look. I shrugged my shoulders, pointed toward the gun, kept the engine running, and hopped out the driver side.

"I swerved to keep from hitting an animal. I'm sure it was a deer. It all happened so fast," the girl said with a desperate, wind-soaked look.

"How long have you been out here?" I yelled.

"An hour, I think. Two cars and a truck passed me. Thank you so much for stopping."

She was drenched and shivering. Jillian guessed that the girl was in her early 20s. Her matted brown hair clung to her face.

She had on a dark blue parka, blue jeans, and running shoes.

"Can I catch a ride to the next town? My car is really stuck."

I nodded as the rain continued to pelt us both, then pointed to the passenger door. Jillian reached down and helped the girl climb up. In her backpack, she carried a water bottle, a bag of corn chips, and a towel. I made sure her car was locked and climbed my way back up into the cab.

Once everyone found their place, Jillian handed out towels she'd found in the back cab. Drying her hair, the girl introduced herself:

"I'm Jenny. Sorry about all this water. It's nasty out there."

As we continued driving, the young woman told us that she was a University of Washington student headed back to Seattle after spending time with her family in California. She wasn't worried about the car; it belonged to her father. Jenny said that she would call her father and let him know the location. She was confident he would make arrangements to take care of the car. She had more concern about whether she hit the animal she swerved to miss.

The city of Ashland was up ahead. We all hoped there would be a wrecker available in the town famous for the Shakespearean Festival.

"Is it to be or not to be?" I said, looking at Jillian who just stared at me with a blank look on her face.

"Ashland, Shakespearean Festival, Wrecker Service?"

Jillian raised an eyebrow at my joke before looking down to check Manny's list of resources for a tow truck.

"Pay no attention to our driver, Jenny. He's been driving way too long today."

Jillian looked from me to Jenny as she said that. Jenny smiled as Jillian asked:

"What are you majoring in at the University of Washington?"

Jenny finished drying her hair and began eating the rest of

her corn chips before answering Jillian's question. Jenny said she wanted to get her core requirements out of the way first, then focus on health sciences. Her mother and father were in healthcare, and she thought it was a worthy vocation.

"Jillian is in the medical field," I offered, continuing to check for oncoming traffic as we picked up speed.

"Really! What? Like a doctor or nurse?"

"More on the level of a Physician Assistant. I went to nursing school for two years and spent six years as an Army medic."

Jenny and Jillian suddenly had plenty to talk about. As they carried on their conversation, I noticed how much they looked alike, despite being about a decade apart in age. I wondered if they saw the resemblance too. Jillian found more towels and handed another one to Jenny. Jillian pointed to the towing service on the sheet and started to make a call for a tow truck.

"Oh, don't bother. My dad will make the arrangements for that kind of thing. It's his car and he'll just jump right in there and make it right."

She didn't sound very convincing to me. Maybe being tired made me more skeptical. Still, Jillian must have felt the same vibe. She asked Jenny if her parents lived in Seattle. Jenny acted as if she didn't hear Jillian's last question, then suddenly came forward with:

"No, they live in Portland. My dad travels around the state. That's why this won't be a problem for him. He knows everyone in the state it seems. It wouldn't surprise me that he knows the tow truck operator in Ashland."

After a few minutes, Jillian looked at me and said:

"Why don't we take Jenny to Portland? It's right on the way."

I held my breath and kept gazing straight ahead. They, meanwhile, waited for my reaction. There were a few considerations, the most important being: The Mob Chasing Us.

"I suppose," I finally replied, still looking straight ahead and trying to smile. Jillian's comment still hung in the air like a piñata waiting to be struck down.

"I don't want to be a bother," Jenny murmured.

Bother? We are chock full of bother around here. We should bottle our bother and sell it. I had to fight myself to keep from saying anything out loud. After a few moments of hesitation and focusing on the road, I checked to see where we were on our adventure. Knowing that we weren't going to be making an unscheduled stop to drop Jenny off made me feel better about our progress. My confidence grew with every mile the further north we drove. And just like the diesel, we kept refilling into the Kenworth, confidence became our re-energizing fuel that made me feel better about our chances of succeeding.

As the drive continued, Jenny turned out to be a fun and engaging distraction. And that was that. As our eighteen-wheeler rolled down the highway, it was unanimous. Jenny, unknowingly, joined our seemingly clever escape. So far, so good.

"I hope I'm not being too forward, but the two of you . . . don't look like . . . like . . . your average truck-driving duo," Jenny offered with a slight smile.

Bingo. Jenny figured something about Jillian and me that did not make sense just by looking at us. What was I thinking? That we could just show up in public, as your average long-haulers, smacking gum, hanging with the other drivers at the truck stop, and blend right in? Not that we really "hung out" for very long at each stop. Did the people we met along the way bust a gut laughing after we left?

"Ah, no, you're right," Jillian admitted, suddenly breaking the silence. "We . . . we are doing a friend a favor," she continued, as I looked at her sideways. This time it was my turn to raise eyebrows.

What's the old rule: The less said, the better? I listened and watched Jenny's reaction in the mirror. Jillian felt she owed Jenny some explanation. Jillian knew enough from the look on my face to be careful, so she proceeded with caution.

"We're hauling building supplies and will make the delivery in Vancouver, Washington," Jillian stated as she adjusted the map in her lap.

"Oh, that's right across the river from Portland," Jenny replied.

"Yes, I see that on the map. Oh, we drive straight over the Columbia River. I always wanted to see the Columbia. I've heard so much about it."

Jenny seemed relieved, knowing that our stop in Portland to drop her off wouldn't inconvenience us much.

A feeling of satisfaction came over the cab as we each sat back into our places, eyes on the road. Jenny sat in the middle seat right behind us.

The big rig began to climb higher into the Cascades on I-5 as pearls of rain now appeared in the headlights. The sound of the rain took over as our conversation came to an end.

My lower back began to seize up. Yoga, deep breathing and muscle stretching timed to the wiper blade movement helped as the road continued to disappear under the rig.

The dashboard lights cast a hypnotic glow which combined with the engine's hum. I felt frozen to the wheel as I began some face yoga. Scary face, relax, scary face, relax. My phone rang – thank God – which brought me out of my scary exercise. It was Bear. I looked at Jillian and asked her to show Jenny the back cab while I took the call. Even though they were literally a few feet away, I wanted this conversation to be as private as possible.

"Wait, you got someone riding with you two?" Bear asked, almost shouting.

"A stranded motorist," I whispered. "I'll explain later. What's up?"

"Rick, you're being chased. No more rescues, okay?" He

paused, then continued. "Alright, we know the BMW boys and some associates are on to you."

Silence.

"Rick?"

"Shit," I attempted to think rather than say anything out loud at that moment. "What the hell, Bear?" Now whispering and not doing a very good job of it.

"They know you're headed north in a big rig. There's still a lot of homework for them to do."

Terrific. I've put everyone in jeopardy: Brenda, Jess, Jillian, Artie, Manny, and now Jenny.

Bear added: "Where are you right now?"

"Just passed Medford, heading for Grants Pass."

"You're making good time, rookie, but be careful up there and be sure to keep in touch with me and the local weather reports."

I half-heard what he said and only had to look at the rain/snow mix coming down to realize that my driving skills were going to be put to a very big test. I really had to focus on driving this behemoth. My grip instinctively tightened. In addition to the weather, we had to keep checking the rearview mirror for fast-moving traffic coming our way.

"Call when you arrive in Portland, and ditch the broad," he said before hanging up abruptly.

Jillian and Jenny came forward, talking about Jenny's plans to visit Italy in the summer. I could tell that they were both opening up and were pleased to have each other's company. I decided not to tell Jillian what Bear reported about the Castillinos, at least not right away. How would I do that anyway with Jenny sitting right there? Bad news could take a back seat for now.

The time came for me to call Brenda and give her our coordinates, which showed we were slightly ahead of schedule. As it turned out, Brenda had nothing out of the ordinary to share. We worked out a call schedule, and she offered to update Jess.

Then Brenda said something I'd heard before, though her tone was more imploring now:

"Be careful, Rick."

Grants Pass could have been worse, judging from the weather report. The weight of these rigs works in the driver's favor except on snow and ice. That's what I'd been told, and something I did not look forward to testing. The roads were wet with slush that flew up past the windshield. Total relief came when we crested the pass and had that part of the trip behind us. My focus now became "incremental driving." We had two more hours before our next stop. Jillian asked if I still planned to refuel in Roseburg. We had it marked as a place to stop to eat and stretch our legs. I told her that we would stop, but she had to make it quick.

The green and white road sign indicated our next exit, where the off-ramp looped around and passed under the freeway through a short tunnel and into the truck stop. This part of the driving – slowing down, gearing down – had become automatic, even in my tired state. The ladies were in charge of food and paying for fuel. Everything went off like clockwork. In the meantime, I took the gun out of its hiding place overhead on the passenger side and moved it under the dash.

Our fuel stop took about twenty minutes, and, without any hesitation, we were gone. A traveling trio of two escapees and one mystery girl.

19. "Watch Where You're Going, but Mostly Watch Where You've Been."

Jenny finished what she was eating and laid down on the bed in the back of the cab. It was time for her to daydream. She drifted, floating over the road, listening to the conversation up front, and then slowly, gradually, she was at home with her parents and friends. They were all looking at her. The one who left. How could she forget them?

No one understood her decision to leave such a privileged life. No explanation would satisfy them: Mother, a former RN, her famous cardiologist father, grandmother, Uncle Stan, Aunt Bernice, and cousins. Nothing should have stood in the way of Jenny making her contribution to the Addison empire. She often wondered like this and then stopped and dug deeper into what life would have been like if Eric, her precious twin brother, had lived.

"Jenny, dear, you're an Addison, and there are certain traditions and responsibilities you must uphold." Those were the last words she heard from her father.

The decision to go against her parents' wishes didn't come easily, but it had to happen if she was to follow her passion for acting. In her mind, she already possessed the entertainment bug, to be on stage or in front of a camera as an actor. She could feel it. There was something driving her, unrelenting, a feeling of comfort when she pretended to be someone else. Taking on a new persona was beyond transformational; it became empowering. She loved it and was a natural. As a child, Jenny would come home from school, close her bedroom door, and that's when a new world would open up. All she had to do was pick up a book, *Alice in Wonderland,* and she was off with the Mad Hatter, chasing the rabbit, avoiding the queen and her guards.

Her family thought it was cute when she was young and selected to play the lead in almost every production in elementary and, eventually, high school. But when it came time to pursue a college, she wanted to go to New York to attend acting school at NYU. They urged her to attend Smith, to be among students connected to their social network.

Her drama at home became an overwhelming burden that prevented her from creating anything dramatic on the stage.

The world of privilege never fit as well as the world of make-believe for Jenny. Whenever there was a social gathering at the country club or at their home, she would socialize with friendly, well-meaning people. She even made a few friendships with girls and boys her age, but they all seemed to have ulterior motives. Their world felt so unbelievably make-believe.

Jenny decided to leave a few weeks ago and head to California to meet up with a girlfriend. With that choice, she felt the possibility of her dream coming true. She could sense her parents' disappointment as she flew the friendly sky to the west coast. These recurring thoughts, distracting her driving, refused to rest.

Her long-haul daydream continued as she watched the scenery go by through the small port-side window. Deep REM sleep would be preferred, but for now, this time out gave her a few moments to ease anxious feelings about her journey as she slowly began to hear the hum of the road again.

Jillian was tired too, so she reclined the right seat and promptly drifted off. We had a couple of hours to go until Roseburg, and I was on high alert, watching the road both ways and listening to Boz Scaggs in my earbuds to keep me driving straight on the down low.

Little towns passed by like islands in an ocean. I continued shifting gears and allowed the truck to rise and fall through the mountain roadway's undulations.

§

Michael Castillino was upset when the small plane landed in Redding, California. The flight had been plagued by strong wind gusts, causing his brother Tony to continually throw up and moan since taking off from San Francisco. Michael led a team of four professionals that he personally recruited. For all intents and purposes, they were business people looking for real estate opportunities.

New information verified that the target had somehow managed to escape Los Angeles in a long-haul tractor and trailer. Several people reluctantly provided the necessary details that helped the Castillinos in tracking their prey. Michael Castillino, the notorious group leader, was the one person who intended to put a stop to what he and his father felt was an infringement on the family business back east. Michael had a personal vendetta against a man he didn't know. At the same time, he reluctantly admired Rick Blaine. It might sound strange to others, but to those in the family, it made total sense. Michael's main purpose in this operation became a duel with a worthy adversary. The goal was to eliminate Rick Blaine and any witnesses, period.

Blaine sales representatives had overstepped their bounds when they suggested to a group of distributors who moved products for the Castillino organization that they change their slotting policy of overcharging to place Blaine items in their system. The Blaine representatives intimated that the distributors could be in violation of federal discrimination law by not allowing Blaine products into their system. On the surface, that may be viewed as a positive approach, making the firm aware of being out of compliance. Michael viewed this proposition by Blaine as the tip of the iceberg, especially if the Feds came sniffing around.

"We deal with this now, before it gets out of hand," Michael said as he entered the rental car driven by his brother, Anthony, who had to change his shirt before getting in the car.

The two passengers, Vincent and Marty, just listened from the back seat. They were the muscle and effectively dealt with issues as directed. Whatever Michael ordered, happened, no questions asked.

Michael's father granted his favorite son new powers prior to this trip as he groomed him for future family leadership. The old man had plans to retire and live in Sicily, a place the family used for recruiting new people and burying five generations of elders. Most of those ancestors belonged to the infamous crime organization known as The Black Hand.

The Castilliinos were headed north on I-5. They had the truck identification, compliments of an overly friendly truck stop cashier who took a liking to Marty, his biceps, and a C note. The further they drove, the more Michael was ready to discuss the issue of "being out of compliance" with the man himself, Mr. Blaine. They also needed to make sure the young lady with him would not be able to discuss her connection with Ms. Liberty Scarelli. Jillian was in the crosshairs too.

§

The city of Roseburg gradually appeared on the horizon. We were ready to take a few minutes to leave the cab and stretch. The temptation to extend the stay and give in to our collective tiredness was evident as I looked around.

"We have to keep moving," I half-whispered.

Call it instinct, but a voice inside my head kept on repeating go, go, go.

A pump opened up just as we made the turn. I climbed down and began refueling. Out of the corner of my eye, I spied a man approaching the rig at a run. Immediately, I tensed up and prepared to do battle by crouching down and freeing one of the tire chains from the back of the cab. When I turned, I saw the guy smiling and pointing toward the middle of the trailer. The guy stopped and put his hands on his knees. He looked to be out of breath and harmless. He introduced himself as a driver from one of the other rigs.

He said, "You got a low one on number eleven."

All my body would allow me to do was stare. I didn't know what the hell he was talking about.

"You alright, buddy? Number eleven tire, on the inside right. It's down about forty percent. Just thought you might have missed it."

Smiling, I thanked him as I replaced the chains.

"Not number eleven," I answered, wiping my hands with a small rag as the man waved and walked off.

Jillian woke up, opened the door of the cab and climbed down.

"Jenny fell asleep. You finish refueling?"

"Yes"

"I'll go in and pay. You need anything?"

"Nope. Let's get going after I check the tires."

I pulled the tire pump hose close and began to work the driver-side tires first. This became no easy task, and as I began to pressure check and fill number eleven, I spotted that same driver working the other side. Speaking through the undercarriage of the trailer, he asked, "Haven't seen you around here – thought you might need some help. I'll take this side. Did you find number eleven down as far as I thought?"

Thankful doesn't even begin to describe how good I felt at that moment. The other driver must have guessed that I was a rookie; I sensed he felt sorry for me and I didn't care. It was all I could do not to feel the same about me. The other tires took time, some needing more air, but I figured we were on schedule and didn't want to risk a flat tire. In the meantime, Jenny joined Jillian, and they stretched their legs by taking a short walk around the parking lot. The air was brisk. We had to stick to our plan and keep moving.

After a slight delay, we were on our way.

20. "One Thing Leads to Another."

The Castillinos checked the refueling transit record at the Grants Pass truck stop after a brief conversation with the manager, which included a hundred dollars being shoved in the man's face.

Anthony, or Big T, a nickname he'd had since grade school, discovered they were on the right track. He said:

"From what that bird told me, the target is four to five hours ahead."

"Good, now drive," Michael asserted while rubbing his temples.

He controlled the conversation in the car, which for now was no conversation at all. Michael wanted time to think. He didn't need to know what the weather was or wasn't going to be doing. All he cared about was catching up with Mr. Blaine and his lady friend. Tony felt sorry for his big brother. After all, the family depended more on Michael; he and he alone was assuming the burden of the family business. Tony could only imagine what it was like to be that responsible. Taking on that responsibility was perfect for his brother, and Big T would be there to help. After all, Michael included his little brother in all sorts of matters. They were close. And the unsaid was allowing Tony to, occasionally, lighten things up.

"Hey, Mike, how about them ducks?" Tony offered with a smile, glancing over to see if Michael might be doing the same.

"What?"

"The Ducks. You know, the University of Oregon Ducks college football team? They're pretty good."

Michael shot a look at Tony that could melt iron.

"What? Just making a little conversation here, jeez."

Michael flicked Tony's ear, and hard. The finger flick dated back to when they were kids together, walking to school or sitting around, and Tony would say something stupid. The thump was felt all around as Michael shouted his feelings. Marty and Vincent, relaxing in the back seat, tried not to laugh: "Shut up about them damn ducks and drive, unless you want to switch with Marty."

"Jesus, that hurt, Mike!"

"Well?"

"Okay, okay. I'm good, sorry," Tony uttered.

He tried to hide his embarrassment, but it wasn't easy. His skull still hurt as he tightened his grip on the steering wheel.

In spite of their internal rift, the Castillinos were slowly gaining on the target. Michael pushed Tony to keep the speed up, even though the near-freezing rain was unrelenting. Marty and Vincent decided to break out some playing cards since the rain cut their vision down to less than a mile. Gin Rummy helped to pass the time.

§

Jenny couldn't stop thinking about a phone conversation she'd overheard with someone referred to as . . . Bear. A strange name, she thought, but that's not what bothered her. Something was wrong.

She could also tell that Jillian and Rick were friends, not lovers, and from what she pieced together, they were on the run. Why? And who from? The more she thought about that situation, the more she worried about what she had to share: The truth about why she was stranded on the road. The feeling hung like a cloud, and was beginning to affect her mood. Her heart began to beat faster. It was time for truth-telling.

Jillian started singing along with Gregg Allman on the radio.

"No, I'm no angel. I'm no stranger to the street. I've got my label."

Jenny quickly commented:

"I love this song. My uncle is a crazy Allman Brothers fan."

She joined in singing with Jillian in the lead and me on back up.

There we were, singing away as the "truck-driving trio." We made our way down the highway admitting, along with Gregg Allman, that we have our story to tell.

I increased our driving speed on the longer stretches. My second wind arrived just in time, and rolling my shoulders around helped me relax. With a loud exhale, I began to feel like myself for the first time in days. Back and leg muscle stretches were easier now in the truck driver's seat. Bottled water followed by healthier snacks helped to satisfy my hunger and keep muscles from cramping.

Our singing felt good too. We were on an oldies binge for some reason. "Good, good, good vibrations," helped each of us rally, so we kept singing, with Jenny taking the lead for almost an hour. One song after another, on whatever rock/oldies station we could find, required some finesse while we rolled through the hills. Note to self: Include some of this music on a new playlist when possible.

Jillian was singing and trying to stay on watch at the same time. She continually monitored the side mirror and checked the landscape for cars entering from a side road. Looking for what? She didn't really know, except for Bear's suggestion that they be vigilant for fast-approaching headlights at night and shiny front-end grilles during the day.

We stopped singing for a stretch. Jenny joined the watch until she fell asleep. I drove, and Jillian continued to co-pilot as the hum of the road became our new rhythm. Driving through the night was a first for me. For some reason, I could feel my heartbeat. Maybe it was the added adrenaline. When the sunrise came in a few hours, it would mark a full day of driving.

The silence was broken as Jenny woke, yelling about needing to get away.

"Oh, man, that was so real," she said, obviously embarrassed.

Jillian put her hand on Jenny's knee and asked if she was all right.

"Ya, ya, sure." She yawned as she asked, "Where are we?"

We'd just passed by Salem and were about an hour from Tigard, a city south of Portland. Our talented and tired singing group was making good time, and I intended on arriving in Portland near sunup. I traded glances with Jillian in my small dash mirror. She knew what I thought about our mysterious passenger having more missing elements in her story. I nodded to Jillian to go ahead and ask. Jenny looked down as Jillian asked:

"Is there something you want to tell us, Jenny?"

She looked at both of us and said:

"Why do you ask?"

It seemed odd that she hadn't called her father regarding the car or the accident. If we were wrong and she already had, then why not tell us?

Jillian looked at Jenny and added:

"Do you have something to share with us, Jenny? We're here to help if you need us."

Jenny took a second and looked straight ahead.

Slowly, Jenny revealed why she had taken to the road.

We listened intently. She dropped out of college to pursue an acting career. Her previous story about her parents, she admitted, was fabricated. Jenny had parents, but they retired in Florida, where she's from originally. Her acting career never really took off in Los Angeles, so she was on her way to Seattle to catch up with some friends working in a theater company. The car she crashed was borrowed, and she intended to call and let her friend know about the accident and the location but left her phone behind.

"Thanks, Jenny. Okay, let's see." Jillian's tone became more serious. "How about first things first. You might make that call to your friend if you haven't already. The State Patrol has probably flagged it by now, and it should be removed. Here – use my phone. Next, it seems like you should stay with us a little while longer while we figure things out."

Jenny looked straight ahead as she removed a tissue from her pocket and wiped her nose. She knew Jillian was right. Having admitted to the truth must have made her feel better; a smile, wider than before, appeared as she reached out and held hands with Jillian. Jenny let out a deep breath, sat back for a few seconds and then sat up. She had some questions of her own.

"So, now you know about me. What about you two?"

Jillian looked at me, and then at Jenny, and calmly said: "Looks like we'll need to tell you the short version. There are some fast-moving headlights coming on strong behind us."

I checked the mirror and sat up straighter. Jenny asked about us again.

"Jenny," I said into the windshield, "we're being chased by some . . . unsavory people who are framing me for rape and murder. They are also after Jillian because she knows the truth."

As I explained our situation at light-speed, Jillian was moving unnecessary things off the dash: maps, a paperback book, mixed nuts. Then she checked for the gun.

Jenny watched in horror as Jillian removed the Glock from the compartment near me and chambered the first round. Jenny then sat up straight, looked at Jillian, and cried out:

"Jesus, who are you two, Bonnie and Clyde?"

"We don't have time to explain, Jenny," Jillian declared as she turned the safety off and replaced the gun back in the compartment.

"Understand this, Jenny, you have to trust us. We are not the bad guys, alright?" Jillian added.

She gave me our exact location and quickly noted that there were no exits coming up for about thirty miles. Jillian tossed the map to Jenny and told her to fold it with our location showing and added: "It's a bitch not having Google Maps!"

Jillian was preparing for battle, a mentality she had intended on leaving in her military past. Who could blame her? The headlights were more evident now. It could be nothing or something. Who knew? Just in case, I asked Jillian if she'd taken the safety off. She answered with a stern look on her face.

"Of course."

§

Tony nudged Michael awake. He almost hit his head on the windshield. Vincent and Marty grabbed the back of the front seats respectively, nearly ripping the seats from their frames.

"Scope the truck up ahead. It might be them," Tony said to his brother.

He'd spotted the rig as they came into a big valley. Even though it was still dark, Tony felt the truck up ahead had the configuration of a rig carrying building materials. Plus, there had been no other truck traffic up to that point. The load appeared to be the size they were looking for: a Kenworth hauling building supplies. They had to know for sure. Michael used the sniper's scope, and even though the car bounded through some dips, the license plate appeared to match.

"It's got to be them," Michael said as a slight smile appeared like an evil apparition.

The rig up ahead had just begun to climb the other side of the small valley as the Castillinos came over the top and headed down the slope behind.

"Speed up, little brother. I believe we've found the runaways just in time. They're slowing down. Perfect."

§

The truck was steadily losing speed as it climbed off the valley floor. I knew we needed to crest the ridge before we could pick up any more speed. My head rotated between the road and the gauges, road, gauges, side mirror, gauges, making sure the engine didn't overheat. It helped that there was very little traffic at this time of the morning. Jenny asked what she could do to help.

"Stay calm and buckle up. Watch me. If we have to return fire, get down low. Understand?" Jillian stated in a quiet tone, simultaneously squeezing Jenny's hand hard enough to communicate the gravity of the situation.

As the tractor's engine gradually reached maximum power, the color code behind the numbers moved from yellow into the last color, red. This was a new experience. The cab shook as if we were going over small boulders in the road. An unfamiliar noise emanated from under the driver's seat. That must be the transmission.

"Is it time to shift and ease the engine pressure? How much slower?" I whispered.

The shift into a lower gear nearly threw all three of us against the windshield. Anything that wasn't secure ended up front. Immediately, I changed my mind and shifted up, which seemed to help the shaking but reduced our speed even more. While the ladies cleaned up spilled coffee and juice, I held onto the hope that the next one hundred yards to the summit would go quickly, and we would begin our downhill run before the fast-moving car behind us caught up. I was swimming in sweat.

My next glance at the side-view mirror revealed slithering snake-like headlights gaining on the rig.

21. On Your Mark, Get Set, Run!

Tony Castillino prided himself on being able to drive in any weather condition at any speed. In his mind, NASCAR drivers were his only equals. Speed became exhilarating the faster he went. Besides, he had on his driving gloves that fit his oversized hands perfectly. His gloves were multifunctional: He wore them in fights and when he touched the trigger of his AR-15.

The Castillinos needed to confirm that the rig up ahead was the target. The scope clearly showed that the license plate matched what they were given, but to be perfectly sure, they needed to see the driver's door with the truck's I.D. numbers. In Tony's line of work, changing license plates was a regular occurrence – there was a lot of crime in this world.

Michael had the name of the freight line and its manifest. He'd be able to finally identify the truck once they were alongside the rig.

"If it is them, let's make 'em sweat." Michael didn't mind playing with his prey.

The steady rain and accompanying crosswind pelted and buffeted the car. Tony did as instructed, hands tight at ten and two on the wheel, ready to pass when Michael gave the word. At the same time, the car's shocks were being tested. It didn't help that each of the four men weighed over two hundred pounds. Plus, the guns and ammunition in the trunk added considerable weight. Tony's mind went into NASCAR mode. He was the middle car, stacked three across, coming out of the south turn at Daytona.

§

I figured if the car behind us contained the bad guys, wouldn't they have to identify the truck before taking any action? How would that happen? Jillian and Jenny stayed low in their seats, making it look as though I was alone. To mask my identity, I put on a baseball cap that I'd found in the back, which automatically made me a Los Angeles Dodger fan. My attempt to become someone else may have come too late, but I had to try. Why was it taking so long? It seemed like forever before the rig crested the hill. Glancing back, I could see them moving closer. Finally, the engine began to hum, we increased speed, and we were off. Then, here they came, playing cat and mouse.

Michael readied himself, checking the truck's number sequence on the sheet.

"Mike, they're picking up speed!" Tony shouted.

Michael yelled instructions to the men in the back to be ready to shoot on his order, then gave Tony the "go" to move out and pass the rig.

Jillian let me know when the car disappeared from her side mirror.

Checking for oncoming traffic, I downshifted a gear as the car pulled alongside like a panther bursting from the jungle. With my right hand on the shift knob, eyes moving back and forth, I was ready for whatever came next. The passenger made eye contact with me as the car slowed to match the truck's speed. We were now playing a highway chess match. My heart started pounding harder, my throat dried, and my hands sweated as the black sedan reduced its speed.

The sedan driver overshot my door-side panel. I figured they were still trying to identify our rig. Out of the corner of my eye, I saw movement on the highway ahead.

Another big rig was coming up the grade from the other direction.

§

"Mike, Mike, we have company."

"How far?" Michael shouted.

"A mile, maybe a mile and a half."

"Pull up again. I need to see the door."

Tony increased speed and eased the car forward. Michael read the door-side panel:

"It's them! Stay here."

"Mike, we have to go or back off."

Michael didn't care and took a moment to stare as the truck driver nervously looked back and forth.

I turned my head and looked straight ahead, watching the oncoming traffic flash its high beams, and continued my normal shifting up through the gears, gaining speed:

"It has to be them," I announced, trying to sound confident, ready to move into action.

Michael had been so focused on the truck beside them, he hadn't noticed how close the truck ahead, on the same side of the highway, had become.

"Michael, Mikey?"

"Jesus, Tony, go, go, pass the damn truck!"

Tony passed in front of the oncoming truck with fifty yards to spare and checked the rearview for the driver's reaction as the passing truck blared its horn. Marty and Vincent couldn't help themselves and watched the driver they just passed out the back window as they kept going.

"We got a clear shot. You want us to take 'em now boss?"

Marty had his forty-five caliber ready.

"Not now. Punch it, Tony. They are shitting their pants, and I want them to sit in it for a while."

They had another forty miles before the town of Tigard, and then Portland close beyond. The goal now was to stop the truck before it reached Portland.

The bigger city of Portland would be too congested and could cause too many complications. Vincent searched the map on his phone for an exit and found it about eight miles ahead. Michael told Tony to speed up and take that exit when it came. The plan would be to wait for the truck to come along and force them off the road. The speedometer climbed: eighty, ninety, higher. Tony's face reflected sheer joy as they took the lead in his imaginary race.

Michael's mind created a new scenario: The wreck would be an accident caused by a less than capable driver, Rick Blaine, who'd needed to escape. They would wait at the exit, and as the rig passed, they would re-enter the highway and force Rick Blaine and company off the road.

"Poor bastard." Michael's laugh had a sinister tone, which Tony and the guys in the back seat knew all too well.

When Michael shared his new vision of the staged accident to come, they began to laugh too.

§

The car gained speed and disappeared from view over the next rise. For a moment, I thought that maybe I could have been mistaken. Was the "body-aching tired" causing me to see things? Jillian tapped my arm and asked if I was okay.

"If it's them, what do we do next?" she asked.

My third wind was beginning to kick in. I took a deep breath, stretched my legs, and as calmly as possible, said:

"We'll find out in the next few miles. Where's the next exit?"

§

On duty, up ahead of both Rick and the Castillinos, was Oregon State Trooper Jared Anderson. Trooper Anderson didn't mind working the swing shift, having only been on the force for two years. It was part of the program. Rookies were known to pull swing-shift duty for a couple of years. SS duty was synonymous with stopping speeders and pulling drunk drivers off the road or out of horrible crashes. It kept him busy most nights, and he needed to remind his wife that it was to be expected. In Jared's mind, his job kept the communities he served safer as he built his career.

The more reasonable day duty would come eventually. He could wait. Meanwhile, life was good, and he smiled as he adjusted the picture of his wife and their newborn son on his car visor. Anderson and his wife, Judy, were transplants from Arkansas who had settled in Forest Grove, a town southwest of Portland, and close to the Oregon beaches. Judy recently made reservations near Cannon Beach to celebrate their third wedding anniversary next month. He couldn't wait.

Trooper Anderson passed the early morning hours by completing paperwork on his computer and watching the highway from a secluded position next to a light beer billboard. The irony of a sign advertising beer working in tandem with the State Patrol handing out DUIs made him smile. The sun would be rising soon, and that fact widened his grin. He was ready to go home.

He heard the oncoming roar of the engine before he saw it. Clicking his pen and carefully placing it in his breast pocket, Jared looked up in time to see a black town car pass, going well over the limit. Jared radioed in his position and announced to dispatch that he was in pursuit.

§

Now that the car disappeared from view in front of us, we were on high alert checking all angles of the landscape for places a vehicle that big could be hiding. The highway opened up, with more flat land visible on either side, making it tougher for a car that big to hide.

The tension in the cab created an odd anxiety, at least for me. I knew firsthand what these mob guys were like and didn't want Jillian or Jenny to suffer because of me.

Darkness slowly gave way to a lighter sky in the east off to our right. The advent of daylight would make it harder for them to hide a big sedan. And then what? I was looking for the car to jump out of nowhere at any minute. No one likes surprises, especially ones that could kill you. Our immediate plan remained the same: I would drive, and Jillian would return fire.

Even with a fake smile, I tried to lighten the mood:

"Hey, look at it this way. They are going to have to come to us if it is them, and we're bigger than they are."

Jillian returned the smile and suggested we call Bear right away. I agreed and could clearly hear as she was sent to Bear's voicemail.

§

Up ahead of the Kenworth, the Castillinos were in for a surprise of their own. Tony's racecar fantasies were interrupted when he noticed the flashing lights appear behind. He gave Michael the heads up. Vincent and Marty were ready in the back seat, both armed with handguns, a sawed-off twelve gauge, and two AR-15s in the trunk, accessible from the back seat.

The exit ramp they planned to take was coming up. Tony confirmed with Michael and slowed down to take it. The disappointment that appeared on his face was apparent, but Michael didn't care. Tony's NASCAR skills were not going to be tested further this morning. This race had turned exciting and, discretion being the better part of valor, he signaled his exit and pulled off. Time for a pit stop.

§

We continued checking, front, back, sides, repeat. That car couldn't have just disappeared. Several cars and a few trucks passed going the opposite direction, no traffic coming along with us on our side of the road. I sprayed the outside windshield to make sure we had good visibility.

The exit Jillian identified was approaching, and I felt the need to pull off and rest before reaching Portland and heavier traffic. The three of us had had a conversation about what to do with Jenny. Her life was now in jeopardy, and we encouraged her to consider leaving us before our pursuers tightened their grip. Jillian told her to call someone to pick her up.

"I understand, let me, wait . . . what's that over there?" Jenny pointed, nearly hitting the windshield.

Each of us saw them at the same time: emergency lights flashing up ahead. We couldn't tell what was going on, maybe a traffic stop. I began the process of slowing down, carefully downshifting as flashing bursts of light filled the early morning sky like fireworks. Then came the repetitive **RAP PAP PAP PAP** of gunfire.

Jillian screamed:

"Rick, you can't go there now! Something's wrong!"

We continued to slow. The speedometer read forty as we watched what was playing out in front of us.

There were two bodies on the ground by the dark sedan. Shots were being exchanged between the State Patrol cruiser and the black town car. I recognized the town car and knew immediately, the shooters had to be the men who passed us a few minutes ago. Whatever emotions I had been holding back suddenly surged forth like a volcanic eruption.

Something had to be done, even if it meant taking fire ourselves. Almost like it had a life of its own, the rig aimed itself directly at the dark-colored sedan. I yelled to Jillian and Jenny to get down and hold on. They moved quickly into the back cab, strapped in, and braced for impact.

§

"Officer down, shots fired. Exit . . . nineteen," came the call to dispatch.

Despite being wounded, Officer Anderson managed to call for backup. Unfortunately, the closest unit was twenty-five miles away, attending to a multi-vehicle accident. When the call went from pursuit to "officer down," however, the entire force of eight additional units was ordered to respond as soon as possible.

Anderson bled from two wounds, one on the upper leg, the other on the left side of his face. The shotgun blast surprised him. Quick reflexes saved his life. Just as one of the men in the back opened his door to fire, Anderson leveled his service weapon; both guns went off simultaneously. The man with the shotgun fell dead out of the car. Anderson was knocked back to the ground by the shotgun blast. He recovered fast, and in running back to the cruiser, he was wounded in his upper-right leg. He managed to recover his service weapon and scrambled back to his cruiser for cover. The officer, with his back to his passenger-side front wheel, returned fire but began to lose consciousness. Out of nowhere, a big rig came hauling ass down the off-ramp and directly at the shooters' vehicle.

§

Ronald Turbine and his wife, Jerri Lynn, retired school teachers, loved to travel. They had just picked up their new blue Subaru Forester and were on their way, looking forward to driving from their home in Eugene north to Canada Island.

Their last-minute decision to drive through the night the first day, in order to avoid traffic, turned out to be a good one so far. They enjoyed being out on the open road without the "crazies," as Ronald often called other drivers. "It was always the other guy that you had to look out for," according to Ron. And Jerri Lynn, his wife of forty years, agreed.

Their first day, night really, included a meal that Jerri Lynn had pre-made for breakfast, which Ron looked forward to, especially the sausage and egg burrito. After this brief stop, they would eat their breakfast while driving near Portland, then catch the afternoon ferry near downtown Seattle. It was a plan that Ron had anticipated for months. Their agenda included lunch on the ferry as they sailed off to Canada Island, then dinner in Victoria at the Empress Hotel around six after check-in. Following a very carefully thought-out plan created a more enjoyable experience in life as far as the Turbines were concerned.

When they came up to the rest stop, there were no other cars around. Ron loved to drive. And finding ways to avoid traffic made him enjoy the experience even more. He busied himself by emptying out their garbage sack as Jerri Lynn made her way to the restroom. Hydrating becomes vital when you spend hours driving, but it went right through her.

Out of the corner of his eye, Ron saw the flashing lights from the patrol car as a big black, limo-like vehicle pulled up crossways in the yellow parking lines. Ron noted with disgust the parking error; it wasn't far from their car in the rest area – somebody could have been injured. Just then, Jerri Lynn called for him to bring her small travel bag. He returned the small plastic garbage container to the back seat, picked up the travel bag, and was making his way to Jerri Lynn as the first shots rang out. She screamed, and Ronald watched in horror as the Patrolman and one of the men from the limo exchanged shots. Ron froze in place. The rapid fire continued. That unfroze him. He ran and dove toward Jerri Lynn. They both ended up crashing through the ladies' restroom door as a battle raged outside.

"Oh, no," he said as they laid there listening to what sounded like a war taking place.

"What is it, Ron? Were you hit? Oh dear God, what's happening? Ronald, quick, do something!"

"Yes, okay, yes. I HAVE to go."

"To the bathroom?"

"No. Not here."

"Maybe not now, Ron. Stay here. It's safer. You can pee later."

"I have to go back to our car. I left the car keys in the ignition."

§

Michael was sure the trooper had been hit and shouted to his brother to look for a way out. The car tires were blown; Vincent and Marty were dead. He thought the long-haul rig might run them right over. Instead, the driver blocked most of the view of the cruisier. Seeing no one in the cab, Michael decided it was time to move before reinforcements arrived for the trooper.

Surveying the area, Tony spotted a car parked near the restroom not far away. Michael watched for any sign of the trooper. Seeing none, he motioned for Tony to go. Tony stood up from behind a large rock and made a break for the blue Subaru. Upon arriving at the SUV, he noticed two things: The keys were in the ignition, and a man was poking his head out of the women's restroom door.

The gunfire had subsided. Ron looked at his wife and decided it was time to check their car.

"Be careful, Ron," she said, her warning echoing off the cinder block walls.

Ronald always prided himself on being careful. And although he appreciated what his wife just said, he wiped the sweat off his brow with his sleeve, grabbed the stainless-steel handle of the door, and slowly looked out toward the parking lot. Seeing one man looking the other way, Ron began to move his feet, trying not to make a sound. He'd planned to retrieve the Subaru keys and check the car for damage when he heard a voice:

"Stay back. Move inside, grandpa, or you're a dead man."

Ronald froze. Had he not decided to pee a few minutes ago, it may have happened right then. He retreated faster than he had come outside. He threw his arms around Jerri Lynn and held on. They hugged tighter as their car's engine revved.

Tony started the Subaru and helped Michael throw several bags containing guns and ammunition in the back of the Forester. They quickly made more room by tossing a couple of suitcases into the bushes, but kept the ice chest.

"Hey, these people eat right," Tony declared as he closed the lid.

"Let's go little brother."

Ronald and Jerri Lynn held each other tight, sadly watching as the men tossed their gear in the back of the Subaru. All Jerri Lynn could think of were her granola bars, sugar-free gum and orange juice left in the front seat.

"At least they'll have something healthy to snack on," Jerri Lynn blurted involuntarily.

Ronald had a different thought.

§

The entire scene played out in front of us. We watched from above in the cab of the Kenworth. The rig was nearly nose-to-nose with the black sedan. I climbed down off the tractor cab as Jillian raced out in front of me, gun neatly tucked in her waistband at the small of her back. She reached the wounded state trooper first. Jillian had gone into "medic mode" the instant the Subaru sped off. While Jillian and Jenny tended to the officer, I ran to help the two people standing by the restroom.

"Are you two alright? Was that your blue car that just left?"

Neither one of them looked at me. The man was mumbling something that sounded like stop.

After a minute or two, they both snapped out of it and asked about the trooper. The three of us walked quickly around the rig's cab to the patrol car.

The rig served as a shield for the trooper's car, which protected him, but also made the Castillinos' escape possible. Jillian and Jenny were working fast to stop the officer's bleeding.

"How is he?" I asked.

Trooper Anderson had taken his belt off, but had passed out before tying it around his upper leg. Once the tourniquet was in place on the upper thigh, Jillian ripped open his shirt in order to treat a shoulder wound. Jenny found a larger first aid kit in the officer's open trunk, which included gauze pads, more ointment, and larger bandages.

"His pulse is light but steady. I think he'll make it. I've seen worse," Jillian said in a confident tone.

"He must have called for backup. Can you hear those sirens?" Jenny shouted.

Two state patrol cars arrived in time to lend support. After interviewing Mr. Turbine, they sent an all-points bulletin out on the Subaru. Jerri Lynn busied herself by making a few calls. Thankfully, she kept her phone in her purse. She made contact with some friends close by that were willing to pick them up. She also canceled their reservations for later in the day.

"Come on, Ron. Let's go home as soon as our friends arrive. I'm tired."

I felt sorry for the couple. They seemed like nice people who got caught up in this ridiculous nightmare. Fortunately for us, they served as a distraction and allowed us to leave sooner than we anticipated.

Jillian and I didn't want to draw attention to ourselves, so we made our way to the rig and left the Turbines with the state patrol. They were happy, playing the role of witnesses who could identify the gunmen and their stolen car. We ended up being bystanders. The troopers were more interested in what appeared to be a professional exchange of gunfire, and were busy taping off the area. Some officers took photos and attempted to identify the dead men.

In the meantime, Trooper Anderson was transported by helicopter to a Portland hospital in stable condition, thanks to Jillian. After thanking Jillian and Jenny for their help, we were free to continue our journey.

Our adventure continued in high gear despite our exhaustion. The next scheduled stop for refueling would happen in Vancouver, Washington, just across the Columbia River bridge from Portland, a few hours away. The sky revealed a bluebird morning.

We made our way north, watching for the two men ahead of us, who were now on the run too.

22. "Eyes on the Road, Hands Where We Can See Them."

Ten a.m. and the gunshots still rang in my ears. We pulled into the Vancouver, Washington truck stop. The bright, shining sun gave us plenty of reason to feel cautiously optimistic. My hands were stiff from the steering wheel, and my back ached. We'd made it this far by being on alert for nearly one thousand miles, and vigilant we needed to remain. I looked over at Jillian and set the brake. It seemed so natural now: the setting of the brake and the decompressing in the cab. What would it be like to sit behind the wheel of my Porsche again? Jillian and I looked at each other and smiled. She was tired too. I could tell. Her smile looked forced now; she'd been through so much in the last few hours, saving the trooper's life topping the list. Our mutual hope was that the bad guys had run for the hills. Ya, right.

Ultimately, we came eye-to-eye with our pursuers and lived to tell about it. It angered me to know that there were people out there, possibly lying in wait, preparing to pick up where they left off. I swore to myself not to let that happen, even if it meant disappearing for more than just a few weeks.

Jenny broke the silence as she burst out crying. She simultaneously rolled forward, swept her hair back, and yelled.

"What just happened? Oh, God. Sorry, I couldn't keep it in," she admitted sheepishly.

"Let it out, Jenny. Holding it in isn't healthy. Besides, think about it this way: What would have happened to that officer if we hadn't come along?" Jillian asked her.

They hugged as the quiet returned, until I pulled on the door handle and slowly made my way down to the pavement. Stretching and looking up into the sun felt rewarding. Closing my eyes, a mental road map appeared leading north. It hurt even to concentrate. Up to this point, I had never been that intensely focused, for so long, in my life.

The ladies quickly shopped, then paid for our food and gas. Hopefully, it'd be our last stop for a while. Jenny, a smoker, stood watch for the blue Subaru or any strangers in big cars driving slowly. Meanwhile, I grabbed some quick shut eye on the bed in the back of the cab. The second my head hit the pillow, darkness swallowed me.

Jillian sat in the driver's seat. Jenny, having just climbed back up, lowered herself onto the passenger seat watching, waiting. Jillian also watched me sleep. Fifteen minutes was all I asked for, which she extended to thirty when she heard the snoring.

Later she told me that she couldn't believe how we managed to take action and intervene to protect the state trooper. If I hadn't made the decision to drive into the firefight, the officer would surely have died.

"What made you react like that, Rick?"

"Why do you ask? Are you upset that I put us in danger? Tell the truth."

"No, absolutely not! I just think it was a pretty brave thing to do, that's all."

I'd become a reluctant hero, according to Jillian. Fine, I thought. I was just relieved that she, Jenny, the older couple, and the trooper were all okay. Now, let's move on and don't stop moving.

§

BOSTON, MASSACHUSETTS – PETRULO TRUCKING

The longer the call went, the worse the news became. Lorretta hated many things in life, but excuses, especially long ones, topped her list. She was ready to kill someone if they didn't stop talking soon. Michael's west coast job had taken a bad turn. As head of her family's largest profit-producing business, she knew something had to be done, immediately, if Michael were to continue enjoying his freedom. Otherwise, he'd have to trade it for an eight-by-six-foot room with bars, or worse: a coffin. Men are only good for one thing, and hardly ever at the right time or in the right place.

Lorretta went into Plan-B mode and called for the private jet. She now planned to make an unscheduled west coast trip. Her intuition was kicking in. And her impulses had never let her down. Get ready, she thought, I'm coming, Michael. It's for your own damn good, baby.

Washington State had approved the retail sales of cannabis, and she was going to check on her new operation, which transferred legal cannabis from Washington State, overland, to the east coast, where thoughts on cannabis were, what's the word for it? More primitive. The whole idea was hers. She had special compartments built to house the weed, creating undetectable space, mid-trailer. Special boxes were welded below Petrulo Trucking long-haul trailers' subfloors that held up to one thousand pounds per load.

Lorretta made one more call before leaving her office. She wanted Michael to know that she understood the killing of Libby; it made sense. But the rest of this, chasing the target, had to end soon. Lorretta had to be careful; Michael's ego was huge. She let him know that reinforcements were on the way, and that she would soon follow.

§

VANCOUVER, WASHINGTON – MILT'S TRUCK STOP

My phone had been switched to vibrate during my deep sleep.

Bad decision, as it turned out. Bear's calls had gone unnoticed and repeatedly went to my voicemail. That was on me, but Jillian decided to take the heat as she later told me. She intervened and took his last call, jumping down from the cab to talk. Bear kept his composure and asked how things were going, trying to get a fix on where we were. She explained what had just happened with the shooting. No response.

"Bear?"

She could hear him clearing his throat, as if he was going to give a speech.

Bear asked Jillian to let me know that, in no uncertain terms, we could not stick our necks out and risk our cover, let alone our lives, again.

He continued in a slow and succinct manner: "I have men in the area who are available to help. One guy is very good. Crazy good. He's on his way to meet you."

Bear gave Jillian specific instructions on who would be in contact and what to do when he arrived. A rendezvous would be planned on the fly, so we had to be flexible. He suggested that she set a time to meet in Tacoma, a city just south of Seattle. Tacoma now became the new drop point for the trailer.

Jillian would also have to contact Jess to let her know where to eventually meet us. Everything from now on would be happening "on the fly" as Bear put it. Jillian arranged everything, which included contacting Brenda. Meanwhile, I was completely zonked out.

Jenny needed to walk outside the rig for a reason other than stretching. She was a smoker, and even though she had tried to quit, she couldn't help herself. She needed to calm her nerves. Jenny had bought a pack of cigarettes when she and Jillian were inside the station paying for fuel.

She had liked the store. It was big and clean, with nice-smelling showers and, surprisingly, fresh produce. What Jenny hadn't noticed was a man dressed in blue jeans, sneakers, leather jacket and knit cap, standing further back in the store. He appeared to be reading a magazine, but was actually watching her every move.

§

Michael Castillino read the text coming to him from inside the convenience store. We have one more person to add to our wanted list, read the message. Michael shifted in his seat. The blue Subaru's car seats didn't fit him, which stressed him out even more. And this new message made him want to put his fist through the windshield. His mind was conflicted. Lorretta and her reinforcements were on the way. The past few hours of turmoil continued to roll around his head. The question became: Should they make their move here, or wait? His instinct told him to wait. Meanwhile, he had to get out and stretch his legs.

Tony had the spotter's scope. They parked the Subaru behind the store, under some overhanging maple branches, where they planned to leave the stolen vehicle. The car was strategically positioned in such a way that he could see the pumps and the long haulers' rest area, where Blaine's rig sat ready to roll. He watched as a young woman came out of the rig. She looked too young to be the other one, Libby's old buddy, Jillian. That's not Jillian. Pretty though, he thought, as she lit up a cigarette. It always amazed Tony when people would light up in a refueling area.

"Pretty, but stupid," he said to himself as he squinted into the scope.

"Go ahead and blow yourself up, girl," he whispered as he followed her with the scope, then carefully scanned the rest of the area.

Michael opened the car door and slowly stretched his legs out the passenger-side door again. The waiting game began to weigh heavy. He could feel his pulse beating in his temples, palms sweating, dark glasses providing some relief from the increasing glare of the sun.

"See that girl by the rig?" Tony said, still looking through the scope.

"Ya, what about her?" Michael replied, rubbing his legs.

"She's with them. Joey says he heard that Jillian dame call her Jenny."

Okay, so there were three targets now, Michael thought. He chewed on another stick of peppermint gum, his favorite.

The game was on, and Tony readied himself for some payback. The deaths of Vincent and Marty would be avenged, and the business threat eliminated. Vincent and Marty had come into the organization six years ago and quickly became like brothers to Tony. That trooper had made two good shots before they'd wounded him. Michael couldn't imagine that he was still alive.

Michael and Tony met six men in a back alley after crossing the Columbia River. Michael placed lookouts at four truck stops along the target's route. He had Lorretta to thank for sending in the additional men. His confidence, along with his endurance, was being tested. But Michael was up for the challenge. He had to be. When the replacements arrived, he felt both deep relief and profound anger. Relief, because of his losses; he needed the help. Anger for having to run and escape. He should have stayed and finished off the targets. Michael removed his shoes and started rubbing his feet.

He'd been monitoring Blaine's rig along with his brother,

when Joey's text arrived from inside the store. Quickly replacing his shoes, Michael immediately alerted his men. His stomach began churning once again as his mind shifted into high gear.

§

Jillian motioned to Jenny to hurry as Jenny walked out of the store toward the rig. Jenny picked up her pace as she made her way to the cab.

§

"They're boarding," Tony said as he refocused the scope. "The tracking device is in place."

§

I woke while crying out as Jillian and Jenny climbed back onboard.

"Where in the hell . . . are . . . we?"

My movements were stiff as I lurched forward toward the driver's seat.

"Sorry," Jillian whispered.

Both she and Jenny chuckled at my reaction.

"You look like a zombie. A nice-looking zombie, Rick," Jenny quipped.

"Got it, thanks," came my reply.

I slapped myself in the face a few times, looked at myself in the mirror, poured some bottled water in my hands and ran fingers through my hair. Looking a little more presentable, I fired up the rig. The ladies were strapped in and ready to roll. My watch read two in the afternoon.

Jillian called Jess to let her know of the latest change on the fly. After dropping the trailer in Tacoma, we expected to be in Seattle later that evening. The present plan called for her to meet us near a major landmark, T-Mobile Park, where the Mariners play baseball.

I suddenly felt conflicted. The thought of using my sister as a means of transportation made me feel guilty. These gangsters were serious and what happened earlier this morning at the rest stop was clear evidence that they were probably not going away. Contacts that Manny Alvarez provided might be willing to replace Jess, but that would take time. It was too late to coordinate that. This is a huge dilemma, I thought. I have to go with people I know and trust. Unfortunately for her, Jess is our number one option.

My mind continued to focus on the two factors behind our escape: the east coast mob chasing us, and the authorities looking for me. We were bound to be found if we made one wrong move. No pressure.

The walls were squeezing in on us. We had to keep moving from now on.

Bear's people were among those looking for us. Having so many invisible threats and helpers in the shadows made me feel like a fish in an incredibly large ocean of creatures, attempting to discern friend from foe.

The anticipation of it all became increasingly exhilarating. I'm not sure that anything in life, other than combat, can prepare you for that kind of feeling. Think. Decide. Move. Our original plan would have us dropping the trailer by now, in Vancouver, which meant we'd be driving the cab only, lightening our load significantly. Why wait to drop it in Tacoma?

"I want to get rid of the trailer now," I said to Jillian without looking at her.

"Makes sense. Hauling the trailer is like dragging an anchor through heavy traffic. Do we have to go all the way to Tacoma?" came her reply.

After checking the map with Jillian, we decided that taking a back route east off I-5 would be faster.

"Instead of going further north through Tacoma, we make a turn and drive northeast and leave the trailer in, let me see . . ." She hesitated and then pointed to the city of Auburn. She then suggested driving the smaller Highway 18 from there to the Maple Valley junction, which connected with I-90 east.

"This route will take us east of Seattle, but it's shorter. I think it should keep us on schedule," Jillian offered, fingering the map. She folded it to the point where I could see exactly what she was proposing.

"Yes, but not that far east. I like it. We'll then turn back west to Seattle, drop the cab and meet up with Jess as planned." When I said this, I was partially trying to convince myself too.

Our collective idea created a roundabout path; still, it might throw people off our trail. We didn't have time to take a vote – we had to act.

"Call Manny, find a location in Auburn to drop the trailer, and hurry, that exit is coming up," I urged Jillian.

This new course of action felt better to me. Dropping the trailer in Auburn rather than Tacoma, and driving just the tractor would make this part of the trip go much faster.

Jess was already in Seattle, staying at the Ramada Inn near the SeaTac airport, awaiting our call. I wasn't going to keep her waiting long; this had to work. Our plan was to leave Seattle tonight in Jess's car, then drive through the night to Spokane. This latest change in plan felt better, and I was determined to make it happen.

§

Lorretta told Michael that additional men would be waiting in Seattle, just in case. These were Petrulo Trucking "contractors" that she personally picked to aid Michael in his operation. Her west coast trucking connections were nearly as important to her business as those in the east, and Seattle was a hub location. As far as Lorretta was concerned, she and Michael were in the same battle with those runaways.

§

"Did you get enough rest, Rick?" Jillian asked as she and Jenny carefully monitored traffic.

"Yes, I'm fine. Thanks. Call Bear and let him know that we will soon be headed to the Maple Valley junction once we drop this trailer. We should arrive in a few hours. Has Manny called?"

§

Michael needed to make sure the three targets stayed aboard the rig, until it reached a more secluded location. There, he could rendezvous with his men and take care of this situation once and for all.

The Castillinos followed at a safe distance behind, tracking the rig. They were just out of sight, yet close enough to prevent any quick escapes. Michael moved his men like chess pieces. He rotated them to several popular truck stop locations south of Seattle. His strategy was to take the targets when they were the most vulnerable, preferably in an out-of-the-way place.

§

No rain today. The sky was a deep blue with white puffy clouds. Perfect for sailing – and hopefully escaping. I-5 presented some busy lane changes which kept my attention. Driving became more like a contest to avoid crashing. This activity tested each of us as we watched out for regular traffic while remaining vigilant for the men who were most likely after us.

Jenny had an idea that she wanted to run by the two of us. She tapped Jillian's arm and began telling her, loud enough for me to hear.

"I have this friend, a guy, and he looks a lot like Rick," she said, sounding like she was trying to sell us a load of Amway.

"That's nice," Jillian said looking at her like Jenny had a third eye.

I glanced at Jenny for a quick second while shifting up through the gears. She went on to explain that if it ever came down to it, she and her friend could serve as doubles for Jillian and me.

"It's just an idea," Jenny offered as she shrugged her shoulders and tilted her head.

When she finished, I couldn't help myself. "That's crazy! I said. "Do you want to die?"

Jillian smiled at Jenny and grabbed her hand. "Look, we're going to drop this trailer, and you with your friends, and hopefully no one else will know that we were here, other than Manny and Jess, of course."

Manny interrupted Jenny's crazy idea session by returning Jillian's call just in time. He provided the coordinates for a new drop location in Auburn right on Highway 18.

Jenny was clearly embarrassed and sat back. She looked frustrated by her inability to deflect the mounting pressure we faced.

"I don't want to be dropped off with the trailer," Jenny stated matter-of-factly.

"That's the plan, Jenny," I said flatly.

"Plans change. I'm not leaving you two."

Jillian looked at Jenny, then at me. Our drop point was coming up.

"There's nothing here for me. I sense something better with you. I don't care about the danger."

With that last comment, Jenny sat back, buckled in and stared at us as if she dared us to try and move her.

"There, over there, Rick!" Jillian pointed, shouting numbers as she followed the addresses along the route.

The fenced-in yard next to a warehouse looked new. Freshly

paved asphalt with bright yellow entry markers made it easy to find. A man came running out when we pulled up. He guided us through a tight opening and motioned me to back up into the drop area, where another person waited to direct us toward another series of long yellow lines the width of the rig. I rolled my window down and set the brake.

"There you go, buddy." The voice came from a woman who took charge of the trailer separation.

She climbed up behind the cab and began pulling the hydraulic hoses and disengaging the trailer.

"I guess you guys are in a hurry," she yelled as I joined her in the effort.

"Yes, we, ah, need to make a connection in Seattle this afternoon."

The whole sequence of unhooking the trailer took twenty minutes. I signed some papers and we were off. How Manny managed to find this location at the last minute was incredible. Thankful and relieved, we were off, weighing much less than when we pulled in.

I climbed up and re-entered the cab.

"Last chance, Jenny," I said.

She sat back in defiance, arms crossed.

"Okay, tighten that seat belt. It's good to have you with us, but know this: Now you're in the crosshairs too. Got it?"

"Got it."

Jenny's fierce eyes defied her smile. Jillian reached over and grabbed her hand. Clearly, she didn't know what she had just agreed to, but she'd stll chosen it.

The Castillinos were closing in at that moment. Michael was happy to be back in a bigger car, thanks to Lorretta. But the traffic became more of an impediment as the freeway led to a highway that ran right through a small city. Unbelievable. And thanks to the traffic congestion, they were unable to stay as close to the target, who had stopped up ahead for some reason.

The truck was moving at a sloth's pace through Auburn, Washington traffic, on its way to the I-90 junction, a distance of about thirty miles. As mid-afternoon approached, the mood in the truck was guarded, but relatively upbeat, even though we were falling behind our self-imposed deadline of meeting Jess by six.

We listened to some soft jazz Jenny and Jillian found on the radio. The sounds coming through the speakers, located in the back of the cab, seemed to mirror the rhythm of the traffic. Grover Washington was wailing on a long note when my phone rang. It was Bear.

"We're in a place called Cle Elum, about sixty miles east of Snoqualmie Pass, just off I-90!" Bear shouted as if he could not hear himself.

I told Bear that Jess was waiting in Seattle, according to our current plan.

"Change of plans, Rick. You'll have to come our way if you want maximum protection. And from what I figure, you'll need it sooner rather than later." Bear spoke directly and seriously.

Jillian went into action, handing one of our two maps to Jenny.

"Quick, find that place, city, whatever," Jillian directed. "Cle . . . something."

She and Jenny found Cle Elum on the map and began charting a new course. Traffic was beginning to open up and we were fifteen minutes away from the I-90 junction, exit 18, Maple Valley. Instead of turning back toward Seattle, we would be heading east.

§

The Castillinos were in careful pursuit. Michael busied himself by planning an ambush. He figured the rig didn't need to refuel, so he wondered whether they'd be stopping once Blaine and company reached the I-90 junction.

"Move up, we're getting closer to the junction," he ordered his brother.

"Which way do you think they'll go?" Tony responded.

"What am I, a mind reader?" Michael shouted sarcastically.

Tony gave his brother a stare that seemed to temper Michael's rough edge. He immediately changed his tone. Tony had been doing a great job of following the rig and doing his NASCAR routine all day.

"Hey, you're doing fine. Just move up, okay?"

§

The Maple Valley junction signs began to show above the larger lanes of the I-90 freeway, two miles ahead. Elevated traffic crisscrossed up ahead, then gave way to a steady flow of fast-moving vehicles. I hated changing plans so many times, but this last one felt right. Normally, decisions came naturally to me, but right now each one weighed heavier than the last.

Jillian could tell I was tense. She put her hand on my arm and said, "Hey, I can tell you don't want to take Jenny any farther, right?" I nodded my head. "Whatever you decide," she continued, "you got us this far."

Sure, whatever I decided was fine with her, but she also felt we should let Jenny out at the junction. It made no sense to risk her life. Jenny heard us discussing the last part.

"I'm a big girl," Jenny pointed out with pursed lips. "I can take care of myself. I'm staying with you guys. We're riding this thing out together." Jenny then reached over and turned off the radio.

My last call with Bear gave us two pieces of information. First, we learned how close he figured the Castillinos were behind. He didn't know for sure, but suggested they were closing in fast, based on the last reported sighting near Olympia. Bear also said his associate, Tom, would meet us in a white SUV at the MP truck stop. We'd know it was Tom by the SUV's sun shield, which had "Hellraiser" written in reverse across the windshield's top. Bear said we had to ditch the tractor and leave with Tom, no questions asked.

The MP truck stop came into view, and I had this nagging feeling that something was about to happen. The truck stop looked to be the largest we'd seen to date. There were big, wide-open spaces, with thirty- to forty-foot trees lining the back portion of the place.

Jillian texted Bear: "Okay, we've arrived."

Jenny and Jillian gathered the few belongings they had around the cab. I made a wide-sweeping turn and checked for parking. As I geared down, we entered the truck stop directly over the bright yellow entry arrow on the pavement. The sun glared through the windshield as I parked the tractor behind the store. When there was no white SUV in sight, my alert antenna went up even higher.

"Text Bear and give him our position behind the station."

Jillian immediately sent Bear an urgent text. Jenny hurried to finish packing our belongings.

I had just set the brake when two large vans came out of nowhere. One tore around in front of us and the other stayed behind the tractor. We were boxed in with no way out. A man dressed in a black leather jacket and a dark blue stocking cap strolled up to the driver side of the truck. Jillian had the gun ready and Jenny held on to the back of my seat, anticipating a confrontation. As the man stopped behind the cab, I reached across for the gun, watching the guy in the rearview mirror. Placing the gun between my legs with the safety off might be considered stupid, but I had a feeling. The man stood to the side and out of sight. Then, it happened.

He jumped onto the lower step of the cab, and with a big-ass grin shouted, "Hey Ricky, remember me?"

It was the same guy I hit with the crowbar a few days ago. The left side of his face was black and blue. Sweat began to saturate my back; my right hand moved for the gun. Without wasting a beat, the man lifted a small pickaxe from behind and took a swing, hitting and shattering the driver-side window. I turned my head just as the blunt side of the ax glanced off my left temple. The gun popped out from between my legs as I dove under the steering column. Jillian went for the gun as the man quit hitting the window and began punching out the sheet of broken glass. He reached in, attempting to open the driver's door. That's when Jenny came over the top of the driver's seat with a punch of her own. It caught the attacker square in the nose and sent him flying backward. As he fell to the pavement, a white SUV came screeching into the parking lot, narrowly missing fuel pumps, the mob's lead van, and our tractor. The maneuver left the SUV facing out toward the freeway.

Jillian, who had been watching for an attack on her side, looked over and saw me curled up and bleeding. I remember moaning and trying to sit up. There were people yelling. Someone tried to open the passenger-side door. Jillian went for the gun. She pushed me back down and took a shot through her open side window, causing the attacker to back off. The commotion intensified with the sound of people fighting and doors slamming. Above it all, I heard a man's voice yelling for us to get in the SUV.

"Rick, Jillian, now would be a good time to haul ass! Get out of there now."

That must be Tom.

Jillian heard the man yelling and saw a tall, lanky, redhead trading punches with three smaller guys who were attempting to take him down. If that was Tom, he was taking care of business, swinging a heavy-duty chain. He caught the man who reached up to open Jillian's door with a vicious swipe, nearly taking his arm off, as two others joined in the melee.

Both Jillian and Jenny managed to exit the passenger door with me in a half-conscious state. My arms were stretched out, one over each lady, as they shuffled as fast as possible toward Tom's white SUV. They pushed me inside. Jillian spun around and saw that Tom might need a hand. She left me with Jenny and ran to help Tom. She leveled the gun at the attackers, then yelled, "Stop or I'll shoot!"

Time stopped. Bloodied and grateful, Tom bashed the heads of the two men left standing, knocking them unconscious. He quickly wrapped the chain around their upper torsos like a calf roper in a rodeo. He grabbed Jillian by the arm, took the gun, and kept it trained on two other men who tossed their guns over to Tom. He pulled the ammunition clip from one gun and took the other.

"Nice work, lady," Tom said as he and Jillian backed away slowly. Then he ran for the SUV with the two guns in hand.

More gunfire sounded as they came closer to the SUV. Scattered shots were coming from a car parked on the other side of the station. Tom pushed Jillian inside as he returned fire, allowing him time to enter on the other side. The engine roared and the Hellraiser sped off, leaving behind a car, two vans, Manny Alvarez's tractor, four severely wounded mobsters, and two others needing new guns. We were gone.

23. "To the Rescue."

After a few minutes of rolling around and hanging on, Jillian found herself in the back seat taking care of me.

"I'm Tom, your driver!" the man at the wheel shouted. "You must be the desperadoes from L.A., do I hear a yes? Cause if you're not, I've made a massive mistake." He laughed, which revealed his blood-stained teeth. Tom must have split a lip or bit his tongue, I thought.

"Yes, we're them," Jenny responded while being jostled from side to side in the front seat.

Tom made his way through traffic east on I-90. He reminded Jenny, who normally enjoyed riding shotgun, of the crazy professor in the movie, *Back to the Future*. He spoke quickly and intensely. His wild-eyed expression made him look like he might know what the future held. He had a black arrow tattoo across the back of his neck, and wore khaki shorts, army-green military boots, and sported a red goatee that matched his ponytail. His custom-fit shoulder holster held a sawed-off shotgun that ran down his left side over a tight-fitting, sleeveless shield of body armor that emphasized his bulging biceps. He removed the holster while changing lanes and handed it to Jenny, who took the weapon as if she had been expecting it. The speedometer read ninety.

"It seems as though I've sustained an obnoxious injury. Blood from my forehead is interfering with my vision," Tom stated as he drove wildly, looking from the rearview mirror to Jenny and me in the back.

"Would you be so kind as to help me? The first aid kit is right there," Tom said as he pointed at the glove box in front of Jenny.

"Yes, of course," Jenny opened the compartment and began looking for something to close the wound. Tom had a generous smile that greeted Jenny as she attempted to treat his facial cuts and bruises with a towel and medicated moisture pads she found in the door-side panel.

"I'm here to rescue you three, so sit back and enjoy the ride. Those boys are mad as hornets."

The speedometer continued to read ninety.

Tom's grin was a mix of gleaming white teeth and cherry-red stains. Jenny gave him a bottle of water she'd found and told him to swish and spit. It took more than one try, but eventually Jenny cleaned the wounds. Meanwhile, Tom skillfully maneuvered through freeway traffic. The weaving gently rocked each of us passengers, side to side. He made it look easy, using all four lanes, heading away from the original target of Seattle, a few miles ahead of the pursuers.

Tom's head wound was hard to close. Blood from the wound prevented him from seeing clearly. Band-Aids didn't help the situation.

"You're doing great . . ." Tom began.

"Jenny," she responded, trying to keep her balance while leaning over the driver, attempting to clean the cut and not block his vision.

"Some people just don't know how to drive," Tom joked as he narrowly missed a car with a sign that clearly read: Student Driver. He smiled at Jenny and suggested a new idea. "Tell you what – reach into that glove box and get out the super glue."

Jenny did as he said, trying to anticipate what was about to happen with the glue.

"You're having a little trouble closing the wound, this glue will help. Believe me – it works. Now pull the skin together, go ahead, yes, oh it hurts so good! Careful not to get some in my eye. It would burn like crazy. I guess that's how it got its name." Tom's grin reflected more pain than joy.

That procedure was a first for Jenny. She had never used glue on a cut before, but Jillian had. Jillian gave Jenny some pointers and after a few tries, while bouncing, weaving, and applying pressure, it worked. She held her hand like a clamp on Tom's forehead. From Jillian's perspective, it looked as though Jenny was driving by using Tom's head as the steering wheel. Crazy.

Tom asked if Jenny was a nurse. She shook her head and pointed at Jillian.

"Well, good to know we have an RN aboard, especially when we're on the R-U-N!"

Tom laughed at his own joke and slowed to seventy-five as traffic began to thin out. Jillian held my head upright while she continued to search for my phone. She needed to contact Jess to let her know our status.

"The fella there must be Rick, so who are you?" Tom asked Jillian, who was bouncing and multitasking in the back seat, comforting me and watching behind for people chasing us.

"Jillian. And thank you for coming to our rescue," she answered.

Jenny released her hold on Tom's forehead, placed the bloody towel in the glove box, and tightened her seat belt. The ladies looked at one another and smiled. Tom, meanwhile, increased his speed as we began to drive up a steep grade on the west side of the Cascades.

My head hurt and my thoughts felt scrambled, like eggs being whipped into submission. Suddenly, Jess came to mind. I looked at Jillian as she talked to Tom and tried to get her attention. I was trying to say Jess's name, but there was no sound. Jillian looked at me and asked if I needed water. I nearly choked because it wasn't the water I needed, it was contact with Jess, now, that mattered most.

I was finally able to speak. "Jess, call Jess . . . and Brenda."

"Yes, okay, I will call Jess now. And Brenda. She may not know about our latest change. Good idea."

Her confirmation caused me to relax and settle into this chaotic ride.

"Hi, Jess," I heard Jillian say. "I'm calling to give you an update."

"Oh my God, is Rick all right?"

Jillian told her that my vitals were good. Jess could tell by Jillian's voice and the disturbing road sounds in the background that something terrible had happened.

"The guys chasing us are bad news," Jillian said. "I'm not sure how this is going to play out, but Rick got us this far and we're going to remain positive."

Jess accepted the latest change of plan and began considering one of her own.

"Where are you headed right now, Jillian?"

It took her a few seconds to respond. She searched for where she'd written down the name of the place, then she answered: "Vantage, the bridge at Vantage on the Columbia River, Jess."

"I have an idea, Jillian. Jillian? Can you hear me?"

"Yes, yes, I can hear you."

Jess told Jillian to stay strong and that she would call or text within a few minutes. She hoped to have an option for us to consider. But first, Jess needed to make another phone call.

Despite my spinning brain, I recalled speaking with Jess yesterday. I'd suggested the option of meeting at the Lake Roosevelt Resort, nearly two hundred miles east of Seattle, and taking a boat up the waterway, then switching to a car and driving the last hundred plus miles from there to the lake in North Idaho.

I had a feeling Jess was now improving on that idea. She'd call Penny at her store and ask her if she'd consider a seaplane rescue. Eastern Washington is full of lakes and waterways, the largest being the Columbia River, which crossed under I-90 at Vantage. But there wasn't much time to decide.

Tom continued racing down the highway at eighty miles per hour now. We were headed for Snoqualmie Pass on I-90, going from a few hundred feet in elevation to over three thousand in a matter of minutes, thanks to our crazed driver, who used all three lanes to his advantage. Tom made it look effortless. Swearing at drivers while driving one-handed, he checked his rearview mirror and carried on a spirited conversation with Jenny about using and reloading his shotgun.

"What happens if the police stop you for speeding?" Jenny asked with a smile. Tom, meanwhile, switched lanes and downshifted in a way that resembled a Hollywood stunt driver.

"From what I know, and from what Bear is telling me in my earpiece right now, we've got company headed our way about three klicks back. So you tell me: fight or flight? Besides, if the cops show up, they'll be on our side, right?"

Jenny nodded. Her impulse was to look back over her shoulder, even though she couldn't see that far. She unbuckled her belt, leaned over the seat, and helped Jillian move me into a more restful position by knocking down one of the seats. They traded looks and both smiled with raised eyebrows in response to Tom's driving. Tom observed their behavior in his rearview.

"Hey, get back in your seatbelt. I know what I'm doing, ladies. Besides, I have a radar detector," Tom said as he quickly changed lanes, smiling as he passed another driver on the right, then moved quickly back to the left lane.

That's about the last thing I remember before checking out.

I tried to focus as I walked in the middle of a wheat field, wandering hungry and alone. Off in the distance, I heard the sound of a train whistle similar to the one I used to hear on our family farm in Idaho. The blue of the sky, and the soft white clouds, made the moment perfect. Warm wind welcomed me and made me want to fly. I took a deep breath and when I let it out, my feet left the ground. I can't remember a feeling like this, ever. With my eyes closed, I soared. I reopened my eyes and kept flying, diving, then finally landed. I crossed my legs and sat down on the ground. Leaning back and looking up, I realized how tired I had become after traveling miles and miles. Tired, so tired, more tired than I'd been in a long, long time. Mom? Dad? There were voices off in the distance. People were yelling. Something was terribly wrong. I told myself to sit up. I jumped to my feet and began running, running from something. What? On the horizon stood our house and barn. Where were the people yelling? By the house? I had to hurry, but with bare feet, running was difficult. And then it happened: I was airborne again. A rush beyond all rushes. Yes, I looked down, and there sat Butch looking up at me. He said something, but I couldn't hear. What? Suddenly, I began to cry, tears streaming down my face. People, coming closer now, appeared out of a fog. Who were they? Something was pulling me toward the crowd. I needed to be there with them, but I wasn't sure how to land. I began to swirl around and around. I yelled for them to wait, wait, wait . . .

"WAIT"

"Rick, Rick, wake up, Rick."

24. "This is the Craziest Dream I've Ever Had"

I wandered out of my dream state as we approached Snoqualmie Pass in the Cascades. My head felt like it had been used as a soccer ball for an entire game.

"What's . . . what's . . . where are . . . we?" I forced my words out slowly and deliberately.

Jillian checked my eyes. Her military training helped her to determine that I was suffering from a concussion. How severe, she didn't know.

"Hey, welcome to the chase, Rick," Tom said as he slowed for some minor road construction.

The SUV came to a stop, which gave Tom time to reach back and shake my hand.

"I don't know exactly who you people are, but from what I know so far, you've managed to stay ahead of some pretty bad people."

My eyes finally focused more closely on Tom and what was going on around him.

"Who are you, and where are we?"

"I'm your driver. You can blame Bear, my employer and confidant. We served in special forces together, just long enough to drop into a lot of trouble. All in the name of our country, of course," Tom explained with a blood-stained smile.

"Here, why don't you try to sit up a little?" Jillian offered.

I adjusted myself with her assistance. The spinning of the SUV's interior slowed as I began to get my bearings. Tom swished water in his mouth and spit out his side window. I decided to do the same.

The road grader that had been crossing the highway finally made it to the other side. The flagmen turned the sign from STOP to SLOW, allowing traffic to creep forward. We were just beginning to move when the back window of the SUV shattered. A round flew through the interior, missing all of us somehow, spraying everyone with pellets of glass and other debris.

Tom accelerated just after the bullet pierced the back window. His quick maneuver sent us into the ditch bordering the freeway. His SUV angled hard to the left, found traction, then shot up and out.

"Hang on people!" Tom yelled as he sprang into action, speeding around the two cars ahead of us. The SUV took off, causing one of the flagmen to dive into the ditch we'd just exited.

"The chase is on again. Heads down low for now. Those hombres are way too close, so it's adios amigos!" Tom shouted with an added "yahoo!" at the end.

We raced past on the shoulder of the road, then gained speed. Gravel hit the vehicle's underside with rapid-fire ferocity as its tires kept searching for traction. The SUV continued to kick up gravel until it finally found concrete, and a much smoother ride, as we raced east down the open freeway.

I looked at Jillian, who continued to stare back behind us. After a few seconds she turned and smiled. We were armed and ready for battle – each of us now equipped with weapons Tom had passed around. Jillian had his Glock special; I had mine. We moved over the seats into the cargo area, taking lookout positions in the back. I pulled away some window fragments to make a slightly bigger opening. The move increased the road noise, but improved our field of vision and allowed us more room to shoot if necessary. Unfortunately, the road noise added to the tension. Hopefully, we didn't have that much farther to go.

Tom tapped his headset and called Bear for directions and an update.

"Gotcha, chief. You bet," Tom responded. "We're past Snoqualmie, heading to Ellensburg and our rendezvous at a place called Vantage, correct? Yes, the landing at the Columbia River. Right. You sure? I've got it on my screen. Okay, hey, they are after us like hounds on a fox. See you there. Over."

Tom now had his game face on and told everyone to stay low as he accelerated to over one hundred.

§

SANDPOINT, IDAHO AIRPORT

"Clear!" Penny checked all around, fired up the seaplane's engine, and slowly began her rollout.

She was as revved up as her plane, and began taxiing down the apron leading to the end of the runway. She and Jess agreed that if Rick and his friends had any chance of escaping, a water rescue could be their only option. A man by the name of Bear had needed a little convincing, but ultimately concurred.

The plane's engine purred as she gained altitude. The wheels folded up into the sponsons as she headed for her destination: The Columbia River at the Vantage Bridge. The distance was 220 road miles. She would cut the travel time down considerably if this little scheme worked.

§

After an hour of car chasing and weaving in and out of traffic, Tom's Hellraiser raced over Rye Pass. From there, the

Columbia River came into view. It appeared to wind along like a large piece of meandering rope suspended between the canyon walls. Each of us, including our driver, tried hard not to sightsee, but it became difficult the farther down the sloping freeway we raced. The view was new to Tom and breathtaking for the rest of us.

"Damn, that's pretty awesome," Tom muttered.

As the sun made its way past the SUV's open back window, I shifted in my seat to try and take in the same view. Tom passed his dark glasses back to me. The glare of the sun made it more difficult to watch for our pursuers. Darkness would eventually work in our favor, but that was still a few hours from now. Tom said that Bear and his men were waiting at the bottom of the hill, ready to defend us. He turned in his seat and asked everyone to listen up.

"We're going to come in fast at the boat landing down there to the left of the bridge." I could barely make out the grassy field and boat launch. He pointed at a spot, on our side of the river, next to the Vantage Bridge.

"We're on the last lap of the race, so get a good grip. Hopefully, the GPS is correct and the roads we need will be there, because this is all new to me. Bear is waiting with reinforcements, including your boy from, what is that company you own?" Tom yelled as he looked at me.

"Blaine."

"Right. His name is Major something," Tom said.

"Frank is here?"

"Affirmative, if Frank is Major. He brought along some additional help. We're going to turn your flight around fast. Then it's so long and goodbye."

It was hard to hear with wind rushing through the SUV's cabin. What did he mean by flight?

§

Two black sedans, both fully loaded with the Castillinos' heavily armed men, began to catch up to the target. The targets' driver must be on meth, thought Michael. He had run out of patience, not that he had much to begin with, and confirmed the kill order for everyone involved, including the ladies. He didn't know how long this chase might last. The map showed plenty of desolate land once they passed the river up ahead. Michael's goal was to overtake the targets and either deposit them in the river or out in the desert beyond. There'd be no survivors; no one involved would ever be found. Night would eventually cover the whole situation. How convenient. Bad things happen in the dark. Michael felt that luck was finally on their side.

§

Penny couldn't get the call from Jess out of her mind. She kept going over the fact that Rick needed to be rescued. He normally escaped, disappeared like one of those Vegas magicians on stage, and enjoyed his time away. Jess's call was quick and to the point. Penny could hear the concern in Jess's voice, not only for her brother but for the others involved. Who were they? And what kind of mess did her buddy get himself into?

Her De Havilland Beaver aircraft purred like a kitten as she made her way out of Idaho airspace and into Washington State's. It should purr – the craft had just gone through its C-check, a normal maintenance routine after a hundred hours of flying. Thank goodness. Penny leveled off at eight thousand feet. It had been less than an hour since her contact with a man by the name of Bear. She was making good time. His name made her laugh.

Penny couldn't help but think back a few weeks ago, to when she and Rick ended up in the lake after falling off his boat with Butch. How carefree and fun that day was for her, for both of them – and Butch.

When Jess had given Bear's phone number to Penny, it came

with an explanation. She said that he was a private detective assigned by Rick's attorney to keep him safe. It sounded to Penny as though Jess attempted to sort out for herself, as well as Penny, who was who and what was what. There definitely would be some explaining to do later.

From Bear, Penny received the coordinates for landing along the I-90 corridor, near the bridge at Vantage. He sounded more like a military sergeant than a private detective. She could tell from the way he spoke that this "favor" had turned into a rescue with life-and-death consequences. Jess had alluded to the possibility, but Bear really emphasized the serious nature of what was happening.

She'd driven over the Vantage bridge several times over the years, even flew past with her father once, but Penny never thought about a water landing there until now. Her course was southwestward, with a heading of two-four-zero, provided by Seattle air traffic control. The ride at this altitude could be challenging, but so far so good.

Timing her flight to land when the group arrived remained critical. She knew it would be a challenge to be there in time for the pickup. Penny had another concern: landing back at the lake when they returned to Idaho. In order to do so, she'd have to make it back before total darkness fell. But for now, she decided to take each step one at a time. Checking the instrument panel and the horizon for general aviation traffic revealed an overwhelmingly beautiful sky. She plotted her course for the Columbia River landing. This would be her most important "touch and go" landing to date.

The rugged seaplane had been airborne for nearly an hour when Penny called Seattle air traffic control a second time. She began descending and estimated it'd be about twenty-five minutes before she landed. The wheels retracted and locked into the pontoons. Anticipation began to take over; she liked it, butterflies and all. Bring it on. Soon she'd be welcoming passengers aboard in the middle of one of the largest rivers in America, with the engine and propeller running. No problem.

This was one of those maneuvers you learn after, not during, flight school. Emergencies will do that. She rehearsed the landing over and over in her mind: landing on the Columbia River without incident and rendezvousing with Bear's watercraft, watching for the blinking light bar of blue and green, transferring three passengers, and then going.

Before taking off, she'd removed a row of seats to ensure the plane had plenty of space for her three passengers and their gear. This created more room for a quick entry. Even though she looked forward to meeting Rick's friends, introductions would have to happen fast. More importantly, she was eager to find out what in the hell was going on.

Penny organized her thoughts by writing down everything Bear outlined. This exercise would test her skills to the limit. Only this morning, she and Butch were chasing geese off the dock and removing bird poop so visitors wouldn't be offended. I can do this, she kept telling herself out loud, as she dropped in altitude, reduced speed, readied the flaps.

25. "Touchdown"

Bear heard the slow drone of the plane's engine before he caught sight of it. Where was Tom? Organizing rescue missions was not foreign to Bear. He easily handled the pressure, and appreciated working with others who did the same, like the pilot of that orange-and-blue plane coming into view. Penny, yes, Penny's her name.

And the other lady, Jillian. She, too, came across as calm and reserved when they talked on the phone, which really made her stand out – especially when plans seemed to be changing like colors in a kaleidoscope. He would bet she had a military background.

His former military engagements involved coordinating with men more than women in life-and-death situations. Business as usual in the military. Both these ladies sounded confident and steady. Steady as she goes, he thought while watching Penny bring the seaplane around on final approach.

Bear had two of his guys near the dock, standing by for the swift transfer of passengers from Tom's vehicle to the watercraft.

Major Connors and his two people were stationed farther up the road, in sniper positions, ready to take on the Castillinos and whoever was working with them. Bear's plan required quick action, with no rehearsal and no mistakes.

"We'll load the three on board the seaplane while you and your men distract the pursuers!" he shouted to Major over the two-way radio.

"Roger that," Major responded.

The seaplane had to remain out on the river and away from any harm. The watercraft, with twin seventy-five horsepower outboard engines and a pair of aluminum pontoons, would rush the plane with three passengers, under Bear's direction.

"Once the three are safely on board, you move away fast, so the pilot can get the hell out of here," he told the man driving the boat.

Bear figured they had under five minutes to make the transfer once they reached the plane. He did not anticipate that they'd come under fire during the transfer; the plane would be nearly a thousand yards out. Sweat appeared on Bear's forehead as he heard the high-pitched sound of the SUV's engine. It was happening. He looked up in time to see Tom doing over a hundred miles per hour as he headed for the freeway exit.

"Bear, do you have eyes on us?" Tom called.

Then Bear heard shots.

"That's affirmative, Tommy, get your ass in here."

§

"This is November 6-8 on final approach for a Columbia River water landing at Vantage. Over."

Penny came out of her turn right over the bridge and located the windsock posted high on the railing. The bright orange cone-shaped sock indicated that the wind coming from the south was strong and unwavering. Small whitecaps kicked up like hungry bird beaks as she maneuvered the descending plane toward its final approach.

"Descending: five hundred, four hundred, two hundred feet."

Flaps down slightly, reduce speed, hard left rudder, Penny thought. The wind buffeted the plane slightly, though it was nothing serious. Penny handled it with no problem. Down, down, one hundred, fifty, ten feet, BAM, touchdown, flaps back, speed maintained.

The plane ran across the whitecaps at sixty miles per hour, then forty as the plane sank lower into the water. Penny turned to taxi and radioed Bear: "Touchdown, clean. I'm on my way. Over."

"Roger that, Penny. Good job. I'll let you know when we're departing. Over."

The surface winds were strong, but she managed to guide the plane closer to the launch area without much trouble. The plane reacted perfectly to the strong wind, bouncing up and down, side to side, with Penny practically standing on the left, then right, rudder pedals.

"No problem," she kept telling herself out loud. "This is the mighty Columbia!"

Out of the corner of her eye, she caught the flashing lights of a pontoon boat waiting at the launch. Penny continued communication with Seattle air traffic control while Bear monitored the same frequency. The orange De Havilland with blue trim and a touch of white lettering came closer.

§

Nice aircraft, Bear thought, just as Tom came barreling into the launch area. The vehicle, driven like a white flash, entered the landing area accompanied by clouds of dust. The SUV spun around and kicked up gravel for fifty feet as the driver door opened. Tom pulled hard on the hand brake. He had his shotgun out, ready to cover his three passengers.

"You look like hell!" Bear yelled in my face.

"It's nice to see you too!" I managed to shout back with a slight grin.

Major's men were exchanging fire with our pursuers. A white van that had been trailing the murderous convoy of black sedans headed for a ditch on the other side of the boat launch not far from us. Bastards.

I caught sight of a familiar craft: Penny's plane. Here, in the middle of the chase?

"Bear, what the hell's going on?"

Bear had binoculars trained on Penny as she taxied our way. He quickly explained that Penny and Jess had formulated the water rescue idea.

"And as it turns out, it's our best option for getting you three out of harm's way. Now move it!" Bear slapped me on the back, and we ran for it.

"Over here, Chief!" one of the men at the dock shouted to Bear. "The boat's ready, sir."

"Let's go, people!" Bear shouted back.

Jillian, Jenny, Bear, and I raced to the dock where the pontoon boat idled. Bear half-carried me as we went. It felt as if we were in a movie, running low as others covered us with gunshots that drowned out traffic noise on the nearby freeway. A few of the rounds that ricocheted off the concrete boat launch surface were too close for comfort. Major Connors radioed to Bear that he and his men were in a battle with the second van, which was loaded with heavily armed men and had just arrived on the scene.

Major had been conscripted by Brenda. She contacted him yesterday, asking for suggestions on how to help me, based on his military experience. It didn't take long before he concocted a plan of his own, then recruited two ex-Navy Seals that were willing to join the effort. After contacting Bear, Major and his men had met with Bear in Cle Elum. Combined, they had enough force to engage the Castillinos.

Bear had the entire crew in defense mode. Once the plane left and we were safely on our way, the battle would become more offensive.

The action happened so fast, no law enforcement had time to make it to the scene. Bear knew that would change soon and was prepared, with the help of Ralph Phillips. When the time came,

Bear would present documents stating that he and his men were working on solving the Liberty T. Scarelli case, a California case that involved the mafia.

§

The confrontation on the Columbia River at Vantage proved to be more of a fight than Michael had figured. The last of Lorretta's recruits had been deployed, a total of approximately fifteen men. They were scattered around in a semi-circle now, and were less able to advance their position. The other side proved to be more efficient at killing. Ammo rounds were at a premium as Michael rallied his troops.

"Keep it up, men! Don't let them get away."

Michael Castillino had not considered the possibility that Mr. Blaine might have a security detail of his own. He sat slumped behind his car, stunned. His brother Tony was dead, shot through the forehead as he closed the trunk lid and stood to run for cover. Michael had to decide whether to kill or be killed. Clearly, the battle's tide had swung in Blaine's favor. His options were fading fast with the sun, especially with the way the opposing force returned fire. Who were these guys?

He aimed his AR-15 and fired to his right, then switched to his left. He watched the plane landing and a boat preparing to head out. The three targets were being rushed to the boat. He had to make one last-ditch effort to keep them from escaping.

Michael had an idea, but he had to act fast. He thought of the high-powered sniper rifle in the trunk. It was accurate at one thousand yards, and the one man who was paid to use it was returning fire to his left. Benny was reloading when Michael grabbed him from behind and quickly brought him up-to-speed. Benny, or Benidicto the Eraser as he was known in the Army Special Forces before his dishonorable discharge, had to stay low while opening the car's back door. He pulled the back seat down, then found the rifle and its high-powered ammunition. Michael covered Benny with bursts of gunfire as the Eraser quickly scaled the rocks behind them in order to get a better view of the seaplane. Benny had his orders: Don't let that plane take off.

Michael then disappeared after sending an emergency text message to his one lifeline.

Shadows were beginning to form, and, like a snake in the bushes, Benny slithered out and around the gunfire, moving up the hillside that overlooked the freeway, boat launch, and the plane as it continued to taxi in circles.

§

Penny steered the plane in a circle at the rendezvous point.

She radioed Bear confirmation that the plane would taxi until the pontoon boat arrived, maintaining its distance from the gunfire. What she found hard to control was the flow of the river that pulled the plane closer to shore than she intended.

Bear's comfort level increased the farther from shore they traveled. Making the switch in moderate wind would be tough, but he felt more confident as he communicated with Penny.

"November 6-8, we're approaching on your starboard side. Over," Bear radioed to Penny.

"Roger that, Bear. Be careful, watch my wing. Doing my best to keep it steady. Over."

§

Michael's men lay dead or wounded. The rest, men he didn't know, were showing signs of giving up. They were through. The Castillino force, outflanked and disillusioned, began to surrender just as the state patrol arrived. The only fighter remaining was Benny. He had scaled the side of the gorge's slope bordering the recreational area, approximately two hundred feet farther from the battle. Just as he had in Iraq, he set the rifle with its tripod base, leveled it, then carefully rotated the bolt action as he focused the scope for a clear shot at the plane. His scope read nine hundred yards. Well within range.

Hearing the boat launch from the dock, he immediately changed direction and lowered himself to the ground as he turned his baseball cap around so he could easily use the scope.

"Ah, gotcha. Ducks on a pond," Benny whispered to himself.

§

Bear took over the controls of the pontoon boat as they came up on the plane. That allowed two other men to help in the transfer. Penny opened the passenger door after folding the co-pilot seat forward to make room. The transfer began as Benny's first shot rang out. It hit the boat's port-side pontoon. The next shot tore into the leg of a man assisting in the transfer. The wounded man collapsed back onto the boat's deck in agonizing pain, just as the plane's door slammed shut. The pontoon boat pulled away with Bear at the controls, radio in hand.

Bear caught Penny's stare. She was preparing to exit and gave him the thumbs up, along with a smile. Bear returned the thumbs up with a nod, no smile, which was more like him. He raised both hands like a referee signaling a touchdown, then bent forward and yelled "GO!"

Penny pushed the throttle forward, and the De Havilland's nine piston, four-hundred-and-fifty horsepower Pratt & Whitney engine revved to max. Both her hands were tight to the yoke as the plane's pontoons attacked the waves, attempting to get on top of the water. Penny asked everyone to lean forward as the pontoons found their grip and began to dance, back and forth, on the waves. The plane was at top speed within thirty seconds. Just then, BAM! A third bullet pierced the wing and part of the windshield.

§

Right as the bullet hit the wing, Penny lifted the seaplane off the water and into a dusky sky. Even though the bullet managed to reach its mark, the plane continued to rise. The distraction did not appear to affect her at first. Penny had to stay focused at this critical stage. She switched the navigation lights on, then pushed the full right rudder against a strong crosswind, and checked for damage. That's when she felt the effects from the shot. Penny was adjusting her dark glasses when the fingers on her left hand felt the head wound and warm, liquid blood. The wound needed attention to stem the flow of blood now coming down her left side.

When the bullet hit the plane, pieces of metal shattered close to her head on the left side, knocking her sunglasses off. The sun had descended to the point where she stared straight into it. Her glasses fell as she tried to adjust their angle one more time.

"I need those sunglasses, Rick."

They had fallen to the floor of the cockpit. I retrieved them and carefully placed them back on her head.

"Thanks."

I noticed Penny's wound right away and alerted Jillian.

"Well, that wasn't in the plan," Penny mumbled with blood painting her wry grin.

"Are you okay to fly?" I asked, reaching across the seat and readjusting her sunglasses. "Here, let me clean those for you."

"Wait, Rick, I'm going to bank to the right and change course first. And, yes, I'm okay to fly."

The plane completed the turn. A slow, steady rush of air came through a crack where the casing that sealed the windshield had separated from its mount.

Jillian checked her wound as Penny leveled the plane's flight at five thousand feet. Jillian slipped a gauze pad under Penny's headset and held it there. Jenny came forward and wrapped tape carefully around Penny's head. For the time being, the bandage appeared to stop the bleeding.

"This is not the look I was going for," Penny said as she whispered. "Thank you."

§

The plane's roar bounced off the canyon walls as the state troopers, with the assistance of Major's men, took control of the situation. They cuffed some and lined others up for body bags, and treated still others for wounds. The Vantage boat landing became the staging area for triage and separating the good guys from the bad. Two medivac helicopters landed and were immediately put into service, taking the wounded to hospitals in Ellensburg and Spokane.

The authorities found Benny three hours later. He had taken off higher up the canyon wall after watching his comrades' surrender play out. Benny had too many criminal convictions to avoid decades in prison. Instead of surrender, Benny decided to go out with a .50 caliber bang at close range. He leveled his rifle at the ensuing officers, and with a big-ass grin on his face, proceeded to open fire. That was the end of Benny, who died in a hail of gunfire, not knowing how much trouble his last professional sniper shot may have caused Penny and her passengers.

26. "Fly Like an Eagle."

Penny maintained control of the seaplane she loved dearly. This flight had become more than her typical sightseeing tour, and she thought she'd prepared herself properly for the trip. Her head throbbed at the temples. It felt like something was trying to get out of her head. What happened? Whatever it was, she would handle it. She had to. Blacking out was not an option, although . . .

Controls, instruments, gas, ailerons, rudder . . . CIGAR. Repeat.

Her thoughts were primarily on flying and, secondly, on what would happen if she couldn't maintain control.

Even though Rick looked rough around the edges, he may need to help fly this bird, the plane, the . . . he often took control when they flew together. He'd never taken off or landed the plane . . . there's always a first time. What's happening?

Jillian noticed Penny mumbling to herself. She and Jenny focused their attention on Penny. It's hard to see the pilot's eyes when you're strapped into the back seats, though. Every few minutes, Jillian checked Penny's wound and her vitals as best she could. With Jenny's assistance, she used the first-aid kit to reapply the dressing around Penny's head. It wasn't easy, moving from back to front, with the plane gaining altitude and fighting the wind.

"That should work for now. We'll keep an eye on that wound for you, Penny," Jillian reassured her.

The co-pilot's seat felt less comfortable than our ride in the Kenworth, though I had more concerns than my comfort level. What must Penny be going through? And what about the plane? For now, a tailwind pushed us along. The ride remained smooth, but my mind was reeling. The wind rushing through the seal on the windshield had to be addressed. My seat area had more room than Penny's pilot side. I rose out of the co-pilot's seat and reached over in order to check out the windshield.

The bullet penetrated the casing that held the windshield on the port side, but the seal remained in place despite the area where the bullet hit the plane. Where did the bullet end up? Did it glance off or go further into the plane? Was there more than one shot? If so, that meant a bullet might have hit the plane in another location, the engine or the wing? Time would tell. For now, we had to put up with a hissing sound coming in between the metal frame holding the windshield in place and the shattered portions of the windshield itself.

"Duct tape," Penny whispered.

"What?" I responded.

"Get the duct tape, in the metal case behind in the cargo area," Penny urged.

"Yes, of course." I finally understood.

There had been too much going on for my rattled brain. Jenny found the case and handed me a giant silver roll. I quickly went to work, sealing the inside of the cockpit area where we'd incurred the most damage. The hissing changed octaves and became much less noticeable. We took that as a good sign and went back to monitoring Penny. Since we were flying below ten thousand feet, pressurization was not a factor.

She seemed to be lucid, but for how long? We worked in concert with Penny's movements as she continued to maintain control of the plane.

Penny looked at me and smiled. Her eyes seemed hazy as she whispered, "Hey, Blaine, want to take a turn at the controls while your friends back there change my bandages?"

I felt a surge of adrenalin. Obviously, yes. The controls were in my hands as the ladies finished what they started, bandaging her wound more efficiently.

The plane became easier to control as we leveled off at just under nine thousand feet. This aircraft had a slight delay in the turns, though it felt smooth and met little resistance. It felt a lot easier than the Kenworth.

"I've got it. We are level at nine thousand."

"Yes. You look good at the controls, mister. Keep it up – I just need a moment with the ladies."

Penny gave me the nod and a few altitude instructions as I brought the nose of the plane down. I kept both feet pressed evenly on the rudder pedals, then moved the aileron control clockwise. That moved the port wing up and starboard wing down, keeping the plane level. For now.

Jillian finished bandaging Penny who looked like she was sporting a large white headband.

"Are you sure you're okay to fly, Penny?" Jillian asked, sounding concerned.

"Yes, just give me a few minutes and some Advil gels from the kit. I'll be fine."

"I need to adjust this bandage so it works better with your headset. Here's the Advil," Jenny said as she located a bottle of water.

When Jillian finished with her third round of bandaging, I looked at Penny with reassurance.

The plane's nose began to descend. I slowly pulled on the yoke to bring the plane back up to level.

"Nice," Penny said.

Jillian and Jenny strapped back into their seats. Penny radioed our position to Seattle control. As she did so, I noticed her left eye twitching.

"How's the headache?" I asked her.

"My head's better. It's the plane I'm worried about."

Penny asked me to help monitor the gauges. She was concerned about the sudden loss of fuel or oil pressure due to the gunshot. If the round penetrated the fuel tank located in the wing, the plane would have gone up like a Roman candle. We dodged that bullet, so to speak. The main gauge indicated we had enough fuel to make it back to the lake, but Penny reminded me that gauges had a sneaky way of lying, especially when a plane has been compromised.

A pilot might switch between left and right tanks for several reasons, and each side has its own gauge. Watching for a sudden loss of fuel in either tank became an obsession for all of us.

"Hey, I'm busy flying," I stated sarcastically, trying for some levity.

"I know it's difficult for men to do more than one thing at a time, but see if you can multitask this once and watch the damn fuel gauges too." Penny's comment made everyone laugh.

While she was checking the plane for damage, I continued to fly. She also made a call to Lannie Culbertson at Harbor Beach.

"Lannie, this is November 6-8. Over."

She repeated the call, there was some static, then: "Penny, this is Lannie, I read you loud and clear. Over."

"Lannie, we are running a little late and we're a little busy up here – I'll have to cut this short. Just wanted you to know. Over."

"Penny, we're here: your dad, Chet and me, on standby. Fly safe, dear. Over and out."

§

The Major and Bear were busy coordinating the cleanup with the state patrol. Bear could no longer hear the engine sound of the escaping seaplane. He immediately felt a sense of relief as his shoulders relaxed and he sat on a bench, awaiting Penny's call on the two-way radio. A few minutes passed as Bear watched the cleanup as the last medical chopper lifted off.

"This is November 6-8. Bear, do you read? Over."

Bear nearly dropped the handset as he responded.

"This is Bear, November 6-8. I hear you loud and clear, Penny. Over."

"We have sustained a hit on the port side of the aircraft, possibly through the wing and part of the pilot's side windshield for sure. Over."

"Anyone injured? Over."

"Affirmative, a slight wound for me from the metal casing around the windshield, but we're fine. Maintaining nine thousand, descending to eight thousand feet in a few minutes, heading three-zero north by northeast, over."

"Can you make it to your destination? Over."

Bear's question was interrupted by Jillian's shout:

"Look – the fuel gauge."

Jillian and Jenny were helping me watch the two fuel gauges. Jillian was pointing to the port side needle, which suddenly started dropping faster than normal.

"Rick, check it out – portside fuel."

Penny looked back over her left shoulder at the setting sun, the mic in her hand. I gently tapped her. Her startled eyes shifted to me. She replaced the mic, left Bear hanging, took back the yoke, and went into action.

Bear's transmission with Penny suddenly and abruptly ended.

"November 6-8, do you read me? Over?"

I answered Bear's second attempt and signed off. Penny took the controls and pulled her pilot seat forward. She pushed the call button on the yoke.

"This is November 6-8, declaring an emergency."

Bear heard Penny's emergency call and stared northeast. "Good luck, 6-8," he whispered. Penny's emergency transmission was intercepted by Spokane's International Airport at Geiger Field.

"November 6-8, what is the nature of your emergency?"

Once Penny explained our situation, the tower returned the call.

"November 6-8, we have your location and landing site options. Over."

Penny acknowledged the response from Spokane and told them to hold.

The mood in the plane moved from hopeful to desperate faster than the fuel gauge needle heading to E. Penny knew her options and began to take action.

§

SOMEWHERE ON I-90 HEADING EAST

Michael Castillino had never been so discouraged, cold, and uncomfortable. The metal box he found himself in had become his lifesaver and for that he was thankful. He followed directions sent to his phone and eventually found his way to the waiting long-haul trailer parked in a public restroom parking lot.

Sunset came early in the canyon, creating just enough darkness. Under its cover, he managed to stumble his way through scrub brush, thorny bushes, loose boulders, and water-filled ditches until he eventually located the Petrulo Trucking trailer. Alone, angry, hungry, dirty, and covered in scratches, he followed her instructions. He crawled under the trailer, then unlatched the hidden locking mechanism, lowered the door flap, and climbed inside. With the door shut, he sent the driver a text, and within a few minutes, they were moving. Now in complete darkness except for the light from his phone, he began to feel claustrophobic. He tried not to throw up. It was as if a giant monster had gobbled him up and was holding him prisoner in its belly. Get me the hell out of here, he thought.

As the rig gained speed, rocks and debris hit the bottom of

the one-inch thick metal casing that separated him from the road. The container was never meant to carry a person, only contraband. The noise became so deafening that at times he had to hold his hands over his ears. Unbelievable. Hurry.

Hiding inside the specially built cannabis container, felt like trying to meditate inside a bass drum during a rock concert. The Petrulo Trucking trailer Michael now inhabited headed east, currently being pulled along the interstate at sixty-five miles per hour. It might have been a thousand miles per hour with all the damn noise and jostling that was taking place. It drove him crazy.

Counter to what he normally felt, he couldn't help but be thankful and ashamed at the same time. His plan had failed. Blaine got away. Tony, his little brother, was dead, as were some of Michael's best men, along with several of Lorretta's armed reinforcements.

All Michael could do was to lay in a fetal position, his hands over his ears, and hope that his escape had worked.

§

Penny turned her head slightly. "Hey, everybody. We're going to be fine. This old bird has been wounded, but she's ornery, like me."

Her comment and smile helped ease the tension. Jillian and Jenny held one another as I looked at them and half-shouted, "Hey, this day just keeps getting more exciting with every minute!"

From that point on, Penny had to decide between landing the plane on the ground or in water. Her decision became easy when a warning light indicated the landing gear inside the port pontoon had malfunctioned.

"Spokane Tower this is November 6-8. We need coordinates for a water landing. Over?"

After Penny declared her emergency, she switched the fuel tank from the port-side wing to the starboard. The tank switch is a normal function that pilots often perform during a flight. It worked flawlessly. The starboard side tank indicated a three-quarter capacity. That provided enough fuel to make the water landing at Pend Oreille if she chose to take the chance.

§

As Penny dealt with flying, her phone received a text from Bear. Major and Bear were told by officials that not all the Castillinos were accounted for. The text read: MICHAEL CASTILLINO IS MISSING AND PRESUMED TO HAVE ESCAPED.

I looked up from her phone and half-laughed at the news. How could that be? He'd been identified at several locations along our route. Bear had verified that more than once. I would have to confirm that news later.

§

Penny needed help. I could feel it. Call it a vibe, intuition, whatever, there's a special feeling that takes over when someone close to you is off their game. It became evident to me that Penny was struggling to keep the seaplane steady and operational. The wind had come up and we were experiencing turbulence as the weather shifted. Penny's head started to roll forward. She was blinking both eyes, and trying to refocus. I reached out and held onto the yoke. She caught herself, looked at me and sat back.

"Thanks. I need another minute."

Jillian unbuckled, reached over the pilot's seat, and began to massage Penny's shoulders as Penny laid her head back and sighed.

The turbulence came on gradually and eventually caused everyone to bounce as if we were performing calisthenics together. The rolling and buffeting must have awoken something in Penny, because she caught her breath and confidently took hold of the yoke. Flying became more manageable with the two of us at the controls. Penny guided me through how to use the control wheel located between our two seats. Rotating the wheel changed the pitch and yaw motion of the aircraft.

"Everyone, take a deep breath and let it out slow," I said, doing my best to relieve the tension.

"Okay, mister yoga!" came a chorus of responses from the passengers.

Penny whispered, "Be ready to take over control again when the wind settles, okay, Rick?"

The sun began its descent past the horizon behind us. I nodded a yes to Penny, and watched the horizon ahead as we flew northeast with Spokane Valley disappearing to our right and North Idaho straight ahead.

Jillian and Jenny were doing their best to stay calm given the circumstances. Jenny had fallen hard on her right ankle when she jumped from the Hellraiser. Jillian helped her by keeping Jenny's foot elevated. She placed it on her backpack lying in her lap. Jillian then wrapped an ace bandage around that ankle, which normally wouldn't take long, but the action required more time now because of the rolling and pitching in the cabin.

"These old buggies can sometimes buck like a wild bronc. Hope you ladies are okay back there," Penny offered, trying to sound reassuring.

My head slowly spun like the propeller humming in front of us. The high-pitched drone of the engine and the occasional air pocket bump added to my discomfort. Mind over matter, I kept saying to myself, as Penny looked at me.

"Rick, go ahead, take over. Go."

The last thing I wanted to do was take control of the aircraft. Instead, I held on tight to the yoke, worked the rudder pedals, and managed to keep the plane relatively stable. Penny then began discussing alternative water sites. The current question was where we'd find the nearest water? We both paused, considering area waterways, when a smaller airfield control tower called.

"Beaver November 6-8, this is Felts Field Tower. Over?"

Penny radioed back immediately, and the tower responded.

"Beaver 6-8, the Spokane River water landing adjacent to the field can be cleared if needed, landing 9-0 degrees. Over."

"Felts Tower, this is Beaver 6-8. Affirmative. Will advise. Over."

Penny checked her pilot's log binder, which listed all area landing sites. That particular water landing was one of the more challenging in the area. The narrowness of the Spokane River at that point and the possibility of floating debris were her main concerns. She told me that she had landed her precious seaplane in that very spot a year ago as a test, which sent river-goers scrambling off their inner tubes as she passed overhead. That happened in the middle of the day. No way would we try that again, given all we'd been through.

Penny made her decision after making a quick calculation on fuel. "We're going for Pend Oreille," she whispered.

We were now northeast of Spokane, heading for our original destination, a water landing on Lake Pend Oreille. Penny's confidence convinced us all that we were finally on the right course. She placed her hands back on the controls as we continued out of Washington and into North Idaho airspace. Both Jillian and Jenny gave the "thumbs-up" sign, causing Jenny to raise her bandaged foot.

Jenny snuggled closer to Jillian and held on. Penny and I worked as one to maintain control and prepare for landing. Making that decision gave us both a sense of relief.

The sky changed from light to darker blue. Pend Oreille came into view, high on the horizon, straight ahead. Traffic on Highway 95 moved along like ants under us. Lights from Bayview at the south end of the lake broadcast the town's presence.

"When we are ten miles out, call Lannie. Tell her we may

need some help landing. Okay, Rick?"

"Help? As in an ambulance?"

"A runway. I need to be able to see the water as we land."

"Right. Lights on the water, in a line on both sides. Got it."

"It doesn't have to be perfect, Rick. But I'm concerned about not seeing a stray boat or two on the lake this time of night. I have to have a clear path. I also have to see the water at impact, as we touchdown I mean. Understand?"

"Got it."

This bird of mine is going to touch down and we'll be home. I love this plane. It's like a business partner I couldn't do without, someone you depend on and know that they will always be there for you – like now. Oh, God, please help us home. The sound of that sweet engine means so much. The lift off the water or a runway, the strength of it all. We are depending on you, my friend. Stay strong, carry us home, and everything will be fine. My head, what's happening?

"Next, radio Felts Field to let them know of our plan to land at the lake." Penny's eyes closed for an instant. When they opened, I could tell she was back. Adrenaline began surging up through my body like espresso shots. This renewed feeling helped me to focus.

Penny was in total control of her aircraft. She turned to me and ordered: "Call Lannie, check the fuel gauges and drink some water." I started to press the call button as I took a sip of water, and then it happened.

The plane appeared to be doing fine until the traditional low hum of the De Havilland's engine offered a new sound. It was an ever-so-slight knocking that was barely perceptible, except for Penny, who caught it right away. She sat up as if someone stuck her in the back with a pin.

"The engine is struggling," she whispered to me.

I acknowledged what she said with a nod. We were now twenty miles out from the lake, with the sun's light fading. We couldn't let that happen to our confidence too. Penny was now saying each of her actions out loud.

"Reduce speed and descend to two thousand. Keep our heading," she told herself.

Penny had one other concern she shared.

"The port pontoon may have sustained some damage, Rick."

"Wait. Oh, yes, the indicator light," I remembered.

We had to hope the indicator light malfunctioned and that the pontoon could support the landing. A hard surface landing at the Sandpoint Airport was never a serious option. If the landing gear indicator was right and the gear failed, we would crash on a harder, less forgiving surface. Her instinct told her we stood a better chance with a water landing.

I was momentarily confused and asked, "Penny, just want to confirm. Which is it, water or land?"

She looked over as if coming out of a trance. "We're going for the water."

Water landings are rarely performed in low light because there are no field lights along a runway. But Penny had no alternative. She now had to stay the course. Besides, it was still technically light enough, she quickly expressed.

She asked me to maintain control while she went through her checklist.

I had been fixated on the fuel gauge and the new engine sound of rum, rum, rum. I hoped my nerves would hold out as I called Harbor Beach to announce our landing.

"Roger that, 6-8. This is Joe Parker. We're standing by, Rick. Let me talk to Penny. Over."

Penny clicked her mic. "Hi, Dad. Over."

"Honey, you've got this. Call Seattle, let them know and go through your checklist. Over."

"On it, Dad. We'll be fine. I . . . I wish we had more light. Over."

"Penny, listen, don't worry about a landing strip. We're deploying boats in two lines to serve as your runway lights. Over."

"That should do it, Dad – very creative. How's the surface wind down there? Over."

"You're fine – wind out of the north at seven, slight chop. You'll have plenty of room between the boats, over."

"Okay, Dad, got to go, we're beginning our descent. Be there soon, over. Out."

Penny choked on the word "out" as she signed off. She switched over to Seattle air control and adjusted her bandage and headgear. A quick check of the aircraft confirmed that everything loose had been locked down nice and tight before we made our final approach. The De Havilland flew low and slow. It was normally a dream to fly, but right now, the controls were tighter and tougher to maneuver as we began our descent.

Penny literally stood on the left rudder pedal now because of a port-side crosswind coming down the river to our left. We were working in tandem, like riding a bike together, only faster and higher. She turned in the pilot seat to face the back and asked Jillian and Jenny to sit forward and fasten their seat belts tight. I cinched mine a little tighter too.

"How's the ankle, Jenny?" Penny asked as both back-seat passengers did as they were told.

Jillian and Jenny were holding hands. They both smiled at Penny, who winked back, then smacked me in the shoulder before quickly returning her hand to the yoke.

The lake, now in full view, looked welcoming. Shore lights around Sandpoint put on a good show. Penny radioed Seattle air traffic control and sent out a general area announcement, declaring our landing just in case there was local traffic.

"November 6-8, this is Seattle Control. We've contacted the local authorities to be on the lookout for you. Over."

"Seattle Control, this is November 6-8. Thank you, we're on

final at eight hundred and descending. Experiencing some loss in power. Over."

"Roger, 6-8. Update us after landing. Good luck. Over."

Penny then took a deep breath, gripped the controls and asked me to radio Lannie at Harbor Beach.

"This is November 6-8," I said. "Do you read, Harbor Beach? Over."

Some static came through, then: "November 6-8, this is Harbor Beach. We can hear and see you. Your landing lights just came on. Over."

"Roger, Lannie. We're two miles out and descending, aiming for Harbor Beach, over." Before Lannie could respond, I added, "Having engine trouble – trying to maintain speed, over."

"Got it. Joe and Chet have boats lined up. Look for a landing area. Be careful, over."

"Roger. Thanks, Lannie. See you dockside, out."

Together, we made a slight turn downwind, then an immediate final turn to land into the wind.

"There, there's the . . . runway." I couldn't believe what I was seeing: a watery landing strip.

"Yep, got it. Hang on everyone!" Penny shouted.

Joe Parker's idea had taken shape. He and Chet each took a row and lined the boats up about a quarter of a mile from the beach. They were spaced about one hundred yards wide, which looked like a postage stamp to us. Joe had twenty boats stationed on the water, ten on each side. Chet's job of keeping boats from going down the middle of the watery runway turned out to be a busy one. It created a watery audience of spectators for us.

"She's on final. Keep your distance from the boat next to you. All boats on her starboard side move out another twenty feet and hold. Good. If the plane comes toward you, get out of the way, fast!" Dave shouted through a bullhorn.

"Here they come," Chet radioed from his position near the lake's long bridge.

The knock in the engine went from a rum, rum to a pounding bam, bam. The oil pressure dipped down to forty percent as we made a straight-in approach over Bottle Bay. I could see people standing on their decks just as the starboard pontoon brushed the top of a tree. Penny worked the throttle to maintain control, begging the engine for more power. It sputtered, then responded as the nose lifted.

"Look, she hit one of those tall pines," one of the men radioed from the Bonner County rescue boat.

Their job was to shine the searchlight on the water approximately a hundred feet from the bow of the boat. The roar of the plane overhead nearly deafened the spectators below as Penny fought to bring her plane back in alignment and hit the targeted spot cast on the water.

"Keep the light there, Billy," came Joe Parker's voice over the headset. "Steady, steady until she's down."

Boat traffic looked as though it stopped at the long bridge. Penny scanned the water, lining up her landing spot. I watched out the starboard side for possible boat traffic. The long bridge leading into Sandpoint looked like a lightsaber out of Star Wars, pointing us toward our destination. Traffic on the bridge had come to a stop, making it a very long parking lot at the moment.

We had just enough contrast between the dark water and the last bit of blue sky. At total darkness, the water reflects the sky and makes it difficult for pilots to judge what's up and what's down. We needed to land now.

"Come on, come on," Penny said, coaxing her pride and joy onward as everyone held tight.

"Come on, baby, you can do it," Joe urged into the mic.

Off in the distance, she spotted the Bonner County emergency rescue boat, its lights flashing and its big spotlight cast on the water.

"Rick, check it out! There's our landing spot."

"Fifty, twenty, ten . . ."

"Hold on tight to the controls. Help me pull, pull . . ."

IMPACT! The hard slam almost yanked the controls out of our hands, then pitched us back up and forward. The engine struggled like a boxer recovering from a punch in the face.

Penny throttled up, needing more power to level out. The plane's engine responded, but not as she had hoped. It provided just enough power to lower the nose of the aircraft. It slammed down, sending water up and over the plane. We pushed the yokes forward with both of us straining in our seats. The plane pitched to port, pivoting the plane to the left and Penny into me. We raced across the water, trying desperately to stay within our lighted runway.

"Hang on!"

27. "All Good Things Must Come to an End, or Do They?"

We hit the water hard, and after the initial impact, we were on a rollercoaster ride. The first two bounces sent us flying as Penny worked the throttle. It was a delicate balance between working the throttle and adjusting the yoke. Penny eventually leveled the seaplane, found just enough speed, and stuck another successful landing.

"Touchdown, baby, touchdown!" Penny yelled out as she grabbed for my safety harness.

Screams followed by cheers sounded as the plane's landing lights streamed out across the water. It was a beautiful sight indeed. Penny and I both popped open our side windows. Car horns could be heard from the long bridge, as well as cheers from the city beach close by.

Through tears, Penny checked the plane for damage. We all unbuckled, hugged each other, and high-fived. Our two back-seat passengers, who looked like they had just been on the scariest amusement ride of their life, had their share of compliments for Penny.

"At one point I had my head down, but when we hit the water the first time, I had to look up. I watched as you fought through everything, EVERYTHING, the landing threw at you! Unbelievable," Jillian shouted over the noise of the engine as it struggled to taxi to the Harbor Beach dock.

The port-side pontoon held steady but had sustained some damage – the plane clearly leaned to the left. With the crippled engine doing its best to keep us moving, Jillian and Jenny looked out the windows at the people waving. Boat horns continued to blast. My body ached from head to toe, but the feeling of euphoria helped to manage the pain. The landing had to be the ultimate adrenaline rush.

Penny busied herself by slowly and deliberately taxiing at an angle toward the main dock at Harbor Beach. Smoke rose from the engine vents in the hood. We were taxiing toward the Harbor Barber and Tavern and home, surrounded by boating well-wishers.

We found out later how the Bonner County sheriff's rescue unit managed to keep the "landing light" boats in a straight line on each side of the watery runway. Two of the unit's smaller zodiac watercraft were able to string a thousand-foot line, used in towing and mountain rescues, along each side, which they completed ten minutes before the landing. Each zodiac then worked to keep the boats in a straight line. And casting that searchlight was a brilliant idea too.

Just as Penny prepared to shut down the engine, the chief pulled up along the port-side of the plane. Penny opened the pilot's door and hooked it to the wing strut.

"Everyone okay onboard, Penny?" the chief yelled out.

"Hey, Chet. Y . . . yes, we're shaken up, but no broken bones."

"That searchlight? You come up with that, Chet?" I asked.

"Did it help?"

"Saved our ass, or what's left of it!" Penny shouted as she adjusted the bandage on her head.

"Is that a new style in pilot headgear?" he said with a laugh.

"Ya, you like it? You're buying the first beer after I get this checked out, funny man."

We coasted behind the rescue boat like a smoking, wounded

duck. Eventually, Penny shut her bird down. There were no flames. Penny figured that oil had leaked onto the manifold, causing the smoke. Once the engine stopped, the eventual silence helped us relax.

A second rescue boat came alongside, and one of the officers tossed a rope over to me. He instructed me to tie it around the center portion of the wing strut, which I did from my position on the starboard pontoon. The second line helped to tow us the rest of the way.

Lannie, looking like a cheerleader leading her fans, appropriately waved the cocktail flag and led cheers as the plane slowly drifted to the end of the HBT dock.

She and her customers had monitored the last few minutes of our flight on the two-way radio, sweating out our final approach. Everybody had cheered and hugged one another, even strangers, as Penny announced to Seattle air traffic control that November 6-8 had safely landed.

"It's about damn time – you're late!" Lannie was barely able to get the words out as she continued to wave the flag, tears in her eyes.

Jillian handed me the paddle behind her seat. After fastening the starboard-side door open, I used the paddle to help bring the craft parallel to the dock. That's when I noticed Jess and her husband. Ryan used a long pole to help bring the plane around as we neared the dock. My sister had her palms over her mouth as she slowly walked forward. I didn't expect to see her and jumped from the pontoon into her arms. She caught me in an embrace that felt so good. We hugged and I buried my head in her shoulder.

"What took you so long, little brother?"

"Hey, if you wanted us sooner, you should have hired a jet!"

Ryan joined in the hug, and Lannie draped the cocktail flag around us as the crowd continued cheering.

Penny stood on the port pontoon and looked as though she was ready to pass out; that is, until she caught sight of Butch. A big smile appeared on her face as Butch came running onto the dock.

Relief can have such an energizing effect, and it showed on Penny. She had to climb back into the aircraft, cross over to the co-pilot's seat, and exit through the starboard side in order to get to the dock. But before she did, Penny sat in the pilot's seat. I could see her catching her breath in the stillness as she stared out at the crowd. I excused myself from the group hug and walked over to the plane, then reached in and touched her shoulder. She held onto her head bandage as tears came. We hugged and I told her she was my angel. We were both in disbelief that the crazy scheme had worked.

Penny, who didn't know all the gruesome details, never hesitated to come to the rescue. Now her mouth was moving. She was trying to tell me something. I leaned in closer.

"We did it, Rick," she said. "We did it."

"Sorry about your plane, Penny. I will take care of..."

"You will let me take care of my baby, and when you're ready, you'll tell me what this is all about, okay?"

We smiled and hugged. Through the cockpit windshield, I saw my sister waving and pointing.

I returned to the dock, put my arm back around Jess's shoulder and whispered, "You're the most amazing person I know." And then it dawned on me. "You must have driven like a maniac to get here," I said. I tightened my hug and pulled her close as she buried her head into my shoulder.

We watched as the EMTs sat Penny down and checked her vitals. Butch, meanwhile, took a dip in the lake, then showered the surrounding crowd with his shaking. Afterward, he walked to the end of the dock to wait for Penny.

More thank you's would follow. Brenda's came next. I called

and thanked her. She had coordinated everything and everyone who came together to help with our escape. Brenda had a bright future ahead with Blaine Manufacturing.

Bear called to check on our status. During that conversation, he confirmed that Michael Castillino disappeared before he could be arrested. Traffic had been backed up, east and west, for miles. One theory was that he had some help waiting along I-90. A full-scale manhunt ensued, but the trail turned cold as the shroud of darkness covered his tracks.

Both Bear, the ultimate private investigator, and Major Connors, my gun-toting production executive, had some explaining to do with the authorities. I had previously instructed Ralph to put a team of attorneys together to defend both men on the grounds that they were working as my security while I attempted to find out more about Libby's death. From the time prior to Libby's death until now, the Castillinos had been on the attack. I remained confident in Ralph's ability to take care of tying up loose ends.

As for the rest of the night, we celebrated and then rested. And counted our lucky stars.

THE END

Epilogue

It took a while for the bumps and bruises to heal, and a little longer to remember every detail of what had taken place in such a short period of time. Remembering takes time. And as the past unwound, I had to write it down, as I'm doing now, in my weather-worn, dog-eared journal. Days have turned into weeks, and weeks into months. No one I cared for escaped without suffering some harm. As for me? The Rick Blaine I knew, or thought I knew, slowly evaporated like rainwater on hot asphalt. Looking back, I've tried to find the exact moment when I first felt a hint of change. I didn't need Ted or several beers to know for sure. It had to be when I was accused of rape. That accusation, as false and misleading as it was, tore at my soul.

Up to that point, my life had been measured mostly on a business scale and not a social one. Honestly, there wasn't enough time in the day to do what needed to be done at Blaine Manufacturing, let alone to develop any personal relationships. I definitely didn't have time for love.

As I sit here now, cataloging what happened, the realization of who I am overwhelms me. It follows like a shadow. People close to me have attempted to help me become a more well-rounded person. I see that now. I'm also beginning to see what I could be in the future. That's where the questions begin to form, the main one being: Where do I go from here?

As I look back on what happened, especially in that frightening three-day period starting in California, I have to share what I have found out from my sources.

§

Michael Castillino got away. He, undoubtedly, will return in some fashion. To that end, I've hired Bear for as long as it takes to keep me and Blaine Manufacturing safe.

My attorney worked diligently on the charges pending in Libby's death. His investigation revealed a tie between Libby and the Castillinos, which, he assured me, would eventually get me off the hook. Nothing had been resolved, but witnesses were coming forward – people who identified Tony Castillino as the man seen with Libby the night of her disappearance in Sausalito.

Major called with follow-up details concerning the "Battle on the Columbia," as he called it. He suggested that I stay put for now. I agreed. He also had another idea that took me back a little. It had something to do with who might take my place if I decided to retire. I told him that he and Joe could run things at Blaine Manufacturing for the time being while I healed. I'm sure he knew I had no plans to retire any time soon.

Penny, Jillian, and Jenny were enjoying one another's company. Nothing brings people together more than sharing a near-death experience. Penny's wound required some minor surgery. Doctors needed to shave off most of her hair, which made her look even cooler in the eyes of most of her admirers. From my perspective, her new look was similar to Sheena, the mythical sword bearer, but I waited for the right moment to share that opinion.

The three of them hung out for about a week. Penny showed them around the area by car, since she and her plane were grounded for at least a month. Jenny fell in love with the area and accepted a position at Penny's store as an assistant, where she learned as much as possible about preparing food, selling retail, and handling the post office.

Business at Penny's store remained steady, and she appreciated how well her new hire was received by the locals. A few days ago, Mr. Small made his way across the flagstone patio that bordered the west side of Penny's store. He made the trip just to introduce himself to the new employee. Lannie came up from behind him as he reached the store's front porch and helped him climb the stairs.

"Morning, J.T. Here, let me open the door for you," she said as she reached around him.

"Oh, thanks, Lannie. Good Morning to you. Say, will you introduce me to the new girl?"

"Jenny? Sure, she should be here."

I was there to witness the introduction. It made me feel good. After the waves from the landing last week had settled, so did Jenny. She was thankful to Penny for giving her a chance here in Idaho. Jenny couldn't help but be nervous her first day, she later shared with me.

"Everyone is so nice here at Harbor Beach. I feel like it took a crash landing for me to settle down."

Acceptance was key for her. And Ms. Parker (Jenny found it difficult to call her new employer by her first name) made her feel right at home. Penny told Jenny that she had come highly recommended.

"From what Rick told me, you're fun to be around, and can think fast. He also mentioned that you have a great right hook," she said.

They both laughed at the thought of Jenny taking down a man twice her size while defending me. Jenny told me that her trip with us was an answer to prayers. All her life, Jenny had longed to become more, to evolve, and be recognized by her family. Growing up, she would sit in her room alone, feeling invisible, afraid that one day she would be made to live a life she didn't like or want. Things are different now. She's found someone, and some people, who make her feel important. Penny normally found good employees in the past, but no one willing to remain beyond the tourist season, until possibly now.

Jillian gave herself a few days before returning to Los Angeles and Venice Beach. She missed her Artie. My long-haul co-pilot promised me that she and Artie would take care of my place and stay in contact with Bear, who had become friends with Artie. Opposites attracting again. Bear would also maintain a lookout for the Castillino crowd should they come calling again.

Jess and Ryan were also impacted by all this. They put their lives on hold to help me. The night we made it back to Pend Oreille, Jess, who had my phone for some reason, handed it to me. The caller was Winston Lamperson. Our conversation is worth sharing here.

"Rick, my boy," Winston began. "I hear you had a real go of it, but are now safe."

"That's right, Winston. How are you?"

"Well, to be perfectly frank, we could use your help. And as it turns out, our firm has an additional business proposition for you, when you find time to be here in London. Hopefully, in the next few months, we can introduce Blaine products to all of Great Britain."

"Really?" I managed.

"We'll dig into this later, my good fellow. By the way, Benjamin sends his congratulations and best wishes."

There are only a few blank pages left in this journal. Guess I'm coming to the end of my story.

My final thoughts were recorded back on the dock that night, staring at Penny's orange, blue, and white pride-and-joy, dock lights reflecting off it like a million tiny fireflies. Soon it would return to the hangar and get refurbished.

I couldn't help but smile at the thought of how Penny managed to bring us safely home. Her amphibious beauty proved to be one tough bird all right, just like its pilot. The plane's final gasp of power was almost human. Penny and her plane had a special bond. I had witnessed it.

That night, I ran my hand along the plane's wing. It felt cold like the nose that touched my other hand at the same time. Butch, tail wagging, smiled up at me with that "I'm ready to go for a walk" look. So we did, while friends – old and new – walked along the beach nearby. It was as if Butch was showing me a new way down an old path. We'd walked this route to my dock many times before, but this night was different. Welcoming and safe.

The people who mattered to me were safe too. A feeling of calm overtook me as I inhaled a deep breath. It felt good to be able to take a moment to even be in that moment at that time. The sky burst with so many stars that Butch gave up trying to count them all. Tiny lights, piercing the darkness, watched over us. Tears formed in my eyes, the stars blurred, and I stood there crying from my soul like unpredictable rain.

Acknowledgments

My wife, Lorrie, my sister, Sue, friends, Gladys and Jerry, as well as Jon Gosch and Kevin Breen: great and very patient editors.

JPR